Starlight Symphonies
of
Oak & Glass

Starlight
Symphonies
of
Oak and Glass

Alexandria Nolan
Copyright © 2014

ISBN-10:0615972446
ISBN-13: 978-0615972442

Also By Alexandria Nolan

SHEARS OF FATE
A NOVELLA OF MEMORY AND MADNESS

WIDE, WILD, EVERYWHERE:
SHORT STORIES FOR WANDERERS

Dedication

To all who now, or have ever, called Michigan home. Its natural, glimmering beauty and fascinating history had me stuck in an almost permanent daydream. It is easy to love a place with so much magic.

And as ever, for Terrence.

Acknowledgments

A profound gratitude for my Michigan roots, and for the many tales of Mackinac that drove the research and my imagination.

For my designer, M. Munn, who inspired my mind with her fantastic drawings and artwork, a heartfelt thank you.

Contents

ARCH ROCK.

She Walks in Beauty —George Gordon, Lord Byron

She walks in beauty, like the night
Of cloudless climes and starry skies;
And all that's best of dark and bright
Meet in her aspect and her eyes;
Thus mellowed to that tender light
Which heaven to gaudy day denies.

One shade the more, one ray the less,
Had half impaired the nameless grace
Which waves in every raven tress,
Or softly lightens o'er her face;
Where thoughts serenely sweet express,
How pure, how dear their dwelling-place.

And on that cheek, and o'er that brow,
So soft, so calm, yet eloquent,
The smiles that win, the tints that glow,
But tell of days in goodness spent,
A mind at peace with all below,
A heart whose love is innocent!

I Know an Isle —Rev. David H. Riddle

I know an isle, and emerald set in pearl,
Mounting the chain of topaz, amethyst,
That forms the circle of our summer seas—
The fairest that our western sun hath kissed.

For all things lovely lend her loveliness;
The waves reach forth white fingers to caress,
The four winds, murmuringly meet to woo
And cloudless skies bend in blue tenderness.

The classic nymphs still haunt her glassy pools;
Her woods, in green, the Norseland elves have draped,
And fairies, from all lands, or far or near,
Her airy cliffs, and carving shores, have shaped.

Of old, strange suitors came in quest of her,
Some in the pride of conquest, some for pelf;
Priests in their piety, red men for revenge—
All seek her now, alone, for her fair self.

Prologue

She looked over the numerous boxes and trunks, uncaring anymore as to their contents. Only a single parcel she clasped tightly to her chest, a talisman to protect her on the journey ahead. Protect from what, though? A rough crossing? The curious eyes of those aboard? Or was she hoping to protect herself from her own nature? Her head hurt to think on it, so instead she clutched the leather-bound book ever closer.

The pages were as yet, unfilled, and somehow, it would be her salvation to mar their pristine whiteness. Somewhere, locked within her own mind lay the answers she was looking for, the secrets that had kept her imprisoned all of these long months. She was alone for now. He would be in the shipping office until after dark, sorting the last of the papers, giving the last of the commands, being certain to leave all better than he had found it, in order to ease his father's mind. In order to present a legitimate reason for their sojourn in Detroit. She could not help but bless him for this. For his constant thoughtfulness, though she could not explain why he was willing to undergo all of this shadow play, for her.

She sighed, and realized, uncomfortably, that she was not alone after all. *He* had returned. Not the 'he' she was thinking of, but the other. The one who plagued her every move. He was laughing at her now, laughing at the face of disgust she was making. He was dancing amongst her trunks, and opening them, lifting out her gowns and messing their clean folds to have a look at them. Then he was next to her, caressing her cheek, bold hands on her stomacher. She cursed him, and he laughed again, and vanished back to wherever phantoms haunt.

She opened up the journal, and decided to make one entry. One entry before she left behind this somewhat-sanctuary, this place far away from wagging tongues and familiar faces that would soon haunt her days.

Diary of Cora Ravensdale-Delacroix, May 1826

I do not think I am deceived in thinking, that amongst women who fancy they are in love, that they each of them believe their love is special. All the women in my acquaintance have come to believe, at least in the beginning, that the wooing and sweet soft kisses that first set their hearts soaring is somehow unusual, or out of the common way.
It is both true and untrue, I think. All love is different, so in that way, they are correct in their tightly held fantasies. But, I also find that because love is such a broken, pricking thing, that there is nothing very special about it at all. I have loved two men, (excepting papa) both with my whole heart and soul, and the pain they have caused me in loving them is more than enough to convince me that I was most probably better off without it.
One heartbreak caused by losing his love, and the other, the agony of finding it.
No, there is nothing unique or special about any one love story. It is just a thousand different ways to describe regret, passion and longing.

But that does not mean that my story is not worth the telling.

She sighed again, heavily, and clasped the handsome brass buckle on the face of it. She had made a beginning, and now she looked to the end.

:1:

Weigh Anchor:
Walter Alberts

It seemed to come from nowhere, as phenomenons like this usually do. Like fog settling over a meadow; it isn't there one moment, and then it has crept in stealthily, a thousand ghosts swirling, dancing, promenading among the green of the morning.

The day had started softly, brightly. The sun had been a thin blanket, not oppressive, but not inflicting the passengers with the slightest chill. They had basked on deck, staring out at the mirrored blue all around them. Lake Huron is an engrossing work of art, her silent, siren song luring and captivating the eyes of all those fortunate to have a clear look at her. Her rolling, steady blue waves, the clean, fresh scent of the water, like so many liquid lapis stones, glittering and sparkling in the sunlight. The water so deeply ultramarine that many seasoned mariners and passengers alike would lean down and dip their palms into the lake, to be sure there wasn't glimmering jewels for the taking, just under the surface.

They had only just pushed away from the harbor in Detroit a few hours earlier, and now all on board were preening forward in expectation of the trip ahead of them, as if leaning would pull the schooner closer to the island if they all tilted in unison. The captain looked on his crew, all but two of the men had been with him on many crossings. He knew their habits as well as they knew his, knew their penchant for strong drink and hard work, and every scar on their knuckles or lash to their back had been in his service, and the service of the *Starlight*.

A strange name for a ship, some said. Most schooners bore names like *Andrew Jackson* or *Dearborn*, but there was something that he liked about his command of a ship with a name full of poetry. He had taken the sailing life as one would take a wife, though he had one of those as well, but he couldn't help but be proud and faithful to his first woman, his *Starlight*.

Captain Alberts stood at the prow of the ship and found himself slightly slanted forward with the rest of his passengers. He sniffed the air and he could just discern the smell of fire, a phantom tendril of smoke seemed to invade his nostrils, and he knew it would be a strange crossing. Things happened on the lake, things those on land would hardly believe, but seemed common to those who spent their lives on, or near enough, to the roiling blue. A slight shift in the wind, which seemed to caress his cheek in warning, a caution he knew he wouldn't understand until the trouble was upon him. Such was the romance and drama of the water, and although he had spent his life riding those soft waves, he knew he would never really understand the lakes of Michigan; they were inscrutable.

He was on the water more than most, but all of the Great Lakes people were water folk. Even if they did not suspect it, there was something about those that lived by the water that changed them, their spirits were more open, more easily affected by the tides or the spirits of the water. To spend your life sailing on the waves means to accept superstition and the existence of the unknown without blinking an eye. Things…happened on the water. Words were uttered, visions were seen, acts committed, things believed, that no person that was tied to the land would understand. The island itself seemed to be a halfway point for most men; white and Indian alike. Not quite land but not quite water, but instead something in between the two. A gate between the worlds, it seemed sometimes to Captain Alberts. It was more of a large floating ship that stayed where it was, even as the world changed around it. It was a place out of time, and had been even in the long-ago days of his own childhood. Many changes had come to Mackinac over the years, but it still seemed steadfastly the same, as if the island itself was everlasting and it was laughing at the ideas of the men who tried to claim it. A man like him, with the fresh blue water of the lake coursing through his veins, could only call a place like Mackinac home—there would have been no rest on any other land.

He turned about to observe those who had boarded his ship for the journey up to the island. It was still a wild place in the north of Michigan, and it was strange to see in the space of one voyage how varied life was from the harbor in Detroit, to the harbor in St. Ignace or of Mackinac. The modern world flowed from that northern place in the form of furs, lumber and fish… but it also seemed to somehow exist outside the boundaries of present reality, stuck in a kind of perpetual past; more raw and rugged, but also more vibrant.

A lot of young men, including the new doctor for the fort, and a few others that may have been new recruits or men hopeful of joining a brigade of voyageurs, had all scrambled aboard this morning, nearly missing the ship. He had been surprised to glimpse the prodigal son of one of the agents of the American Fur Company. The captain knew the family well, and had heard the rumors about this youngest boy, remembered his disgrace of the past. He would enjoy making a study of him on this trip up, in order to give an account to his wife and daughter when they made landfall on the island. Just as he was imagining how these tales would light up the eyes of his girls, the same mocking scent on the wind filled his senses. An eerie reminder that the spirits of the lake had their own plans.

Captain Walter Alberts had lived on Mackinac all of his life, and so it was with a bit of dread that he had encountered the other young man that captured his eye. The son of the head of the Cross Shipping Company had appeared on the dock that morning, and since then Alberts had barely been able to take his eyes from him and his young wife.

If the boy from the fur company was gossip, then Jean-Luc and Cora Delacroix had been a scandal. The beautiful daughter of the fort's commandant hastily marrying the heir to the island's shipping company...and under the circumstances— it had thrown the island in a veritable uproar. But it looked as though some of those tongues had wagged for naught, because there was no cooing "bébé" in her muslin covered arms. The face he had remembered gliding around the island on her father's arm had been bright and merry, and in contrast the countenance he saw now, appeared drawn. She carried a deep sadness, the cause of which he could not begin to fathom. It only made the mystery of the hurried marriage and departure more of a puzzle than ever.

With the family's flourishing trade, it was always expected for Jean-Luc to marry well, especially with his sturdy, broad shoulders and handsome face, but the commandant's daughter had been a shock to the townspeople and fort families alike. The family had noble connections across the sea, and even if everyone pretended that it didn't matter in this new country, they still took notice of bonafide aristocrats.

The Delacroix family had operated their merchant shipping, and later passenger shipping business, from the island since the first Delacroix had arrived in the late 1700s, and the Alberts' family had served as captains on their fleet of vessels almost since the beginning. The current Captain Alberts had been brought up to the command of a ship, and had made this same crossing with his father many times since his boyhood. He had sailed on salt water only once as a younger man, and could never quite twist his mind around the desire some sailors had for a briny sea. The salt water had hurt his eyes and the scent of the ocean had seemed dank and dirty compared to the beautiful pristine blue of these northern lakes. He remembered sharing his distaste for the ocean with his father, and how much it had seemed to please the old man.

Aye, to sail on the lake took skill of a different kind, but she was a more faithful lover than the wide sea. She was familiar and beautiful, and he felt sometimes that he knew every inch of the lakes, only to find a twist, a turn, or a sandbar that he didn't recall from any prior journeys. A sudden storm, an unexpected hike or drop in temperature. These were all common occurrences that only a seasoned captain could feel coming before anyone else had even begun to chill, sweat, or feel the warning to take cover.

He did not have the time to dawdle and imagine the circumstances that would return this tempest of news to Mackinac all on one voyage, the machinations and dramas of society fell away in the face of his duties to his *Starlight*. These things had a way of revealing themselves in time, and so without a backward glance, he went to check on his crew and his coordinates. Captain Alberts could still detect that strange shift in the water, the same acrid smell on the air, confirming this would be no ordinary crossing.

His long strides carried him past Mme. Delacroix, and as he caught her eye, he felt her flinch, as if he had struck a sharp bodily blow to her. He stepped back, stunned at her reaction. Surprised at herself, she offered him a weak smile, and nodded in a way that seemed to apologize and dismiss the encounter all at once. He stared for a moment longer and felt his features soften. It wasn't often that anything, or anyone could divert his attention away from the demands of his ship, but there was something about the former Cora Ravensdale that had always seemed to pull people in. It reminded him of a book his father had read to him as a child about a Greek hero and his crew that were captured by a siren's song. She had been captivating even as a child, and it wasn't just to do with being fair of face.

She had a mysterious, solitary way about her. Her father had been known to remark that she would have made an intimidating son, if only she had been born a man. She was known to have a quick mind, and a sparkling wit. Though her features were not as fine and delicate as some of the other fort ladies, her face had character. Long, dark, curling hair, black as a raven's wing, an aquiline nose, a large mouth with full red lips and golden eyes. Eyes the color of the sunset, or a field of goldenrod, edged in soft green. They were not quite cat's eyes, but they seemed to spear into one's soul the same way, as if she were seeing your secrets.

There had been strange talk on the island a time or two, and he seemed to remember her being called a "seer" and an "enchantress" along with the French-Menominee

6

woman who had been her nurse. He had always dismissed those as mere stories or the idle talk of jealous women when his daughter had come home with tales. But, now, seeing the lake reflected in her eyes made him wonder. And now, no longer a Ravensdale, but a Delacroix. Although her face did not have the happiness he would have expected from a sudden, romantic elopement, it still seemed that marriage suited her. It added a depth to her beauty, a bridle to her wildness.

He smiled back at her and continued on his way toward the stern. It was then that he felt it, or perhaps ceased to feel it. He licked his finger and stuck his hand out dumbly before him, something even a new sailor wouldn't dare to do. It was gone. He looked up at the sails to see them hanging dejectedly, deserted by the soothing touch of the wind. It had simply stopped, suddenly. Sometime in that moment when he was lost in the eyes of Cora Delacroix, the wind had ceased to blow. They were becalmed, and as he heard the shouts of his men calling out to alert him to the situation, the light taps of their soft-soled shoes dancing along the planks of the schooner to receive their commands, he felt his lip tremble. The burning smell on the wind, that alteration of the roll of the waves, and he found that the fire of her eyes had burned black into his mind.

.2.
Cora

The past is a place we invent ourselves. A place that never existed the way we remember it, and is rewritten with every passing day. It was with these thoughts that she sighed, and realized how much she longed to crawl into a shell of a former self. A version of herself that didn't burn with the pain of experience and regret. To inhabit the husk of a former Cora and curl up into that past, disappearing from reality forever.

She hadn't always been this way. For most of her life she had been consumed with happiness, an easy rolling sequence of curiosity and the adoration of her close friends and family. But now? Now, she was plagued constantly by that same happiness of her own past, and the destructive consequences of her choices. She dreamed nightly of that other Cora, the carefree, reckless girl that was naked without her broad smiles and laughing eyes.

Her father had been sent to Fort Mackinac from Fort Independence in Boston. The change had been a great one, adjusting to the wild of this small island from the bustling thrum of the streets of the big city. Her father was the commandant of Fort Mackinac, though, and so her position as a leading lady on the island had been established early on.

Still, she had been quite young. She could not help but wonder whether anything might have changed, had she only known the outcome of those first days. She guessed not. Cora knew that her devil-may-care, fearless attitude and feelings of imperviousness would have led her straight here, like an arrow flying to its target.

Cora sat in her ship's cabin and wondered vaguely where Jean-Luc might be. She knew that he, and perhaps a few others on board had probably guessed what she had done. She had felt the ship cease to move the moment she wished it so. She had always tried to be careful with her wishes, knowing full well how disastrous the consequences of her whims could be. Spells was a strange word, and not at all how she thought of her powers. Indeed, they were more like desires made real. But, none of that seemed to matter now, and looking around for her little leather bound tome, she sighed, opened up her diary, and began to write.

It seems strange to be keeping an account of myself again. I always kept a diary when I was a girl, and now, again as a married woman. It was somehow appropriate when Jean-Luc came and brought it to me in my morning room yesterday, as I was overseeing the packing of the last of my things for our return home. He always seems to be reading my thoughts, or picking up on my whims. He had been the one to give me the first journal, too. Perhaps it is cyclical. All things are.

Home! What a strange word. Once I thought nothing of it, but I have learned all too well the power and succor that it can conjure when one has been taken away from it. I know I should think of poor, dear papa, and of my little Rosalind, my darling sister who I have missed so tenderly. But, I cannot help but picture the forests of

Mackinac when I think of the word, for there was the place I was always my truest self. I know in my heart, though, that it will never be as welcoming as it once was. It will never be a place that envelops me in the comfort and love that it had always used to. Not since that day. And never again.

My thoughts seem to continuously float back to the beginning, when all of this began, for it seems my life itself began on the island, and all of the pleasure and pain that has occurred since.

When I had only first arrived in Mackinac, it felt very foreign. It is odd now to think of it, as it is the only place I could imagine calling home. But at the time, for a young girl not yet nine, it was terrifying. I had never seen a native before we came to the Island, or the strange dresses of calico all the women wore. In Boston, we had been fashionable, and Mackinac was savage. Cut-off. It was almost as if we had stumbled into a different world entirely.

The most noticeable difference was the noise. In Boston, there was always comings and goings, gossip and animals, arguments and singing. The sound of so many footsteps in such a small place, the din of life resonated through me, so that it had become a part of me. In Mackinac, life and it's hustle and bustle went on in the same way, but it was...calmer. Less hurried. And just a few steps from town?

Freedom.

We had only been on the island for a few days when it happened. We had settled into our house, just down the street from the fur company, "the biggest house on Mackinac" my father had told us, merrily. Rosalind had clapped her little hands and kissed him, but my eyes had always drifted toward the never-ending blue spreading out on all sides, and over to the deep, haunting shadows of the trees. One of the fort ladies had sent over Waseya. The woman had called her a "chicot" and explained that she was half French and half Menominee. She was dressed in neat calico, her hair was brushed into two midnight braids. Her eyes caught mine and seemed to glimmer. She had kneeled down to shake both of our little girl hands, and we had known in a flash that she was special. She seemed exactly how a mother would, at least to us who had never had one.

11

My father had begun explaining our needs and workings of the house to Waseya, and I had simply walked out the door when no one was looking. It didn't occur to me to gain permission beforehand. The coolness of the forest was calling to me. I walked, on and on, my head pointing straight up into the branches of the trees before me, and I marveled in their height and in the intensity of the secret stillness of that place. I had never felt so at peace, and so wild at the same time, as if another part of myself was forming in that precise moment. That's when I heard it, the sound that would change my life. I wonder, if I hadn't been so bold, would I have run away from it and avoided this heartache? Would I truly want to have avoided it?

The sounds was twigs breaking under the feet of two boys that were of an age with me. The younger of the two had hair to match my own. Raven ringlets and eyes the color of a storm at sea, an azure blue that was almost blinding. The elder was taller and broader of shoulder, with sandy waves like the beach on a windy morning, and eyes the same green as the Mackinac pines. One light, one dark; one water, one earth. Two boys walking my way in the woodland clearing and I was frozen to the spot, intent on making friends.

The smaller of the two, with the dark curls and laughing eyes was bolder even than I. He met my gaze unflinchingly, and held it as long as I could bear it. As I think back, I see that he was daring me from that very first moment, that everything that would come between us was a series of challenges answered and dares given. But then, as young girl, every dare was a fantastic adventure, and so instead of seeing the warning, I saw the chance to grasp onto something extraordinary. He and the other boy stepped close to me in the clearing. The taller boy gave me a small, quick bow and smiled at me kindly, and a little nervously. He was glancing over at his brother as if he was used to his boldness, seemingly holding his breath for whatever fantastic thing he would say next.

Looking at them both closely, it was easy to see they were brothers. The same facial structure, the relaxed way they stood together, as if they had never been apart. But besides the physical similarities...it was plain even then that they had very little in common in their characters. The dark one reached out and grabbed my curls, inspecting them closely. I had been so alarmed, never having been touched by anyone outside my family besides, perhaps, one of my nurses. But, brazenly, he pulled the curl gently, until it was straight and let go, watching it twirl back into it's rightful shape. His older brother made a disapproving click with his teeth and exclaimed, "Mon dieu, Philippe! You cannot touch a girl's hair. You will apologize before you disgrace yourself any further. This is the daughter of the new commandant at the fort. My apologies mademoiselle, my brother is young, and poorly behaved."

Even then there was a kindness there. In those dark green, forest eyes, an understanding, a desire to obey the rules and do what was right. But, I didn't think much of it then. I never did. I thought more of young Philippe for rudely sticking his tongue out at his older brother, and then looking back to me with a raised eyebrow, gauging my reaction. I smiled conspiratorially, and a bond was formed.

"Jean-Luc, you must be mistaken. The great commandant at the fort would not have daughter so cloaked in dirt that she looked like an Indian squaw. This must be some girl of the forest."

He laughed merrily at his own joke and my mouth hung agape, unused to being treated thus, and unsure if it bothered me or not. The older boy, Jean-Luc began apologizing in earnest, but any confusion as to whether I was a lady or not disappeared when I shot forward and knocked Philippe straight to the ground. I had stilled my mind, and the forest around us had grown silent, the very birds responding to my temper by quieting. The boys had looked around, dazed at the idea that I had caused this. Both brothers eyes' met, and they shared a secret smile. Philippe had popped right up, looked at me appraisingly and said to his brother, "I think she'll fit in very well." He grabbed my hand, and they both pulled me into the woods, two sets of black curls bobbing like ocean waves, and a tall boy with hair like sunlight running along behind.

I found myself venturing out into the forest whenever I could sneak away from my father and sister. As for Waseya, I had seen her keen, knowing eyes following after me deep into the wood. It seemed that she knew my secret without me having to speak it aloud, and she silently acquiesced to the wildness inside me, as if she herself knew what it was to hide her spirit under the garments of polite society.

I would amble through the boughs and branches, snagging my skirts and catching brambles and burs in my midnight curls. I would hear them in the clearing long before I would see them. Playing their war games or building fortifications with fallen limbs, as Philippe pleaded with Jean-Luc to tell him stories of adventure and daring. The boys would beg me unceasingly to use my magic for other tricks. To turn the leaves from green to red, as a mock autumn surrounding our play. Or to call down the birds to rest on my shoulders and the rabbits to eat from my hands. My powers lay only in nature, I could command the whole of it, asking it kindly for its blessing, which it eagerly bestowed upon me. Mackinac was a flower waiting for me to request it to bloom, a gift from the spirits. I suppose, I was a girl favored by the manitou. I do not remember when the magic within me began, but it must have been in those first days on the island. Now it seems such a part of myself that to try to think of the beginning is like trying to remember the first time I breathed. It is impossible to know. One day, it just simply Was, and I couldn't recall what my life was like without it.

We would spend our days traipsing through the bracken and playing hiding games with the Rast brothers and my sister, Rosalind. Enlisting the trees and leaves to bend in such a way as to hide us from whomever was looking, so that we could never be found during the games, except by Nicholas Rast, who seemed to have a kind of power over the island all his own. The trees would sprout branches for me, as I climbed higher and higher, never having to fear finding my next hold. I would walk through the sunshine surrounded by butterflies and the admiring smiles of the brothers Delacroix. Magic seemed to be everywhere, surrounding our play, as much a part of the island as the moss that grew or the squirrels on the branches. I think still that it was because of them that my magic got stronger as I grew older, allowing me to help with ailing children and sick animals, giving me healing powers and goodness that I was proud to possess.

I felt at one with the island, the moment I had first plunged into its leafy depths. And so too, I had felt one with my new friends, for they seemed a part of the island, and soon became a facet of my *everyday life. I often have trouble remembering a time when my whole body did not hum with the rhythm of the pulse of Mackinac. My wishes becoming a weave in the fabric of the wilderness surrounding me, calling me to command it and bend it lovingly into the twists of my fancy, creating beauty and communion with the lushness of my surroundings.*

I look back on the simplicity of those days and my breath catches in my chest...such dreams we had! Such lives we would lead! And I, but a girl, but immediately an accepted comrade in all of their plans. I wished for both of the boys to like me; I wished so hard for them to need my company, and like the rest of my magic, the wishes seemed to come more and more true. Their faces lit up when I would approach their games, their diversions were that much more diverting...

The sound of the cabin door opening brought Cora out from her reverie of remembrances. She pulled her ringlets away from her face and she was met with the startling green clarity of her husband's eyes. He always looked like he was searching her for something, trying to plumb the depths of her to understand her mood, her wishes, her needs. He was...kind. He was always kind, and it drove her mad, because he had no cause to be kind to her. Not after all that had happened.

"You've stopped the boat." It wasn't a question, and he seemed to not need an answer. It still seemed strange to Cora sometimes how easily he accepted her powers, she almost wondered if he would understand if she explained how she had used them in the past. If he would, or could forgive?

"Cora, I know you do not want to return to the island yet, but...it is time. Please, bring an end to this calm, before you drive all of the sailors to mutiny and the passengers to desperation."

He said this all with a smile, and he stepped to close the gap between them. He leaned forward and kissed her forehead, lingering just a moment longer than was necessary. Before she even had time to reply, he had stepped back toward the hallway, tipped his hat, and disappeared out the door, closing it softly.

She looked back to the diary lying open, and frowning, closed it. That was enough remembering for now.

.3.

Nicholas

Nicholas stood on the starboard side of the schooner and gazed off into the glimmering water. The sunlight caught every ripple of the blue as if trying its hardest to gather the power needed to move the ship. He sighed deeply and looked down to the object he was worrying in his hands. It was a wooden pipe, the wood grain worn in places from constant use. Though, Nicholas Rast was not a smoker, and had never been a smoker. The pipe had received more use than many, as to him it had served as a kind of talisman. His brother, Edward, had given it to him almost ten long years ago.

It had been a day like today, but mercifully with more wind, ensuring that he would be on his way to his new life quickly. Not so, now. Every remnant of that life, that other life, had been snatched away. Nicholas peered over the side and shook his head with disgust. Of course the wind had given up! What other way to welcome his return to this rude, primitive place amongst people who were his family, but as much like strangers as it was possible to be. His only connection to them was this same red blood he could feel pumping furiously through his veins.

He missed London and the diversions of the continent already. His sunlit tours through Florence, Turin and Venice, sampling all of the Renaissance masters and grasping at the opportunities for moonlight masquerades. He recalled the golden hours spent in the villas of visiting nobility, and had cultivated relationships with men of importance. He had studied the writers that everyone was discussing and earned the reputation of a "Man on the Rise", a man "in the know". Through his mother's relatives and their connections, he had just enough money to be fashionable, and just enough mystery to be avant garde. He had been a cultured colonial returned triumphantly to a fawning Europe whose rules he had learned perfectly.

He thought of his roaming adventures in Madrid and Vienna, the young ladies of accomplishment and beauty, the architecture of the most brilliant masters of any age… this world was closed to him now. He was the second son, the extraneous, the prodigal, the profligate, whoring, spendthrift who cared naught for anything but leisure— and now it was gone.

His easy sunshine life had been ripped from him the same moment his brother Edward had been ripped from this world. The second son no more, but instead the *only* son. The keeper of legacies and bearer of responsibilities.

When he had first received the letter, he had ignored it for a week. He could feel the evil news inside of it. It fairly burned his hand to hold the envelope, as if it were infested with a pestilent, dark spirit who would cause him bodily harm. He'd had these strange feelings all of his life, a "gift" he'd never fully understood. He had grown up with tales of Indian magic, the connection with spirits and the The Great Manitou governing all things. Most of the white children had heard the stories from the Ojibwe, Huron or Menominee people who lived in huts near the water. The stories were one part of his past that he had never forgotten, perhaps because it was a part of his past that had nothing to do with his father and mother, or their expectations for their extra son.

He had opened his escritoire at his Uncle George's manor house every day, and had simply stared at the missive, before closing it all back up again, forgetting all about the nefarious letter as the day unfolded with its usual pleasures. Fishing with his uncle in the brook, or reading with his cousins Catherine and Maisie. But finally, he began to hear the whispers in his mind. His brother's voice, pushing the pipe into his hands, his brother's voice, calling out to him as he boarded the ship that would take him to New York, and then to London. His brother's voice as they played with the Delacroix brothers in the woods, building with the fallen branches and marching like the soldiers in the fort. Although it had burned his fingers so that they were red and tender for hours afterward, he had finally opened the letter.

He had not thought much of his family in the ten years he had been away. He had been sent to live with his aunt and uncle to guard him from the consequences of an unfortunate occurrence on the island, and it also served as an attempt to keep the Rast family involved in English fashion and society. His aunt and uncle didn't have a son of their own, and he had always thought, perhaps, they would adopt him and make him their heir. He had taken to his new home almost immediately, with only flashes of the winking blue of the Great Lakes, or a brilliant green bursting unbidden in his memory. But staring at his mother's writing on the page brought it all back. All of the memories, all of the heartbreaks and the scandal. The pain and all of the remembered pleasures. His brother, Edward was dead. He had died with honor, swimming out into the harbor to help sailors during a brief but mighty storm. Strange things happened in the water near Mackinac Island, he remembered. Something about the mixing of the lakes and the nature of the winds on the water. His hands came up to hold his face as the tears streamed down, and he found that the wetness of those traitor tears was the only healing salve for his burned hands. He thought of his tall, dashing brother. His kind, intelligent hero, and he was stung with the realization that he was the greatest man he had ever met. In all of his travels, in all of his adventures, he had never met a man equal to his brother in civility, or in character. Nicholas may have learned all the court etiquette, the latest dances and was as comfortable discussing art as he was politics, but he would never measure up to his brother Edward. His dead brother that he would never know as a grown man. And this was the sharpest cut of them all.

His eyes were gazing angrily out onto the water, not a ghost of wind tickled his russet hair. Not a single cloud fought back the intense stabbing of the sun's rays on his neck. The pipe was in his hand, he could feel the smooth, comforting weight of it is his palm. He had come here to the side, alone, to throw it out into that infuriating blue. To be rid of this ghostly amulet that seemed to hold a piece of his brother's soul within its wooden bowl. He scowled. He could not bring himself to be rid of it. He drew too much of his strength from it, a silly idea he had cultivated from the day it had been gifted, as if it retained a piece of the giver inside. Sighing, he replaced the well-loved pipe back into the inner pocket of his double breasted coat. Just as he was bringing his hand back to the schooner's railing, he heard the distinct sound of chuckling behind him. Spinning around rapidly he scowled at the first man he saw.

"Is there something humorous about me, sir?" Nicholas spat angrily. He realized that he recognized the man, but could not recall his name. Someone from the continent, surely.

"Might I ask the name of the man who uses me so ill as to make me the source of his private amusement?"

He could feel the anger within him burning, he knew he was overreacting, but was hopeless to control it.

"Steady, sir. 'Twas not I that was laughing, but some members of the crew".

The man gestured behind him to two smirking sailors who quickly went back to pulling at the rigging as if they hadn't been looking at Nicholas at all.

"My name is Jean-Luc Delacroix, and I believe, we are known to one another. If my memory serves, you were great friends with me and my brother, Philippe, and I had always been on good terms with your late brother, Edward. May God rest their souls."

Jean-Luc looked up to meet Nicholas's eyes, and found confusion there.

"I see, sir, that you hadn't heard. I too, am in mourning. My brother, like yours, has left this world. He died at the end of last summer, nine months ago."

Death was always close by, in Nicholas's experience, but it was strange to think how many young men were lost. He wondered briefly what other playfellows from his youth he would never see again. Philippe had always been a wild boy, too wild for young Nicholas even to keep up with, but he realized now that his laughing eyes and bawdy jokes would be missed. He thought to inquire how he met his end, but thought better of it. His own anger at his perceived slight had bubbled down to a manageable level by this point, and he didn't want to risk any more bad feeling. Sometimes, it was almost as if he had an evil trapped within him, a rogue spirit that caused his moods to blacken at the slightest offense. In an effort to soften the confrontation, Nicholas inquired after the Delacroix family and the business of shipping. When he inquired if Jean-

Luc had been on business in Detroit long, and if he had travelled alone, he noticed a raw grimace of pain dart across the man's face.

"No, I've brought my wife."

This was all he would say, before offering Nicholas a small smile and leaning against the railing next to him. He studied Jean-Luc's face as unobtrusively as he could. He knew that he was a few years older than himself, and remembered his steady, quiet demeanor even as a child. He had always been strong, and big for his age, which only made him more formidable as a grown man. But there was a kindness in his face, and a constancy in his character that could be heard in his carefully chosen words, and seen in his warm green eyes. A handsome man. Nicholas wondered briefly what sort of woman he had for a wife. Out of the corner of his eye, a shape moving toward them caught his attention. He could just make out long, wild, black hair like thorns in a wood, and even from several yards away, he could see the golden-starshine eyes in the woman's face. His mouth hung open, in shock. Not so much because of her beauty, it was something else. Something that he hadn't seen in any of his travels. A sense of character and strength, a sense of power and magic flowed from her. He felt again that he was back on the island, listening to the stories of the Indian women on the beach. Nicholas felt almost that he was face to face with the Great Manitou himself, and the feeling of this marvelous woman coming nearer to him with her billowing skirts and flowing hair, was almost too much for him to bear. He reached out and grabbed Jean-Luc's arm,

"My God, man. Is she real? That is the most magnificent woman I have ever seen."

He could hardly stop the words from tumbling from his mouth, they came unbidden and unwanted, but he was powerless to hold them back.

Jean-Luc looked at him strangely and looked at the woman approaching. Then tipping his head backward he let out a loud, hearty guffaw that brought Nicholas straight out of his fascination. He grew hot with anger again, at being laughed at, for letting his guard down around this man from his past. But, before he could say anything more, Jean-Luc reached out for the woman's hand and pulling her close to him, said,

"Mon ami, this captivating woman is my wife! But you may know her better as Cora Ravensdale, eldest daughter of the commandant of Fort Mackinac, and our former playfellow."

Nicholas felt his face grow warm, not for the first time that day, but this time it was with an odd feeling of confusion and embarrassment, instead of anger. He stammered out a vague apology and tried to reconcile the woman before him with his memories of a small, wild girl that had seemed to command the games of the boys even as a child. She had held secret allure then as well, but it had ripened into something else with womanhood. What was this woman's power? What did it mean? What other surprises were waiting for him on this journey?

:4:

Jean-Luc

Jean-Luc could feel Cora's arm stiffen in his, and patting her hand absently, he let it go. She gave him a look which told him that she wasn't bothered by his touch, but rather was in a hurry to get somewhere and did not wish to be held back. These little wordless signals between them felt natural, as they had grown up together and children have a way of communicating that is too often forgotten in adulthood. A soundless, subconscious conversation between them that somehow becomes untranslatable as we get older. This language that existed between the two of them was slowly returning, a mother tongue spoken after years in the foreign land of adulthood. He linked his arm back through hers, and tipping his hat to a bewildered Nicholas, he walked on with his wife.

His wife! As if he had ever imagined that he might marry the belle of the isle, the keeper of his heart. He had known her for what she was from the moment he had set eyes on her as a twelve year old boy, the same moment he had lost his heart to her. It had been strange because up until that moment he hadn't realized that there was a romantic heart in his chest to be given. Even then, at his young age, he had been reared in equal parts Catholic Church and Indian legend. And while he had never skipped mass as Philippe so often did, instead fulfilling his role by his mother's side, singing hymns and genuflecting with the congregation, still the Indian's stories meant more. It was difficult to ignore the tales there on the island where every thread of nature felt like part of an intricate weaving in the tapestry of the Great Manitou.

The island, sometimes, seemed to live inside of him. The golden sand interspersed between the rocks of the beaches was his hair, the summer leaves in his eyes and the sing-song of the chickadee sounding the rhythm of his heartbeat. Which is why he already knew her when he saw her, for Cora was a piece of the manitou spirit itself, and so she commanded him the same as the island did.

He was fascinated by her. Not because she was perfect or unflawed, but because it seemed to him that in a shake of her jet curls was the dancing spirits, that her laugh was the sound of the rippling Mackinac waters, her anger a storm on the lake. She *was* the island, and the island was a part of him, and so he too, had been a part of her from that first moment so many years ago. Enchantments sprang from her eyes and floated from her fingertips, as comfortable with ravens roosting on her shoulders as she was making the leaves swirl in a cyclone around her as she walked through the forest. The word "witch" had never been one he associated with her, because it was the island itself that was an extension of her somehow, and anyone that knew her could feel there was nothing evil in her power, only something raw and earthly. Something beautiful that had drawn him to her from that first sight and had never let go. It was this same power and enchantment within her that she had seemed to hide from him of late. He sensed her drawing a veil about herself, shutting him out, and any associations he might have to the unhappy past.

Jean-Luc glanced back at Nicholas Rast dressed like a European dandy, which, he was certain, was exactly what he had been. His elaborate dress was still eliciting chuckles from the rough and tumble crew, who had doubtless never seen man nor woman dressed in such finery. He pitied Nicholas. He knew what it was to lose a brother, though, Jean-Luc was the first born and so had always had the family responsibility resting squarely on his shoulders. Turning around once more, he thought he could see something of the lost little boy in the man's eyes, the same lost look he had carried the morning he had been sent away. It had been such a scandal at the time, but now, compared to his and Cora's behavior, he wondered if Nicolas' transgression, committed so many years ago, would be overlooked. He wondered if the man would be equal to the tasks his family would set him, and at the same time, Jean-Luc missed the steadfastness of the late, older brother, Edward. Never bosom friends, the two had enjoyed a quiet, easy friendship, built on common temperaments and expectations. These traits, however, were not echoed in the younger brother; Nicholas seemed to move to a different beat entirely.

Their progress came to an end near the prow of the ship. She was leaning forward ever so slightly, trying to catch the breath of the lake on her face. After a time, Jean-Luc came out of this happy reverie to realize that he had been watching her for a long while. She simply stood, immovable, her face remaining impassive, except for moments when her lips would move strangely, as if she was speaking to someone he could not see. And, perhaps, she was, but the question was—who?

The months before Philippe's death had been filled with secrets. Three souls who never had an unspoken thought from each other, had, quite suddenly, fallen silent. They had probably thought he didn't know, but he was neither stupid nor naïve. He was connected to them both after all, and so what they imagined to be secrets, was to him painful screams of admission. A wall of lies loudly being built between them. Since Philippe's death, Cora and Jean-Luc had become in some ways more closely tied, and not only through marriage vows. Instead, tied by their mutual grief and hopelessness, and their mutual deceptions. At the same time there existed a bridge of connection between them that neither one was willing or able to traverse. Separated by secrets she thought he didn't know, and by his inability to confess that he did.

"What are you whispering into the wind?" Jean-Luc asked, smiling more broadly than he truly felt.

Her eyes shifted toward him, suddenly alarmed. "Whispering? Nothing. I wasn't speaking at all."

He tried to make light of it,

"Ahh, but you cannot fool me—your lips were moving!"

She looked as if she was about to protest, so he hurried along adding, "But never mind that now, you can tell me some other time. I have been wanting to ask you, what type of animal do you think our old friend Rast has turned out to be?"

His green eyes glittered in the rays of the setting springtime sun. The corners of her mouth began to lift, ever so slightly.

This was a favorite game of theirs. Her nurse, Waseya, would have them all by the kitchen fire when Cora's father was away with his duties at the fort. She would tell them the legends of her people, and the legends of the island. They would soak up her words like a dandelion drinks the rain from the earth. There was something ethereal about this small woman with her deep copper skin and straight black braids. Something indescribable, she belonged to no time and every time, and he could just as easily see her telling stories to the children or swirling in the wind through the trees. Neither old nor young, pretty nor ugly, it was her voice that held them captive as they peered into the fire. Magic, the legends would come to life, dancing in the flames.

One part of the creation story that was shared by many of the tribes on the island, told of the Great Manitou and his desire to create more men on earth for his son, The Great Father, and his wife, who came from the people of the wind. She was said to be as bright as the sun, beautiful as the moon and playful as the whirling stars.

At this point in Waseya's story, they all would glance at Cora, thinking that this first woman must have been the image of this glimmering girl in their midst. Cora's cheeks would turn the color of the spring moss roses, and Waseya would continue, telling the children that a time came when the Great Manitou came down from the sky and saw the need for more men. It was said that he created these men from different four-footed animals, and this explained why even today, the men of the earth retain traces of their animal being. Some men are cowardly and skittish, they came from the rabbit. Some are bloodthirsty warriors, like soldiers at the fort; these men are descended from the wolf. This explained the ways of men, brave, cowardly, fierce, nurturing, traits lent to them from the animals that gave them life.

As children they had played at the game almost constantly, deciding which animal every man and woman on the island had come from. So, it was with this childhood game on their minds that they turned their eyes back to Nicholas Rast. Cora took one look at him and pronounced,

"Stoat. Obviously. Jean-Luc, that is an easy one!"

Her eyes laughed back at him. He so liked to bring the sunshine back to her visage. For a moment he was hypnotized by her, how he would love to rush back to Detroit and keep her away from any memories of the past year, or any ridicule she was bound to encounter back on the shores of Mackinac. He knew from the letters from his mother that the whole island was in a state of shock by their hasty marriage and rapid departure, and on the heels of Philippe's death…he couldn't think of it now. He would lose himself in her eyes, for just a moment longer.

Her smile lost its sweetness and began to fall back into a frown.

"I think I will rest again in our cabin before we eat dinner. Things are beginning to feel a bit restless here on deck. Excuse me."

She turned to leave, and before he could stop himself, he reached out and grabbed her hand, squeezing it tightly, saying,

"Cora, please. I do not know how much of a hand you had in this, but please send the wind back to our sails before moods become strained on the ship. Please."

His eyes were full of pleading, and it was because of the kindness in his face, in his entire attitude that she snapped.

"You could not begin to understand the powers at work. This ship will move when it is time, and not a moment before. In fact, I suspect circumstances will become much worse before they improve."

Her eyes blazed with the fire of the rising sun, and she spun quickly on her heel, clenching both fists. Before Jean-Luc could consider the meaning of her words, or go after her to calm her down, the shouting began. The angry words of restless men, carrying loudly over the silence of the unmoving lake.

.5.

Walter

If he was made to confess, Captain Alberts had been discreetly checking and double checking his instruments, and had by this point in the calm, adopted an attitude of impatient acceptance. Every seasoned mariner knows that the weather cannot be controlled or cajoled into doing a man's bidding. He had a very foolish glimmer of hope when Jean-Luc had suggested offering a little tobacco to the Manitou, as is legend. However willing he was to oblige this fancy, he noticed that both men looked doubtful as they each emptied the contents of their snuffbox onto the motionless blue glass.

After the initial hours of waiting for wind, Captain Alberts had taken to pacing the length of the schooner slowly, as if he could delay the time passing and somehow keep this ship on schedule. Although he knew no man can force the wind, it did seem eerily unnatural how long this calm had lasted. He had felt that initial shift in the air looking into the unending sunset of Cora's eyes, and it was as if the water itself had copied the depths inside of them.

He could have sworn she had something to do with it, but that was nonsense, wasn't it? She was a woman, not a sorceress. No matter the cause, he was terribly off schedule now though, and he could hear the men discussing supper. An entire day, lost. His cargo would be ripening below decks, fish from as far away as Maine would all spoil if kept out in the growing heat of the mature spring. Many of the barrels had been packed with ice in lieu of salt, a preference and expense requested by a few of the fort families, a choice that the captain now thought ill-advised.

He had been in calms before of course, but none that seemed so malevolent. A ship becalmed in the ocean may sit for days or weeks, but generally the winds of the lakes were kinder, only leaving a ship stranded for a few anxious hours. The men on board seemed more out of sorts than he had ever remembered them, and all around was an attitude of despairing hopelessness. It was a trial indeed to keep his spirits up, much less that of an entire crew wanting to return home. Their journey generally would only take a space of three days or so, moving at a steady clip. Any delay at all, however, could prove catastrophic for the business of the shipping company.

Shouts on deck. The angry sound of too many bored men, reveling in the opportunity to be insulted by each other. Captain Alberts felt his blood begin to sing in his veins. As much as he wanted to avoid discord on his ship, he found that there existed a part of him that was relieved that he now had some task to perform. The roaring shouts grew ever louder, indicating that two men had been singled out to fight and were probably now circling one another, their anger fed by the excitement of the onlookers. The captain stomped towards the fracas and at first could not see beyond the crowd of sailors. He nudged a few aside, pushing and pulling his way to the front. When he got to the center, however, he could not believe his eyes. One of the fellows fighting was a sailor, but the other was a passenger. One of his most trusted men, Big Charlie, was swinging again and again at the jaw of a man whose lip was already split and bleeding. The other man was doing a fine job of blocking most of Big Charlie's jabs, though the captain was alarmed to think what one good hit could do. For a split second, he got a clear look at the other man. Disbelieving, Captain Alberts felt all the blood rush from his face, and he was glued to the spot. It took him a few moments, but the sound of a familiar voice and hand on his shoulder brought him back to the import of the moment.

"Bon Dieu, Alberts! This cannot go on. We must stop them before Rast is pummeled to death!"

Jean-Luc yelled aloud over the clamor of the fight and the shouts of the sailors. Something in his tone had shook the captain from his stupor, and he charged in to the melee and gave both men a hard shove, simultaneously, in opposite directions. Big Charlie, immediately recognizing his captain, and realizing his error, put his hands up in submission, as if blocking the blow of his superior's disappointment.

When Captain Alberts looked to young Rast, however, he saw with some dismay that he was laughing. Thick red blood fell from his mouth and dripped onto the pale cravat tied, just so, at his neck. His eyes looked at everyone and no one as a strange hollow laugh tumbled from his mouth. Then, a terrible, disconnected voice coming from Nicholas shouted,

"Animals! Savages! I have left the majesty of England, the Empire of empires, to be locked into a zoo!"

The laughter continued as the men who had gathered for the fight had begun to disperse at the sight of the captain. Some seemed entranced by the mania exhibited by this wealthy, foppishly dressed, bleeding man who was hurling insults not only at them, but on the entire culture of their home territory. Nicholas Rast's laughter petered off into nothing and it seemed to the captain that he was swatting the air near his ear, as if a fly were buzzing into it.

Captain Alberts turned to see Jean-Luc cautiously approaching the young man, and as he did, Nicholas looked to Alberts like a drowning man disappearing beneath the waves, tied down with an anchor of unswimmable weight. Nicholas collapsed bodily into M. Delacroix's arms, creating a striking scene of weakness giving way to strength. A scene Alberts had watched many times with Jean-Luc and his younger brother, Philippe.

He sighed in disbelief that young Rast was the man who would replace Edward at the fur company. That the hopes of the entire Rast family and the future of the fur trade in Mackinac fell on this sad, confused, broken man's shoulders. At the same time, he had a guilty feeling of relief that Jean-Luc was the brother that had survived in the Delacroix family, the man who would someday be his employer. Strange how destiny had chosen which brothers to take. During the chaos, he had thought for a moment he saw Philippe, heard his laugh, heard him cheering along with the other sailors, goading the men to hurt each other. But no, Philippe Delacroix was dead and buried, and done making mischief. It had been a long day, and obviously the captain needed rest.

He made his way to his own captain's cabin, and poured himself a glass of fine imported spirits, a gift from Alexander Rast, the unfortunate Nicholas' father. He took a small sip, as he wasn't much of a drinking man, and put his head into his hands. It felt heavy, carrying far too many cares and worries within its creases and drooping from his mustachios. He cast the drink aside and left the cabin, feeling abruptly an itch to be outside, with his eyes toward the horizon line.

As darkness began to to creep in on tip-toes with the yawning of the day, the sun began to close its eye and coax any passengers still on deck to the safety and monotony of their close cabins. The good captain noted the air had taken on a staleness, almost a rot, and he shook his head in wonderment. Dreading whatever else this strange voyage had in store for his *Starlight*.

:6:

Jean-Luc

That night, Jean-Luc lay in bed so close to Cora that he could hear the rhythm of her breathing. The calm up and down cadence of her inhale and exhale mocked his own soul, which was a violent torrent of emotion. A swirling tempest of conflicting feelings that whispered voiceless, only heard by his own ravaged mind. The chaos of the fight, the strange words Nicholas had spoken, the look in his eyes—he couldn't understand or explain any of it. And then, there was Cora. Lying next to her was a kind of sweet torture. He turned again and again under the thin blanket, hot from passion for a woman he longed to hold to his chest, yet frozen by the chasm that lay between their hearts. A chasm created by his own brother.

To Philippe, everything had been a kind of cage if you looked at it the right way. When they were young, this had meant their stately home on the main street of town. Their father always said it was close enough to the harbor and Cross Shipping to keep him in the know, and just far enough away to enable him a break with his business. Philippe, though, was a penned animal, only really himself when they could steal away into the wilderness of the island. Indoors he would be nervous and quick to anger, and it was always a relief to their mother when Jean-Luc would pull him out of the house and away from her china. They escaped to the green of the trees, or the crunch of the new fallen snow, and always to Cora, a bird as wild as he. The two of them needed the outdoors to feel their freedom, but for Jean-Luc, the forest was a place of connection, not abandon.

As childhood gave way to adolescence, and then adulthood, Philippe's cage had expanded to include the entire island. He reminded Jean-Luc sometimes of their mother's pug, clawing helplessly at the door to get out, as if his whole being depended on what was just outside his limits. As the years went by, Philippe would grow distracted when the friends would gather in the wood, he was no longer interested in the simple pleasures they had found there in childhood. Instead, every nerve seemed to be straining somewhere beyond, a part of him already deserting this place.

And so, it was natural that Philippe would seek the life of a voyageur, with Jean-Luc to take on the weighty mantle of the shipping company. His parents were frankly relieved for Philippe to find an occupation that would feed his recalcitrant, vagabond, spirit and allow him to survive by his own means. Trapping and tracking the best and most elusive furs, the hardy, harsh life of a man in the wilderness, surrounded by his comrades, this was the life of a voyageur, and a perfect fit for Philippe. There had been a time when their father had imagined that the two brothers would front the company together, presenting solidarity, a true family business. But as the years wore on, and Philippe grew ever wilder, their parents had simply accepted it was not to be, and slowly had begun to release Philippe to his own wishes. And with that release, came a tighter grip on Jean-Luc, as if it was possible that in taking their expectations away for even a moment, it would be giving him time to reconsider their hopes for him.

Foolishly, as lonely as he knew he would be without his unpredictable younger brother, he couldn't help but hope that his absence would offer him more time alone with Cora. Alas, this too was not meant to come to pass. For, the voyageur leaves when the temperatures begin to fall, and as the cruel, white grasping hands of winter came to Mackinac, he saw less and less of Cora in the woods or around Arch Rock. He would hope to glimpse her near Devil's Kitchen where a cobbler had set up shop, and in the past had looked on their meetings with secrecy, and plenty of winking. But, after many cold afternoons of walking through the new fallen snow, hoping to find her, one night he had come home and found her at his dinner table.

Not in his home, but instead news of her, from his mother's eager mouth, over dinner. She had heard from the women in town that Cora was now assisting with the nursing at the fort, and also with the village children when illness would sweep through, a cruel wind on the island. The women in town had clucked their tongues in surprise that Cora's father had encouraged his eldest, prized, daughter to sequester herself with disease and sorrow. Jean-Luc's own father had given him a pointed look, communicating approval at her generosity and bravery, and Jean-Luc had to turn his head in order to not be caught blushing. Her fierceness in the face of tragedy did not surprise him at all.

Then, there were the society parties, though, because of the sickness on the island they had been much more subdued that year. The Delacroix family was often included in these gatherings, the men in town and at the fort hoping to curry favor with M. Delacroix; each wishing to be the first man he thought of when all of the fine

Cross Shipping imports came into harbor Upon entrance to the fête, Jean-Luc would rush right to her side; she would smile graciously, offer him a few meaningless words, and then move on to the next person with whom her father wished her to speak. Indoors she was a fire that had been snuffed out, sitting calmly with her sister, or dancing with an officer, or a visiting banker from Detroit or New York. She was but a spark of the blaze of the woman he knew from the forest or standing atop Arch Rock, black hair whipping in the wind, a goddess of the island. She was not made for the smallness of these parties. But she was loath to admit to the closeness of their friendship, for fear it would be taken away or disapproved of, so he demurred. For her to reveal her true self away from the crush and crowd of this small society would have to be enough for his fool heart to feed on.

With the growing heat of the spring came a return to their walks through the middle of the island and to their games. He had immediately sensed a change in her, where she had left him in the fall but a girl, during the harrowing months of the winter she had matured into a formidable woman. What had been foolhardy meetings as children, would appear to be totally improper as they had grown into young adults. He felt in those first sun-kissed evenings a shift in himself too. He had always burned for her, but the flames had now been fanned to a feverish height. His thoughts grew bold, and his interest could not be hidden. But still, he bridled them, reigning them back into his heart. The timing hadn't felt right yet, but looking back he knew it had been a mistake not to act sooner. It had all been so new, and they both fully knew that both the Delacroix and the Ravensdale families would have been in hysterics to learn the truth of those clandestine, stolen days.

Jean-Luc's river of thought dried up momentarily, as Cora turned in her sleep to face him. Her forehead was creased with worry, and her cherry lips moved quickly in agitation. She then began moving as if running. Instinctively, he reached to caress her cheek, whispering,

"Shh, mon coeur. It is merely a dream and I am here." Though she didn't wake, her fretting ceased and her breathing slowed. Her forehead lost its line and she seemed to rest easier. Rest, though, would not come to Jean-Luc. She was so close to him, and still he could not begin to guess the thoughts that whirled around in her mind. How was she able to control so much of her life with her whims, her connection to nature, her conjurings and enchantments, and yet not see how easily she could save Jean-Luc? How could she not see how a touch of softness from her would be the making of him? If she could only consent to knock down the walls in her heart, to lay bare the truth of her feelings, to begin to heal the cutting pain of last year, then they could rise above it. He felt the truth of this, and wished he knew the words, or had the courage to say them.

There was something about that summer, though. Could it really have been just this past summer? Jean-Luc almost sat straight up, he was so shocked by the thought. This whole past year in Detroit he had busied himself so much with Cora's health, and the running of the company that he had not so much as paused to reflect back on what had brought them there in the first place. Now, all of the forgetting was catching up to him, so that it was now the only thing that flowed through his mind. So much could change in a year. Jean-Luc sighed, if only Philippe's brigade would have been delayed, even for just a week, perhaps it would all be different. If only.

He had truly believed in those first steady warm days of May that he could make her love him. Something *had* shifted between them. She noticed his attentions and seemed to return them, her eyes lingering longer and longer than they had used to. Their walks carrying on until twilight, leaving both of their families demanding to know their whereabouts, the same worries echoed in both households. The breathless excitement to reach the clearing near Arch Rock and see the other already waiting there. It had all been falling into place. With enough time, he was convinced he could have shown her father he was a suitable match, that he was true and worthy of her.

But, Philippe and the rest of his *hommes du nord* were not delayed. In fact, they had been the first back for the season. And not only that, but somehow his impetuous younger brother had managed to win the black feather of his brigade when Clement, the old brigade leader, had died that winter during a fierce storm. Philippe was now the Lake of the Woods Brigade leader, and he would take all the spoils. His younger brother returned, and to anyone on shore that day, he would have appeared as the King of Mackinac itself.

Jean-Luc could not have recognized the trouble that would come from those two heads of curling black hair embracing as he came upon them under the trees. He had seen a beginning of something in that moment, but if he had looked closely, he would have seen something concluding between them all as well.

Letting out another loud sigh in the prison darkness of the cabin, Jean-Luc looked to the figure of his wife, held cocooned by a single shaft of moonlight. How he had loved this woman, and how passionately he still did. He swore quietly at no one, his words unheard in the world; wishing violently, for the millionth time, that all of this madness had not been on his path to her.

·7·
Cora

It is said that the island of Mackinac came to be only after a great fog had shrouded the straits for three suns. When the haze finally lifted, there lay Mackinac, adorned like a glittering treasure with its share of limestone cliffs, majestic trees, and blooming flowers. When he saw its rare beauty, the Gitchi Manitou came to dwell on Mackinac and claim it as his home.

She had dreamt of the legend the night before, basked in wonder at the contentment of the Manitou, marveled at his masterpiece. She had found it only fitting that the aimless, drifting schooner should awake to a fog so thick as to be like smoke from a great fire. She had spied it through the porthole in the early morning light of the cabin, the smoky fingers of the mist bidding her come on deck. Cora had quickly donned one of her oldest gowns, dove gray with puffed sleeves, and for a brief moment remembered her father's proud face when presenting her with the fabric, fresh off a merchant ship, so many years ago. She wondered if it had come on this very schooner. Dismissing the thought, she crept out to experience the anonymity and brief respite from memories that a walk in the swirling fog granted her.

Each step on deck resonated with a deep, oaky thud. She felt that she was swallowing the fog with every breath, or perhaps it was slowly consuming her. She opened her mouth to laugh aloud at the insanity of her dream made real, but it died on her lips, she knew that laughing at destiny would only bring sorrow.

It was an odd kind of freedom to roam in the fog. Voices were muted, and she realized that besides some brave crew members, the rest of the sailors and passengers had stayed safely below deck in the warmth of their own cabins. She wasn't afraid though, for this was of her own making. A delicious escape from the turmoil of their journey and the questions she saw hanging from her husband's lips. She cursed herself softly for her selfishness in delaying the voyage, for bringing on such a dense fog, but, she needed more time. Time to think and consider how best to repair the ripping seams of her life.

What's more, she knew that Jean-Luc wondered if she'd had anything to do with the brawl on deck last evening. He was too kind to ask, and she was too proud to profess her blamelessness. They rarely spoke of her power, of her magic, of her nearness to the manitou. She knew he believed, and that he held her in a kind of awe, accepting her gifts as part of her. But, it didn't mean that he never questioned how she used these gifts, deep in his heart of hearts.

A chill passed through her, a shiver of ghostly wind through her jet black curls, a long forgotten lover's touch. She tensed to realize she recognized that touch, could almost hear the throaty laughter of the man it belonged to. No, the disruption on deck yesterday had naught to do with Cora, but instead was the doing of the dark passenger who had climbed on board with her in Detroit. The same that had dogged her every move since last summer; the phantom of the man who had once been her heart's desire. For all of her gifts, for all of her traffic with the Manitou, Cora was cruelly haunted, body and soul, by Philippe.

She realized she had been holding her breath, and as she slowly let it out, she heard again the same mocking laughter. She had felt his disdain for her when she had taken his brother to husband. He had laughed at her as they fled the island in the wake of his death. Cora had woken mornings to feel the weight of him pushing on her chest, so that sometimes she felt as if her lungs were full of water, and that she was a woman drowned. She had seen him in the face of Nicholas Rast last evening, the man's young confused expression twisted into the hateful sneer she knew to belong to Philippe. She could not believe that Jean-Luc did not see his own brother there, tormenting Nicholas, feeding off of his doubt, his despair. She shuddered to think of what other mischief he would get to before they reached Mackinac. Which was yet another reason she had to prolong this voyage. To free herself from him, to loose the bind he had on her. To be sure that Philippe could trouble no one else, and allow her to repair the damage he had done, they both had done, to Jean-Luc.

No longer feeling liberated by the fog, but instead confined, she picked up her grey skirts and strode purposefully back to the cabin. She needed to make sense of how she had arrived here, in this moment, in these difficulties. She needed to write. And although Philippe had driven a wedge between their hearts, she still took great comfort in the steady nearness of Jean-Luc's presence.

Returning to the room, she was surprised and disappointed to find him no longer abed, and no longer in the cabin at all. Shrugging off the thin shawl she had carelessly draped over her shoulders in her morning haste, and shaking her hair from the confines of its pins, she sat down to her small writing table, smoothed the front of her gown, and opened her book. Hoping fervently to pour some of her despair into it, so that it could no longer plague her heart.

Looking back over the pages I have already written, it is easy to trace the dangerous path I was travelling. Two brothers, close in age to myself, both my bosom playmates and closest confidantes. One, a mirror of my own heart; the other, my truest foil. It is strange, the clarity that comes from reflection, which can never be seen or detected in the moment. Even after our years of companionship, when Philippe was first leaving to become a voyageur, it did not hurt my heart to lose him. No, instead it had tugged on my soul that he was as free as the crow to wander the world, but I, I would only venture as far as a man had consented I would go. My spirit raged at the Manitou, raged at the unfairness at making me but a woman, wishing fervently that I too, might know freedom.

It was then that illness came to the island, carried on swift cruel wings. My days and nights were spent nursing the soldiers at the fort, and the children in the make-shift hospital that only days before had been their school. But the illness would not take me, could not. In that horror of wasting bodies and the wails of frightened children, I came to understand freedom. The sickness took the children of French settlers, the children of the fort ladies, the children of the Potawatomi, the Ojibwa, the Huron, the Fox and the Menominee. It took their old men and their new mothers. It took brave soldiers at the fort and the cowardly as well. The evil spirits even sank their teeth into the life of my sister Rosalind, but the Manitou sighed, and the sickness let her go, although leaving her forever with the scars of the malady. In the midst of this madness, I remember one day, after many hours of working in the hospital, I had returned home heartbroken. My father had but a moment to embrace me, before he too, left the house to help with his soldiers. Waseya, my nurse and only mother that I could remember had gathered me close and whispered that there was freedom in every breath, freedom in every rustle of the wind, and that I was blessed. Blessed to be precious to the great spirit, as dear to him as his own daughter. And I knew that this was the Manitou's answer.

Those dark winter days slowly melted away, and with them, the angry cloud of illness drifted from the island as quickly as it had come. We would learn later that fewer lives were lost on the island than in any of the other nearby settlements, and I breathed a whisper of thanks to the sky. The days grew brighter and bolder, and I felt myself bloom with happiness in the coming of the spring. The steady warmth of those days found me out in the newness of the season, flocking to the first buds of long sleeping flowers, to the green shoots of life springing to the Earth. And not for the first time, I bowed to the wisdom of the spirits, for granting me my wish for this freedom, even if it wasn't in the manner I had originally hoped for.

My constant companion that spring was Jean-Luc. At first, he had been as familiar as my own shadow, never for a moment did I think of him as anything but a part of myself, my playfellow. But with the warmth of the spring came the growing heat of my affections. He was no longer the boy of my memory, but a handsome man in his early twenties, grown more handsome since the last summer. His eyes reflected the green of the new spring grass, and the golden rays of the sun, and he too, became a ray of sunshine, warming me with his smiles, bringing blushes to my cheeks. His compliments were like soft kisses, his hand on mine the faintest flutter of my heart. If only it had carried on that way. If only I had guarded myself. If I'd had the courage to truly see the man who was offering himself to me, tenderly and completely. But ever as wild as the wind, when Philippe returned, the calming spring warmth boiled over into desire.

How can I explain it? I do not fully understand the feelings myself. His boldness challenged the passions already burning in my wild heart. His soul was magnetized by mine, constantly circling in attraction as if by its own force, unable to be controlled.

Like any other day, I had been waiting in the usual place for Jean-Luc, every last fiber of myself quickened with joy for our meeting. I had spent the morning with Papa, coaxing him to eat, and with Rosalind, pinning her hair just the way she liked it, so that it covered an especially deep pox-mark under her ear. But as evening drew near, I could already feel my spirit detaching from the comfort and monotony of my life at home with my family. My eyes would take on a glazed expression, and my heart would already be running *full speed into the arms of the trees I loved so well. The woods were mine, and the time I spent there belonged only to me, and to Jean-Luc. I looked forward to our walk and his tales of the shipping company. Stories of drunk sailors and strange cargoes, the sound of his even voice and his hearty mirth at being able to relate these stories to me, as if he saved them up all the day long in a treasure chest, and then handed me the key to this happiness. But most of all, his familiarity and comfort steadied me, buoyed me after a winter of so much loss.*

From behind where I waited, I heard the faint snapping of last year's twigs on the ground. My skin prickled in anticipation—but I did not turn. I wanted to enjoy every last moment of the expectation of the meeting. I wonder now, if all circumstances would have changed if I had spun around. If I had taken a little more control of my destiny. But, that kind of thinking has been the springboard of my sorrows, because I did not turn. I felt a hand untie the ribbons from my heavy hair, and a sword of sunlight pierce through the trees. Then, a warm, confident man's touch on my arm. This was not the tentative gentleness of Jean-Luc, and so I should have been alarmed, but when those blue eyes bored into the golden warmth of my own, I stared back, brazenly, accepting the implied challenge within. Drowning in the pools of our eyes, feeling my chest tighten for lack of air, but I continued to stare back, the same smile on both of our lips. And this was the first of my blunders.

The sound of the cabin door opening brought her back to reality as she slammed the book shut. He gave her a strange look that asked nothing, but she felt the guilt in her blood rushing to her cheeks to reveal her.

"My apologies, mon amour. I was gone to check on our old friend Rast. He is not himself he claims, though he has been gone so long, I can barely remember how he should be!"

He laughed heartily and smiled at her, chasing her worries away, before continuing on.

"Very strange happenings yesterday, non? And today, the fog is so thick it is like the whipped crème on Grand-mère's tarts."

She found that his own brand of magic had taken hold, for his easy conversation and cheerful words had restored calm to her troubled mind.

He paused for a moment to look at her.

"Mon Dieu, but you are beautiful"

His eyes filled with admiration. Cora could not help but glow. He was often so affable that she sometimes forgot how deep and soulful he could be. What power kindness wields over those with heavy hearts and heavy consciences.

"I think the fog should clear by midday, and perhaps the wind will pick up around the same time."

She looked at him askance, measuring the way he took in her words, hoping for approval, but in his eyes she saw only love, which caught her off guard as always. How could he bear to look at her? Would he feel the same if he understood the whole truth? Would she ever have the courage to tell him? She knew she did not have the heart to confess that the winds would only take them so far before they died away again. She had much more to write before they arrived at Mackinac, and could not afford a swift journey if she was to do and say all that she needed.

:8:

Nicholas

At the sound of his cabin door firmly closing, the dull finality of wood on wood, Nicholas breathed out heavily. He hoisted his weakened frame over to a looking glass to see the damage on his once handsome face and to again wonder what had come over him the night before. His lip was cut and a deep mauve contusion seemed painted onto his fine aquiline features, marking him, in his eyes, as a common brawler one might find in any tavern in London. The very idea made him laugh. He was far enough away from London now, wasn't he? No longer would he fit in with the quality gentry as he had in England. He would instead return to a place where all knew, or thought they knew, his sinner's past, and all judged the misdeed that had banished him from the beginning. All the world, and especially his father, could think what they wanted about the might of Astor's American Fur Company, but working in the agency would not be the making of him as his family believed. Rather, it would be his undoing. He reached up gingerly to touch the angry split in his lower lip, cleft nearly in half from that scoundrel's brutish fists, and he traced the outline of the purple shadow on his cheekbone. Wincing and cursing with the pain, he gave one last hard look into his own cold, grey unforgiving eyes, then he fell back onto the bed, hopeless.

Why had Delacroix come to see him? Jean could have no real interest in him, why, the two had not seen each other since they were mere boys! Even then, Jean-Luc had always been his brother's companion, while Philippe was quick to show Nicholas the many ways he was not suited to their games. Besides, the man's affability sickened him. Nicholas wanted to scream that he would never be Edward, wasn't like Edward, but that he was better than Edward, better than the whole lot of them put together. But, it wasn't true, was it? Edward was the best of them, and not even Nicholas could say a word against him. He found that in Jean-Luc's presence the hateful words would not come, as if M. Delacroix had bound him in a spell of gentleness. His laughter came easy, and he never once alluded to the past, as if sensitive to Nicholas' worries, and trying very hard to make him feel welcome. But as soon as he had left the room, the bitter vitriol returned, a loyal but obstinate pet of his mind.

Jean-Luc had told Nicholas tales of Edward as a man. How he looked so very much like his elder brother that he would have recognized him anywhere. He told him of Philippe's death and life as a voyageur, but never once did he mention how he died, or a word about his own charming wife. It was as if she had cast a silencing spell on him, Nicholas thought. He wanted to know everything about her. He remembered little of her as a child, except that the older boys had seemed to worship her. He had a dreamlike feeling that he and Cora shared some secret he could not quite remember. He had thought to ask, but as the question was forming, a warning look had come into Jean-Luc's eyes, as if he was anticipating the unwanted inquiries. A look that reminded Nicholas that he had his own secrets, his own reasons for being sent away in the first place.

Yes, sent away. It's strange how easily the mind forgets that which it has no desire to recall. In the posh sitting rooms of the English countryside, and the French dinner parties given in an outrageously wealthy widow's salon, he would never have had any cause to remember his disgrace, his crime, his hurried exile from the island, his mother's tears. He was extraneous anyway—they had Edward! But it troubled him as he lay on his cabin bed, blankets strewn about him as if they were wind tossed. It burdened him to consider that perhaps his parents were not as glad to be rid of him as he had imagined them to be, and that perhaps he hadn't been as eager to leave as he had since convinced himself that he had been. His fingers fumbled for the familiar smoothness of the pipe, clutching it to his chest like a life preserver on the open sea, and he fell into a troubled sleep.

He awoke hours, minutes, seconds later, Nicholas had no idea of the time. His blanket had been pulled over his head and was being held tightly over his arms and legs, effectively pinning him to the bed. He struggled, tried to cry out, but the only sound was a muffled moan. He could smell alcohol and sweat and he could feel the presence of men, though none of them seemed familiar, only the vaguest outlines could he discern through the coarse blanket. He struggled a moment longer before he felt the sharp shock of a fist in his gut and the dull pain of surprise. His eyes watered, and while he helplessly tried to make out the figures around him from underneath the blanket, a deep voice spoke.

"That's enough of that, Rast. We know who you are. We remember what you did. Some folks may have forgotten, some may have forgiven. But we've done neither. We remember."

Another thunderbolt to his stomach and the sound of feet leaving the room, his door softly falling back to closed. Nicholas blinked away the tears he could not control, he choked back the sob of unfairness, of fear, the sob of self-loathing. For he knew somewhere inside him, that the men's anger with him was justified.

He rubbed his stomach and felt his face grow hot. He had been but a boy! Just a boy! He hadn't done it to be cruel, it had been an accident. He had never intended anything serious to happen! His hands came up to his mouth in an attempt to drown out the sob that was fighting its way to his broken lips. He carefully stood up, and tip-toed to the door, locking it decisively. He wanted no more visitors today, kind or threatening. He needed to be alone with what he had done, what he had lost, and to prepare himself to face what awaited him on the island.

He groped about the bed for Edward's pipe, and held it to his heart. The only link that remained between himself and his brother. He wondered if he would even recognize his parents, as much could change in ten years, and he knew they may not recognize him, either. He felt his mind wandering, and he realized that he could no longer shut out what he had done, and the pain that came to him in that moment was just as fresh as it had been ten years ago. The scab had been ripped off, and the rich, dark lifeblood of his crime seemed to course cruelly through his body, sickening him, twisting his stomach into knots, and forcing sticky, hot tears from his eyes.

All of them, Edward, Jean-Luc, Philippe, Cora, her younger sister, and a group of Indian boys and girls from the beach huts had gathered around Waseya. She was telling them a story, and no matter how rough the boys played, or how daring their games, it seemed everyone had an ear for her tales. He remembered that he and Edward hadn't played with the other children much that summer, their mother had been sick, and their father had trusted them to help her at home. It was a rare day to be out around other children his age, and the legends the strange woman spun took a hold of all of their imaginations. She told a story about a brave indian girl named Willow Wand and how the Gitchi Manitou protected her and her grandfather from an evil spirit on the island. Willow Wand had then found her beloved, a young warrior from another tribe. The Manitou was pleased, and so gave her magic, to continue to protect those on Mackinac. The Manitou had been careful to teach her how to use the powers for good, and warned her against using them selfishly.

Waseya had looked carefully at all of the children as the story came to an end, her eyes coming back into focus, as if the spirits themselves were speaking through her, instead of the story springing remembered from her own mind. But she had looked longest at Cora, an unspoken warning that seemed to burn her, its meaning lost to all but her and her nurse. She had gotten up quickly and kissed Waseya, before running off in one direction trailed by Philippe, Jean-Luc and Edward. Nicholas did not want to run after her, there was a strangeness in her that wearied his own spirits. Her sister Rosalind had made an excuse to go in and practice her sewing, a model of the dutiful daughter, and Nicholas was left alone with the children from the beach. He had followed them into the wood, deeper than he had ever been before. They played for hours, hiding games and racing games. One by one the children had smiled at him and nodded as they took their leave. They understood English, but many were not confident enough to speak it themselves, and so each left, until only he and one other boy remained. His name was Beshkno, and he was of the Potawatomi tribe, they that they call "the keepers of the fire". He was lithe and strong and had a good command of English. Nicholas had played with the boy before, but had felt then, as always, that no one could notice him when his brother and the Delacroix boys were present. He was the youngest, the smallest and the least daring. But this time he was alone, and he remembered being very happy to have the attentions of his friend to himself.

The sun crept its way through the trees, dappling the trunks and patches of the earth. Nicholas could not remember a day he had smiled more. Fortified by the story of the Great Manitou and the chosen, precious people that received his gifts, Nicholas had asked Beshkno for more stories of the Manitou. But, the boy seemed unwilling to answer, dodging his questions and instead asking about life living in a big house, on the main street, and about the food that the Rast family had for dinner. It was strange to think that this boy, not much older than Nicholas, living only a few hundred yards away, had a life so very different than his own. But, in our youth it is difficult to consider life from outside your one's experience, except to assume another's life is better or more exciting than one's own.

Nicholas had pleaded for more stories, at first in a friendly way, but soon impatience and anger began to take over. He demanded to know more legends. He was sure the boy was laughing at him, secretly delighted at holding on to his secrets.

"Tell me! Tell me of the manitou and his gifts! It's not fair and I won't have you lying to me, you who live off of the scraps of my family!"

He spat the words, and was quickly more wounded by them himself than Beshkno was. He hated his own temper then, and he still did, but it was always impossible to control until the moment he said something he regretted. He felt the tears coming to his eyes, and his friend's face had turned cold. All of the smiles and laughter they had shared during the day had disappeared, the sun under a thundercloud.

"My family and my tribe do not owe anything to the fur company. My father catches the best beaver on the straits, with an arrow shot so clean, you cannot find the hole. If you must know, it is bad fortune to anyone who speaks lightly of the gifts of the manitou, one who does so is likely to be cursed. For the Great Manitou has blessings in one hand, and misfortune in the other. Better to let your deeds decide which hand the manitou passes over a man's life."

Nicholas swallowed hard, and mumbled an apology, tears still coursing down his fool cheeks.

Beshkno's eyes turned warm again, and he moved forward to look into Nicholas' face. His own eyes, were as rich and dark as the earth in the middle of the island. Nicholas', he knew, were grey like stone, as hard and rigid as his stubbornness and his anger. Beshkno clasped his arm with his hand, and said

"I see you, brother."

The moment was over as soon as it begun and before Nicholas could speak, Beshkno had turned and fled, yelling "Chase me!" gleefully. Nicholas was glad to have been forgiven so easily, and felt a lightening of his heart. He shook his head at himself, ashamed of his words, but relieved Edward had not been there to be disappointed in him. He gave chase to find that Beshkno had climbed, snakelike, up to the top of a tree. It was a birch tree, and difficult to climb, for it did not have many branches near the bottom. Nicholas had marveled at the other boy's agility, and shook his head in amazement. He was frightened of heights and could never climb so high. Beneath the tree was a pit made of bracken and dead roots. An older tree had used to stand in the spot, but had died, and slowly the deep, dead roots had washed away during heavy rains or had been gutted by the weight of the snow. The deep pit remained.

He looked from it up to Beshkno, still shaking his head. The boy was smiling at him, encouraging him to climb. Nicholas put his hand on the tree, and just before he hooked his body around the trunk, he looked from Beshkno to the pit and wondered with a shiver what it would be like if his friend were to fall. His arm reached up and he jumped to attach his body to the tree, and he heard the sound.

It wasn't a scream, and even now, laying in his bed in the ship's cabin, the same sticky tears on his face, he couldn't explain the sound. It was a groan, or a despairing sigh. He looked to see the boy falling, falling, just as he had in Nicholas' imagination a moment before. A nightmare made real. The boys eyes locked with his own grey eyes, seeing and unseeing, terrified, yet accepting of the fate that was to be assigned to him. Nicholas had watched the fall, and he had not moved. He could not. He could not believe what he was seeing, certain at any moment he would look up and see the smiling eyes of his friend, so very high in the tree.

All sound had ceased. He could not remember hearing the dead roots breaking the boy's fall or even the solitary birdsong of a whippoorwill. He heard nothing. He rushed to the edge of the pit, and the only sound was of the soft moaning of his friend. His leg was twisted so that the bones were breaking through the skin, and his arm was laying at an unnatural angle. The boy's collarbone had broken, and he could see the white of the bone and the red of the boy's blood jutting grotesquely from the skin. His face was unmarked, and Nicholas recalled thinking that if he could just put a blanket over his body, that Beshkno would be well. If only he could not see his brokenness, then he would survive. But one more look at the boy's bones and blood, and Nicholas could feel Waseya's honey cakes rise to his throat from his stomach. He was sick at the foot of the tree. Beshkno was speaking the language of his people, speaking Potawatomi, and Nicholas was sure he was asking for his mother.

Nicholas turned and he ran. Ran back to Mackinac, ran further than his house, ran away from the bleeding, dying boy. But he did not run for help. He ran instead to a hiding place near a cove in the beach. Just a small space that adults didn't notice. And he stayed and he cried. He knew he should tell his father, that perhaps he could have helped the boy. Deep down, he had known already the boy had been dying. Was probably now dead. But he was afraid. Afraid of the manitou. Afraid that he had been cursed, afraid that his own mind had caused his friend to fall. Hadn't he imagined it, however innocently, in the moment before it happened? Hadn't it come true exactly as he had foresaw it? His whole body was racked with shivers and sobs. He stayed there until nightfall. Something in his gut told him to go home. A warning, a presence in that small space with him. He was drenched with cold from squatting in the water, and he knew his face was swollen with his heartbroken sobs, and he was heavy with guilt. Guilt for his imagination. Guilt for his cowardice.

The moment he opened the door to his house, a general uproar began. His mother was screaming, loud enough to alert the entire island. When Edward had come home without Nicholas, hours before, they had been concerned. When Beshkno had never come back to his lodge, his family had become worried. His mother had known he was in danger. She said she could feel he was in pain. The men of their tribe had tracked them both.

His brother Edward would later tell him the story, and he had told it kindly, which had surprised Nicholas as he had expected no kindness from anyone. When the search had begun many of the the men from the fur company had joined their father to aid in finding the lost boys. The men had been talking in disgust about the natives of the island and how uncivilized they were in habit and in their practices. Waseya had suddenly appeared, had volunteered to come along with the men. She, being half French and half Menominee, had never been easily accepted with any group, but this did not seem to trouble her. She had spoken soothing words to the white men, telling them of the kindnesses of the Potowatomi tribe and how they had treated her family when hereditary young brother had wandered into the woods, many years ago. She calmed the white men, using the magic of her words to convince them. She reminded them how the young men of the tribe were able to follow a trail in places over solid rock that no white man could see, places where there was no footprint or animal's track in sight. It was as if they could feel some energy that had disturbed the forest floor, some leaves turned in a different direction. A sign pointing to something that had swirled over them, a difference that went unseen by eyes that could not feel the energy within them.

The tribe's leader, Grey Wolf, had accompanied Waseya, and it was he who had heard something amiss in the sounds of the birds. A note that betrayed something wrong. And following the signs, they came upon the contents of Nicholas' stomach, and eventually the cold body of Beshkno. It was clear he had fallen, but how, and why? And where was Nicholas? Was he hurt somewhere too? The men had looked and looked, but they could not find him.

Edward had then laid a hand on his shoulder and grasping it firmly said, "And now, little brother, you are safe at home."

After the initial relief at his returning home unhurt, the questions began. Where had he been? How had it happened? Had he seen the boy fall? And why didn't he get any help?

How could he explain to them, that he had caused the accident? How could he explain that he had imagined it happening moments before it did, and in his poisonous mind he had caused the death of his friend? He could not. And so he did not. He told them the truth, mostly. He told them everything but his imagining of the event. His hollow answers seemed to haunt them. The Potawatomi were angry with the fur company. They were angry that this young white boy could possibly have saved Beshkno's life if he had ran to get help in time. If he had not hidden like a coward, if he had not so easily walked away from the tragedy.

His parents did not understand it either. No one did. No one could understand why he would not try to help the boy, and what's more, Nicholas couldn't understand it himself, except to say that he knew there was no help to get, that it had been too late. Only Edward had not seemed to look on him with an accusation of guilt in his quiet brown eyes.

Nicholas had known in the moment that the boy would die. Was meant to die. That it was already decided. He had ran from the truth of that realization and from any part he may have had in it. After a few weeks of refusing to leave his room, his nightmares still came every night, still woke up his family with his screams. Repeated phantasms dominated his dreams where screaming Beshknos fell again and again, their earth brown eyes falling into the bracken, down, down into the pit, young bodies breaking, over and over again. Nicholas would awake wailing, his brother Edward holding his body as it collapsed into sobs. His parents had talked in hushed whispers by the fire, but he could hear them. The confusion of the people in town about his inaction, whispers of doubt saying he had pushed Beshkno. Anyone who had seen the body knew this to be false, but people liked to talk, and without his side of the story, without proof of his emotion, they were free to invent their own version of events. Soon, his parent's fireside whispers turned to plans. And before the month was out, he was packed and on a ship, bound for London.

Laying in his cabin bed, sheets still twisted about him like a shroud, Nicholas thought back on the small, scared, eleven year old boy that he had once been. He remembered that day with a clarity like no other day, save the day he sailed from Mackinac. He remembered his brother's hand holding his, although both of them were too old for such a display. He remembered Edward's tears, and his doe-brown eyes. Though he was sixteen and already practically a man, his brother had looked as lost and scared as Nicholas was. He had embraced him warmly on the dock, for all to see, clearly unashamed of his brother.

It was then that Edward had reached into his pocket and brought out the wooden pipe. It had been a strange thing, even then, for the Edward had no smoking habit. But, reflecting, Nicholas figured that to a sixteen year old boy, it had probably seemed a very manly present to give to a younger brother. He had given it to him without a word, not needing to attach more importance to it, neither one of them knowing it would be the last time they would ever see each other, the last gift they would ever exchange. Nicholas' mind drifted over the terrible memory of those days, the days that had changed him forever. Remembered the pain on Beshkno's face, the pain of Edward's frown. He reached to feel the dried blood on his lip, and to hollowness of the punch he had received in his gut, and he knew it could not begin to equal the torture of his soul, or the hollowness of his heart. He clutched the pipe firmly in his hand, and closed his eyes to the memories, unable to bare another moment in their company.

·9·
Walter

His legs felt as if they had sunk in sand, his steps painfully heavy. The men had resumed their fight on deck, but the brawl was different. He could not see who was fighting and his legs refused to move. He heard his own voice shouting, or rather, could feel his vocal chords vibrating with the effort, his yells lost over the cacophony of men's jeering and cheering. The sky had blackened, the air was still rotten and stagnant, but black clouds had rolled in and there would be no sailors to help him ready the *Starlight* for the impending storm. Captain Alberts could feel the tightness in the air, a strained bow about to snap, a powder keg about to catch the spark of the fight, and the hatred happening just before his eyes.

One more glance down at his leaden legs, and his fears were confirmed—he wasn't moving at all! He shouted again and again until he was certain his throat must be bloodied from his futile efforts. The noise around him faded, and he heard the weeping of a woman. Not the scared weeping of a disturbed onlooker, but the anguished sobs of a woman who has had her heart torn out, and is made to watch the pain of the moment unfolding before her own eyes. Captain Alberts was familiar with the sound. He'd heard his wife utter the same mournful tones when their youngest daughter was lost to the fever that fateful winter. Suddenly, he found his steps, and bursting into the fray he found the forlorn figure of Mme. Cora Delacroix, crouched on the deck, her skirts spread about her like a shield. Her hands were covered in fresh, red blood, and the sound of her wailing was terrible. The lament sent ice into the beating of the older man's heart, though he still did not understand what was happening. Her eyes were bright, piercing sunlight and menacing, as she held the bloodied and broken body of her husband.

The Captain reeled at the sight, and bending over, reached for his hand. Trying desperately to call out to him, but his voice had still not returned.

"Jean-Luc", he somehow managed to whisper, and it was a kind of prayer.

"Why? What man would dare to offend you? What man could find ill humor in your company?"

His whispers went unheard over the unchecked wailing of Mme. Delacroix. Captain Alberts felt the first drops of rain as he struggled to understand how this had happened. Who would have engaged him? Surely one of his sailors, his crew, they would have put an end to it? Still clutching the cold, dead hand of the boy he had greeted on nearly every arrival into the Mackinac port, the boy who had been the delight of his father's eyes and of all those at Cross Shipping Company. The Captain turned his head to see who had brought about this tragedy. He suddenly felt the animal desire to face whomever had cursed his darling *Starlight*.

Captain Alberts stood and turned, his whole body filled with a shaking fury, and stared straight into the icy eyes of Philippe Delacroix, who threw his head back and laughed heartily, before darting forward and sheathing his dagger in the Captain's stomach. Walter Alberts clutched his abdomen and watched as the deep red blood seeped from the wound, a fiery hateful sunset to his life. Just before his eyes closed he heard the refrain of a favorite voyageur song escape from Philippe's curling lips. Forcing his eyes open, he watched as Philippe kneeled next to Cora Delacroix, singing the words into her ear,

By the clear running fountain, I strayed one summer day,
The water looked so cooling, I bathed without delay;
Many long years I have loved you, Ever in my heart you'll stay.

Captain Alberts had awoken screaming in the great cabin. The nightmare had left his body covered in cold sweat, his blankets tossed around, indicating the thrashing struggle had been physical, while at the same time lost in the land of dreams.

He stayed in bed a few minutes longer than was his wont, breathing heavily. He was attempting to make some sense out of why a dream would come on that violently, or leave a deep, throbbing pain in his gut. A pain precisely in the place he had dreamed he was stabbed by a man he knew to be dead. It certainly had not felt like a dream. He could still hear Mme. Delacroix's cries, could feel the first fat raindrops on his head, the blood in his mouth and the warmth of it in his hands. He remembered the curling smile of satisfaction on Philippe's face as he tormented his brother's wife. What could it mean? What was happening on his ship?

The fog of the morning had allowed him time to reflect without being seen too closely by his crew. He was grateful for the distraction of the fog and the clanging of the bell to warn other passing ships of their presence.

Although with no wind, all other ships were just as helpless as they.

Mercifully, he had not seen Mme. Delacroix this morning since he had been on deck. He had decided to run the ship as if it was progressing on schedule, in order to maintain good humor aboard and keep the crew active. He had no desire to have a repeat of yesterday, or heaven forbid, a repeat of the horrors of his dream. Still, he felt his eyes continuously darting around the deck, searching for a sudden disaster, and the presence of Jean-Luc was unsettling. The heir to Cross Shipping was gazing into the slowly receding fog, and the sight of the young man brought bile to his throat. Walter Alberts discovered that although he could not tell his dream to this quiet, amiable young man, he was genuinely worried for him.

There had been a time, only a few years ago, when both boys had affectionately called him "Captain Walter", and had eagerly listened to tales of his voyages (only slightly exaggerated) at his knee. Those times were gone, of course. Jean-Luc was a man, the future owner of the company he proudly served, and in appearance, deportment, education and prospects—the most desirable young man on the island. He wished he could speak to him as he had when he was a boy. Captain Alberts had so many questions. Why had he fled the island? Had there been bad blood with Philippe? What was the coldness between he and his wife, when any fool could see they were mad for each other? All of these questions burned inside him, but they died on his lips—for he could never ask them now. He watched his crew and looked to his instruments from time to time, though any sailor worth his salt knew there was nothing to be read from these tools. As long as there was no wind, the fog could pass and return as it pleased, and the *Starlight* would still be frozen in place, her brightness diminished with worry and disuse.

A few other intrepid passengers had come up on deck, apparently unwilling to be trapped any longer by the suffocating fog. Some of the men were those he had guessed to be recruits for Fort Mackinac, and one couple was the new fort surgeon and his young wife. The Captain stepped forward to speak with the man whom he'd only had a brief introduction on the the morning prior, the same dawn they had set sail.

"Dr. Gordon, well met. Ghastly fog, I'm afraid."

The younger man smiled sweetly at his wife, and looking kindly at the Captain replied,

"Not at all, sir! Isobel and I were just speaking on this very topic. For all of it's inconveniences, there is a certain charm in coming to one's new home slowly, giving it a moment to know you before one springs oneself onto it, hm?"

The Captain considered this a moment,

"I suppose there's some truth in that, especially coming to live on Mackinac after a life in Boston. You may find island life difficult to adjust to, though I can't exactly say, having grown up pure Mackinac myself. But, you might speak with the commandant when you get to the fort—he originally hailed from Boston or thereabouts. And come to think of it, his eldest daughter is on board this very ship, and if memory serves, she spent a few of her first years there."

The captain turned his head to include the surgeon's wife in his last statement, but the doctor was already speaking.

"Unfortunately, Isobel will not find an affinity with the commandant's daughter in discussing Boston, as this is her second move in a fortnight. I'm from Boston, born and bred, but my dear wife is just recently arrived from England, and now I have most cruelly uprooted her again. This is her very first experience of the west."

Captain Alberts nodded understandingly, a laugh on his good-natured lips. He could not prevent, however, a darker feeling from clouding his heart. How would this woman find Mackinac? How would any of his passengers? So many dark and strange happenings, so many mysterious occurrences, and they were barely a day into the journey. The captain did not hold himself to foolishness, but a man had to be a little superstitious to work on the lakes. These waters were known to set seasoned ocean sailors to sickness, turning upside down all things that men understood about the sea. The waves of the lakes did not so much roll, but tumble. The winds did not blow, but instead swirled in a rolling, dizzying dance. Things *happened* on the water, and things were happening now. He would have to keep his wits about him, and not let the spirits of the lake trap him in their spell.

The surgeon had been speaking about their passage into Detroit, and about his decision to serve in the American Army. He seemed a good man, and for a moment, Captain Alberts allowed himself to engage in this normal, average conversation between newly acquainted strangers. He even thought briefly to ask him if he had heard of the fever that had come to the Great Lakes region two winters ago, but shaking his head, thought better of it, no sense in inquiring about events that could not now be changed. Better to focus on the things that were within one's control.

Still the man went on, affably, speaking of things of little import, when suddenly the Captain's attention was caught by the surgeon's wife. She was leaning out over the railing of the schooner, peering into the ghostly mist. A hand, appeared out of the fog, and then another to match it. The captain turned his head, incredulously, unsure of what he was seeing. From somewhere within the fog, or maybe inside of his own frenzied mind, a remnant from his dream came forth, and he recognized those hands. The same hands that had held a dagger, the same hands that stroked the hair of his brother's wife with a lover's touch. The hands of Philippe Delacroix, but this time phantasms, a dream made flesh from the drifting fog. He heard it, quietly, as one hear's the far off crying of an infant from a bassinet in another room, or the lowing of the cows during a storm, he heard the laugh. Quiet, so quiet, he was straining to hear it. Was it inside his mind? Or was it coming from the fog itself?

He felt the touch of the surgeon's hand, gently clutching his shoulder. All Captain Albert's could see was the hands, all he could remember was the laughter, the mocking singing voice and the blood. He stepped forward quickly but measuredly. Placing his hand on the crook of the eager elbow of Mrs. Gordon.

"Pardon me, Madame, but we wouldn't want anyone tumbling overboard, and 'tis easy enough to do in this confusing fog…it's enough to muddle a man's mind!"

All in one movement he moved her away from the railing and back to her husband's care. He doffed his cap, respectfully and made his apologies, asking their leave and declaring he was obliged for their conversation.

As he walked toward a group of his crew members, he began to smile at his own foolishness, shaking the strange images from his mind. He found that he could not completely clear them though, for he had seen Mrs. Gordon's face as he pulled her from the railing, and it had been the visage of a woman in a trance. Try as he might, he could not shake it.

:10:

Jean-Luc

The fog lifted. Slowly at first, so many wisps of smoke disappearing into a chimney. But then all at once, as if the manitou was inhaling it into the sky. The clouds were now settled comfortably high up into the blue where they belonged, seemingly the only remnants of the ghostly morning.

He had walked the ship, bow to stern, starboard to port. All the while admiring the pride with which Captain Alberts took in maintaining the morale of his crew and how lovingly he served the *Starlight*. It *was* a beautiful schooner, made of strong oak and M. Pierre Delacroix, Jean-Luc's father, had been delighted to add her to his fleet of merchant vessels.

It had been a flash of whimsy, however, to christen her *Starlight*. Jean-Luc thought back to the night the new ship had appeared in the harbor, and smiled to himself in the recollection. The timing of the ship's arrival had been unusual, and the harbor master's man had come knocking on their door as the family was sitting companionably near the parlor fire. His breath had been fast, a combination of the exertion from the run, and the man's preference for his wife's celebrated maple cakes. His hurried knock was followed quickly by the man himself bursting into the room. Sweat ran from his rosy-red forehead, and in a flash he produced a well-used handkerchief, swiped it across his puffing face and stowed it back into his pocket before Jean-Luc could blink twice.

His first words, when he was able to regain the power of speech, were a labored (and somewhat dramatic) declaration,

"She comes, Sir! She comes by starlight!"

His father had clapped his hands, and gesturing excitedly to both Jean-Luc and Philippe, he followed the portly man out to inspect his new schooner. Even with Philippe's disdain for everything relating to Cross Shipping, Jean-Luc noted that his younger brother could hardly check his excitement.

Both Jean-Luc and Philippe had suggested a slurry of ideas to name the ship. *Michigan, Cadillac, Lewis Cass, William Henry Harrison, John Quincy Adams, Detroit, Huron, The Mackinac Queen,* and even names from their dog-eared book about the Trojan War, *Helen of Troy, Ajax,* and *The Odyssey.* Their father had smiled broadly on both of them, believing naively that one day these two sons of his would work together in the company he had created, still arguing over what to name their new ships.

They came upon the schooner, sliding almost silently into harbor, gliding and glittering by the thousand lights of the night sky. Her sails were a breathtaking snow white, a true lady of the lake. After taking one long look at her, their father had turned to his sons, clapping them each on the shoulder, and declared to the harbormaster's man,

"Mr. Catesby, I believe you had the right of it, sir. She is starlight itself, and there is no other name for her!"

Jean-Luc remembered the chill of the night and the

incredulous look his brother and he had exchanged at this singsong name. But, on this strange morning, as a grown man, looking at the ship under those whipped cream clouds, the sails just slightly inhaling in, gathering the smallest breath of wind in their white mouths, he saw how right his father had been.

Collecting himself back to the present moment, out of the glowing memories of the past, he felt suddenly the gnawing desire to be at home begin in the pit of his stomach. Guilt mixed uncomfortably with words left unsaid. It wasn't that he hated so much to be away from Mackinac, although he was certain everyone thought this of him. Most assumed he was a Mackinac man through and through, but no, there was a time that he had dreams of adventure. He'd followed closely the news of the settlements in Australia, and of the men and women who volunteered to begin a new life there. He read closely and repeatedly the reports of the expansion, ever westward, into his America. Some of the natives, including a few of the Huron men he knew well, told of lands across the western water. They spoke longingly of the different lakes that could be found in those lands, and of the game, and of the lack of white men.

He dreamed of exploration, but in his heart, had known his place and his home was on Mackinac. He had felt lucky with his lot, and was proud of his father's hard work, earning the family respect and good reputation they enjoyed. For a time, he had been content that Philippe could live the dream of a wanderer. And it could have been enough.

But, with Philippe's death he had taken his new wife away. Away from the whispers, away from the gossips and prying eyes. Though the decision to marry her was not a hasty one, he knew her decision to marry him, *was*. Though he wondered if it was one she regretted.

The temperature of the day seemed suddenly blistering. Beads of sweat poured down from his hairline and ran into his eyes, and a kind of burning, salty sadness filled him up. Jean-Luc was growing increasingly uncomfortable. His eyes danced around the ship wildly, and for a moment, everything was oppressive, pushing into him, weighing him down. His responsibilities were overwhelming, his damaged wife, his duties to his father and the shipping company, the whispering busybodies waiting on the island. All this stress combined with whatever was portended by young Rast's return and the mounting concerns for the fur company's continued success. He was plagued too, by this whole homecoming and what it had cost his father to keep their secret. Yes, their secret. He had somehow blocked it out, hadn't he? He had made himself believe it would disappear somehow, but now he was faced with it, head on. The wood on the ship's railing was biting into his flesh, his blood was pounding, sweat pouring down his back, and instead of friendly, the sun now seemed threatening. He looked about, breathing hard, and saw that none of the men on deck were having the same reaction. He ran swiftly, fleeing below deck, found his cabin, and sat down to watch his wife sleep, exhaling ragged breaths that dissolved into stillness at the sight of her sweet, slumbering smile.

Some time later, he awoke, lying uncomfortably in a heap on the bed. Cora was smiling down on him, wiping his face with a cool cloth. He smiled back at her, his head buzzing for a moment. "There, then. Get the demons out" she cooed, her usual reserve lifted in the pleasure of nursing him. He made no move to get up, enjoying this brief, private intimacy. They'd had so few in this strange marriage, that he found he felt no guilt in lingering over this moment. They'd had a few sudden, passionate embraces, some stolen kisses that spoke of longing, but had always left Jean-Luc wondering what or who exactly she was longing for. And then, there had been that one night—the only night it could be said their marriage could be called a true marriage, a night neither of them spoke of.

A night he almost could believe never happened for the mystery that surrounded it. Yet, he could not but remember the softness of her skin, the warmth of her body against his own, he could not forget, but it was such torture to recall.

He'd had fits like this recently, the sweating, the physical pressure bearing down on him keenly, a yoke around his neck. Cora was convinced it was a dark spirit hanging over him, taking advantage of him in weak moments when he was filled with doubt. And although Jean-Luc was more inclined to believe it was merely a result of anxiety or an over-stressed mind, he couldn't help but wonder if she might be right.

Finger-combing the hair from his forehead, a light of something like desire flashed in her eyes briefly, and he knew it was reflected back in his own. She reddened, and looked away.

"How would you like a turn about the deck? I believe you'll find the ship is once again moving—albeit slowly."

A look of satisfaction glowed on her her face as she extended a small hand to him, and he could not help grinning like a child.

"Oui, lead on, Mme. Doctor." which made her laugh. He wondered why it could not always be like this, so easy. He made a mental note to take ill more often if it softened her thus.

Emerging into daylight he felt the corners of his mouth still lifting. The ship was, in fact, sailing once again. The elation seemed contagious, as all around him were happy passengers and crew, buzzing optimistically about the sudden turn of events. Jean-Luc had known most aboard were male, and in so knowing had understood that the tempers and moods of men could be dangerous in a calm. Looking to Cora he said a silent prayer of thanks that she had called back the wind, before anything worse than the fight of yesterday could break out. They came together to the stern, and watched as the ship left each new wave tumbling merrily behind them.

Looking up from the rolling, tossing aquamarine of the lake, Jean-Luc was pleased to see the new surgeon, whom he'd met briefly over a swig of whiskey following the fight on deck, and his wife, whom he hadn't yet been acquainted.

"Bonjour, Dr. Gordon. I am glad we meet again, and with better tidings this time. Allow me to introduce my wife, Mme. Cora Delacroix."

The doctor introduced his wife around in turn, and she expressed her joy at making a female acquaintance on board. Jean-Luc was at first nervous, for Cora was strange in the company of women. She was a caring and kind nurse, but had always preferred the company of her male playfellows, or the comfort of her family. She was not one for gossip or idle speech, and because of this, many women did not know what to make of her, and so made her the topic of their private conversations. But, he was relieved to see her flash Mrs. Gordon a brilliant smile, and then inquire if this was her first time to Mackinac.

Dr. and Mrs. Gordon shared a secret glance. To a casual observer, it was hardly noticeable, but to Jean-Luc and Cora, who spoke mostly in a secret language of glances and gestures learned from childhood, the look between the couple was endearing and spoke volumes about their bond.

"We are only newly married, Madame, and truth be told, only newly re-acquainted. Jasper and I are second cousins, but I have not seen him in many years. We were bosom friends as children, before his family moved to Boston." She paused, her eyes flitting tenderly to her husband's face before continuing.

"I am only just come to your shores, and had only heard of Mackinac Island for the the first time, but a week past!"

She laughed merrily, auburn curls bouncing with gaiety. Jean-Luc found the sound contagious and the rest of them joined into the laughter, knowing all the while that nothing particularly humorous had been said. It was a moment of released tension, from the uncertainty of the calm, and a small escape for all of them on their way to face reality on the island.

Jean-Luc felt a stab of jealousy for the smooth warmth of this young couple, adventuring to an unknown land to make a life together. He missed Cora's easy smiles and careless laughter. He missed the days of tramping through the forest, her arm in his, and their discussions of places, books, poetry. The whole world had been in her eyes and every dream had been a possibility. He longed for the private affinity that belonged only to their hearts, an intimacy that had begun twelve years ago, and had only bloomed more brilliantly in his soul with every passing year. Until last summer, when all withered with death and despair.

Dr. Jasper Gordon only knew that he was to take over the surgeon's post, but he had not heard why the post was vacant. Cora clapped her hands, her golden cat's eyes took on a fevered gleam. This was a story she found fascinating. The surgeon and his wife tilted toward her as she began to tell the tale. Jean-Luc could hardly keep himself from throwing his head back in laughter, he'd heard the story before, many times, and it was discussed in tones ranging from disgusted shock to inquiring wonder back on the island. Cora, ever a skilled storyteller, reared on Waseya's legends, smiled, looking up at the hungry sails, getting their fill of the cool lake wind, and exhaling smoothly, began her story.

"It is strange, is it not, how one man's story touches so many lives, and like a pebble falling into a stream, the ripples of any event can touch any number of shorelines. For, if there was no story of Alexis St. Martin, then I would not have this tale to share, or have you both to tell it to now."

She paused, her voice moving in a steady cadence, matching the lap of the waves on the ship, her gaze pouring into the eyes of each of her audience, gathering them in. Pulling them under the whirling flow of her easy storytelling. The brilliant eyes flashed in Jean-Luc's own, lighting him up for a moment, before she spoke again.

"It was a sun-filled day in early June. My sister, Rosalind, had just left to bring our father some cold mutton for his midday meal. I remember, I was practicing languages with Waseya on the front porch. The day was fine and we were both content to be comfortably out of doors. Usually, it was my place to take father's meal, but Rosalind had offered, and I had acquiesced, feeling lackadaisical in the sunshine. She had been gone to the fort for no longer than half an hour, when we had looked up to see her come running back, her skirts billowing behind her, face ruddy with confused tears. I had stood up to pull her bodily into an embrace, and I waited patiently, as Waseya had taught us to do when confronted with someone who was in distress, until her heart was calm enough to allow her to speak.

"Cora! Terrible! I was speaking with father, when a soldier burst in, 'Commandant Ravensdale! A man has been shot at the fur company—they are transporting him to Dr. Beaumont directly, sir!' Father was away in a hurry, and bid me run home to you, so that you might come to aid the doctor, if you can."

She then told me she had seen seen the fur trader on her way back to deliver father's message,

"So young! No more than twenty, his face as pale as moonlight, his abdomen naught but a red stain"."

Cora looked about, weighing the effect of her words. Mrs. Gordon looked pale herself, and was holding her hand over her mouth, as if trying to hold it closed. Dr. Gordon, Jean-Luc assumed, probably knew some of the studies released by Dr. Beaumont discussing his patient, but knew that the man did not have the benefit of these human details.

"Dr. Beaumont was much admired for his skills by the lieutenants and officers at the fort, and my father, since his appointment, had been impressed with his knowledge and dedication to his patients. However, the musket had fired from just inches away, and no one thought that the young man would live. By the time I arrived, his face was grey with death, the hole in his gut as large as my fist.

I had helped with the nursing of a few soldiers at the fort who had taken ill, but had no experience with injuries such as this. I had never known there was so much blood inside of a person, nor that one could lose so much and still breathe. Dr. Beaumont brought the man to his own home, where as the Manitou would have it, he lived.

But, he had healed strangely, with the hole from the musket shot staying open— a window to the inside of his body. I visited every few days to offer assistance, then every week, then less and less. The young man was growing in strength, even though his wound was still visible, he somehow made a full recovery. It was on one of my visits, that I came to observe the doctor tying different foods to a string, perhaps a piece of fruit or a hunk of whitefish, then inserting the food directly into the hole, and removing it again every few hours to learn how the stomach digested it. At first, it was unusual, and it seemed…perverse. But when Dr. Beaumont explained what could be learned, what incredible opportunities for understanding the processes of the human body could be gleaned, it was difficult not to see it the way he did. To be fascinated by something we cannot see, isn't that the greatest of mysteries?"

During this break in her narrative, Jean-Luc cast a worried glance to Mrs. Gordon who was beginning to look a little green. Dr. Gordon, however, was enraptured and spoke out in wonder.

"Just so. Just so. That's exactly what excites me about

medicine! I'd read about this case in a letter from a colleague, but not in such detail! Imagine having witnessed these experiments! I envy you, Mme. Delacroix, Dr. Beaumont will change everything we know about the digestive and gastric systems, he is seeing the unseen, as it were, hm? But, pray, Madame, do go on."

Cora smiled, approving of all of the reactions she was receiving.

"The doctor was relocated last August to Fort Niagara, and St. Martin has gone with him in order that he may continue his study. The last I had heard in a letter from papa was that Dr. Beaumont was to write a work on his findings, but I daresay he will not finish it for some time. He is exceedingly meticulous and thorough.

For my part, what I have observed, M. St. Martin is simply pleased to be alive, and cares not about the studies. His wild heart is growing restless with the doctor's tests.

But, it is miraculous, the human body can lose so much. So much blood, so much sweat, it can be riddled with bullets, or survive with little food. It can best the highest fever, it can go on when a heart is broken, or when a musket has torn a hole right through it. But, at the same time, a man can drown so easily, or fall from a high height..."

Her voice trailed off, but Jean-Luc could have sworn he heard very strange words from his wife's cherry ripe lips. While the doctor and his wife discussed the story of Alexis St. Martin and the good Dr. Beaumont, Cora looked distractedly into the glittering blue, the sun beginning its first descent. She had seemed so glowingly alive when recounting the tale, feeding on the fascination of her listeners. But now that those troubling, final, quiet words had slipped from her mouth, she looked slightly diminished, as if in saying them aloud she exhausted herself.

Jean-Luc could only hear the replaying of those last whispered words, words his wife had not intended anyone to hear.

"Or fall from a high height…or be murdered by the selfish wish of a broken woman…"

Disturbing words, words that chilled him to the bone.

For, Jean-Luc knew it was *he* who was responsible for his brother's death. He, who was the murderer.

:11:

Cora

She came out of her storytelling, trance-like focus to see a puzzled look on her husband's handsome features. At first, the look startled her, for he looked so much like Philippe in that moment that it fairly took her breath away. His face was missing the curling sneer she had last seen on her dead lover's face, though, and Cora checked her surprise before it could spill over onto her countenance.

The surgeon and his wife both greeted her with warm smiles, the doctor, she could tell, still caught in the snares of her tale. He was mumbling softly, "Fascinating…simply fascinating…" and shaking his head in wonder. All at once, he clapped Jean-Luc on the shoulder, shaking her husband from his strange reverie. Jean-Luc's eyes shifted back into focus, like a cloud drifting from the treetops to reveal the vibrance of the once-hidden sun on their green boughs.

"A fine tale, and I must admit that I am sorry to have missed it! What do you think of that Isobel, my dear? It sounds as if we have no call for boredom on this island, hm?"

Still beaming, he turned to face Jean-Luc full-on, and began distracting him with other questions of the island's inhabitants and goings on, and the two men wandered a pace down the deck. However, before he completely immersed himself in the steady attention of the excited surgeon, Cora felt a heat on her cheeks and raised her eyes to meet her husband's. They bored into her, speaking to her in the secret language they were both so used to speaking, but unable to translate as well as they used to. He was searching her, a code-breaker reading symbols he couldn't decipher. His eyes flicked away, suddenly, as if they had never been on her at all, and she felt strangely lonely. But, remembering herself, she offered a quick smile and nod of her head to Isobel Gordon, who was standing close to her, sharing her view.

Besides her sister, Cora was unused to the company of women her own age. Waseya had been like a mother to her, and the women of the town had been kindly when they weren't gossiping about her strange behavior. But, there was something bold and warm in the bearing of Isobel Gordon. Something that intrigued her. She came to stand closer to her, both of their gazes turned fearlessly toward the soft, somersault tumbles of the waves, and to the island that would be their home.

"It is very much different from my long crossing on the ocean, but there is something, *more* to it, I think. The lake seems…more welcoming, but also more secretive than the sea. Pardon me, am I talking any sense?" Isobel looked to Cora, her forehead creased in the attempt to find the right words.

Cora smiled deeply.

"Yes, it does. I was young when I left Boston, but the water of the Atlantic is a different blue altogether. There is something unique about the lakes of the Michigan territory, just as you say. Something…hidden. A treasure that is revealed very slowly."

The two women shared a brief expression of understanding. Cora suddenly feeling a sharp twist of loneliness in her breast for her island home. Though the house she was raised in was her home no longer, but instead her home would forever be with Jean-Luc. But no, that wasn't true either, for she had to admit her home had really always been in the forest, sharing the wilderness with him and Philippe. All the same, she was lonely for the happier times, for the moments she had perched atop arch rock, ruling the straits below.

"What is it like? Mackinac, I mean. Please, tell me everything, I must know!"

Although Isobel smiled with genuine interest and adventure, for a moment Cora went cold. Everything? She could never tell a single soul *everything*, not even he that her heart yearned to confide in. No, she could never tell everything, and the realization chilled her. Sometimes she could hardly admit it to her own heart, and she was ashamed that she still could not completely understand her own magic, nor how to use it properly. Especially as it was this ignorance that had buried her in sadness in the first place. That, and her recklessness. She understood her powers less than she understood her connection to the island itself, and to the spirits there, living and breathing inside of her, as if *she* were their home.

But the expression on Isobel's face was all sunshine, waiting for Cora to tell her of the island that she would come to dwell upon.

"It is difficult to explain, Mrs. Gordon." Cora began.

"Oh, please, call me Isobel. I long to hear my christian name spoken from a friendly face."

Cora smiled, knowing exactly how that felt. She longed to be simply, "Cora" after a year of being only "Madame Delacroix" to everyone excepting her husband.

"Very well, Isobel, but you too, must call me Cora."
She paused to collect the words she would need to make
this starry-eyed young woman see the island as she did.

"The island is small, but for someone of the right
temperament, life on its shores is somehow...very rich.
Full of variety. There are the sharp pebbled beaches, and
the dense, unnerving green of the forests. A green
speckled with golden sunlight, flecking and dusting the
forest floor with its warmth. Each bright puddle a chance
to warm oneself in the coolness of the never-ending
viridescent woodland. The island is many worlds. The calm
of the forest and the bustle of town, and the mysteries of
the rolling inland sea. The town is lively, and as I said, the
forest is impressive. There are rock formations so majestic,
and so large, that, if one squints their eyes just right, one
can almost see the Gitchi Manitou setting the stones where
they now stand. It is a wild place, where it seems anything
can happen, and often does."

Cora couldn't help but breathe out a long sigh of
memory and happiness, her aurelian eyes lighting up with
the sun. Isobel was considering her descriptions, and Cora
could almost see her painting the pictures in her mind.
"It sounds lovely, and your love for the island shines
through every word that you utter. I wonder that you could
leave at all..."
Cora turned away quickly, and sensing her blunder over
a tender spot, Isobel pursued a different topic.
"What is this 'Gitchi Manitou'? Jasper and I heard
some other talk from an Indian in Detroit, though we
could hardly make sense of it."

"Ahh, yes, well, I forget myself sometimes. You won't
hear much of it from the townsfolk, except in laughter
from behind their hands. Nor will you hear of it in the fort
either. But, the manitou is an important part of the tribe's

beliefs, and the legends of the island. Jean-Luc and I grew up on my nurse's legends, she being part native herself. For whatever reason, the spirits of the island always seemed... very real and present to us. You will find that there are some on the island that are a little more in harmony with Mackinac, and they are often those who keep these legends close. The soul of the island seems to hold them in its thrall. It is again, difficult to explain, and I'm certain it sounds exceedingly silly, a lot of hocus-pocus and all that, but it *is* true, somehow. Perhaps you will see for yourself when you arrive on the island. There is something singularly unusual to be found."

"Are you one of those who is affected by this strange sensitivity to Mackinac?" Isobel cast Cora a knowing smile, the words tinged with a hint of mockery. But, Cora was used to this, and so hardly noticed.

"I always thought so, but this past year I find that any sensitivity I had has numbed, and has in some places, gone frozen."

Offering her new friend a quizzical glance, both women resumed their quiet observation of the glimmering water. Cora was lost in thought, but her contemplation was soon broken by the hasty appearance of Nicholas Rast, his lip still broken and his features marred by a deep violet bruise. There was something wildly desperate in his eyes, and she realized she could not bear to look at him without pity, without an apology on her lips for the memories of him on the island. He strode quickly to her husband's side, and gave him a quick bow. Jean-Luc broke away from Dr. Gordon, calling a brief expression of regret at the abrupt closure of their conversation. She watched these two men, both boys from her girlhood, walk quickly together, their heads bent earnestly toward the other.

It was then that she felt the first raindrop. It was then that she smelled the strange, wet-earth scent of a coming storm. An unnatural storm. A storm that she had not called, but knew instantly who had.

*   *   *   *   *   *

Cora had made her way back down to the cabin. His voice had begun whispering in her ear as the first clouds had begun to darken. She had bid a hasty farewell to Isobel and had all but run back below deck. Her head was throbbing with the sounds of his urgent whispers. She felt his hands all over her body, invading her with his unwanted touch, both thrilling and repulsing her in turns. It was always that way with him. No middle ground. No compromise. The whisper in her ear grew fervent with longing, and it blocked all thoughts, all wishes, all communication to spirits, all reason. Dulling her magic, her wits, her resolve. The moment he had been ripped from the earth in death, he had become her shadow. To torment her, to attempt to seduce her, to inflame her passions to his bidding, as he had in life.

But she had fought. Ever day, she fought against him, struggled for herself, for her powers, for the happiness of a man she did not deserve, a man she had deceived for her tormentor.

She stopped, stilled her body and her thoughts, and screamed inside her mind,

"Get out! Get out! You have no power here!"

A bit primitive and immature of a command, but she hoped the anger and feeling behind the words would communicate. And as soon as he had invaded, he vanished.

Cora tilted her head back, smoothed the front of her gown, as blue as the troubled water, the color of the lake in a storm, the color of Philippe's cold eyes, and she began to write. She wrote to breathe. To cleanse herself of the memories, to burn them onto the page and out of her heavy heart.

"The memory of those first brazen challenges Philippe issued, his eyes on mine, I am ashamed to admit, still sends tiny jolts of

lightning up and down my body. Painful to remember, but pricks of raw energy all the same. Being with him was always that, raw, crackling energy that seemed to fizzle from my fingertips, and shoot from the ends of my hair. A life force I could not control, only blindly obey.

I wish I could say I felt guilty for what damage I was doing to Jean-Luc's tender heart, but I cannot, because I did not. I did not think of him at all, he had ceased to exist in my selfishness. So focused was I on the trembling excitement of the clandestine meetings with Philippe. If Jean-Luc was the steady solidness of Arch Rock, then Philippe was the straits of Mackinac. He was a roaring fire that set me alight, and delighted in watching me burn.

He was everywhere to me that summer. He surrounded me always, never even a thought away, as he was continually on my mind. He was in the air that I breathed and his heady scent, the coolness of the water mixed with the freshness of summer invaded my senses. He was in the food that I ate, and his fingers played through my hair in the wind. I know now that this was all poison. But, of course, then, it was different. I shake my head and am filled with the lamentations of a thousand sighs at my own foolishness. Do I sound hysterical? I hardly recognize the woman who writes words such as these. To always have been so strong in my own beliefs, to have earned the respect of those around me through my deeds and hard work— and to then abandon all of this without thought or question, all for the desire of a man who was a stranger. Yes, a stranger, for I did not know this dark, handsome, rake. The mischief and daring of childhood had transformed into something very different in his time on the rivers, and in the cold of those voyageur winters.

It is as if the spirits had deserted me, but I know in my heart it was I who deserted them, and myself. In my choice of Philippe I had strayed far from my magic. But those summer nights, just after the gloaming, we would meet in the clearing of the pines, the first haunting hoots of the owl beginning and last notes from the warblers coming to an end. I was always the first to arrive for our rendezvous, and soon he would come swaggering up, and the sight of him would singe me with fever. His unruly black curls, the twins of my own, carelessly falling over his forehead, obscuring his wolfish grin, until he tossed them backward. He looked so grand in his new finery, purchased with the money he earned from trading in his superior furs from the previous winter. Any man could bring in a stack of beaver pelts, but only Philippe could produce a stoat of the purest white, the trap laid so expertly that it only caught the animals paw, so as not to mar its perfect coat. There was some type of his own magic in it, and the men of his brigade held him in a kind of reverence.

For myself, to watch the happy beavers building their homes, splashing their mighty tails in the water, warning their families of danger—fur seemed a sad kind of business. A disruption to the harmony of the forest.

But on those nights, I found no fault with anything that Philippe could do. He would step right into me, inches from my face, I breathed in that intoxicating scent, new leather and clean lake, and his hot breath, hungry for me in the coolness of the night. He kissed me hard and sudden, another challenge I met unhesitatingly. His face would flash into that cruel smile, and he would call me his "wild one".

He was never interested in my daily life, or my family, my dreams and sorrows. I was simply a fire to warm himself with, though I did not know this then. Then, I knew nothing.

Taking my hand, he led me to the water, peeling off our clothes nimbly, his eyes never leaving mine. "Cat's eyes." He would say, astonished by my eagerness, but pleased. "Your eyes, they are golden starlight." We would sink into the dark water, two great fish, feeling at home in the caress of the lake.

Those midnight swims leave me breathless and shame-faced, even as I write these words. To imagine myself so…so…wanton! I blush to think of it, but I also cringe. It is not the passion that shames me, but the man I shared it with. If it had been another, someone more worthy of my love, I think the memories would bring only pleasure. But instead, my cheeks burn hot, and my stomach sinks in guilt.

As it is, I can still feel his expert hands sliding evenly down my naked back, to the curve of my waist and lower, as the soft waves lapped against us like a lover's tongue. His hands moving slowly to the curve of my hips, and despite the coolness of the water, all was heat. Blinding, burning, urgent passion, drinking each other in beneath the all-seeing moon. There were no promises made, but to me, *the gift of myself had been my pledge, and naïvely, I had imagined it was his as well.*

One night, as I lay on his strong chest, my black curls still wet coils, I told him that I believed that Jean-Luc had wanted to marry me. I do not know what prompted me to say it. Did I hope to make him jealous? Did I seek confirmation of his feelings for me? I do not know, for it was the inspiration of the moment. But, I did not expect the response I received.

He began to laugh, raucously and with abandon. The force of his reaction startled me, and I quickly stood up, backing away from him. Something in the sound of his laughter was disturbing, and somehow made me remember, briefly, that I did not know this man as well as I imagined. That he was not the young boy with laughing eyes anymore, but a man. A man with stormy eyes and a heart full of secrets.

"Why are you laughing like that?!" I had cried. "Philippe, you are frightening me!" Wiping the tears of hilarity from his face, he reached for my trembling hand, ignoring my hesitation, and pulled me back down to him.

"Ah, my beauty. I am sure Jean-Luc would love to get his strong hands on you—but I have beat him to it! As always, he has failed to take what is right in front of him, and so it has gone to me instead. No, my wild one, we both have wanted you, and now you are mine. But neither of us shall ever marry you. You are far too fancy and fine for us poor Mackinac men."

He laughed again, a hideous, hollow, mocking laugh, and I puzzled hopelessly over his words. I had not imagined there to be any enmity between the brothers, but here it was, glaring me in the face. And I, an instrument of that ill-feeling. The words he had used had been ugly. He had spoken of me as an object, a prize, and as the minutes moved by, I felt the anger rising in me. I gathered my powers to bend him to my will, but they had lain dormant so long in disuse, and the sound of his sweet slumbering brought me back to the moment. In repose, his face was the Philippe of my childhood. Sweetness and the love of fun, the playfellow of my youth, and now the object of my desire.

I must have misunderstood him, I thought. There must be a mistake, I willed myself to believe. Our meetings had been regular after that and I began to think I had imagined his strange words. After making love to me each night, as if he was a lost lover returned after a long absence, he would regale me with tales of trapping. Of surviving cold northern nights and the strange magic of the other tribes. He would hold me close and stroke his fingers through my curls, singing his voyageur songs in my ear. Kissing the base of my neck in between verses, his lips brushing the tops of my shoulders, his warm breath on my naked flesh, telling his tales of untamed northern nights.

But one night, as the end of summer neared, I grew terrified to see him leave. Terrified, as I had a tale of my own.

We were sitting near the shore, as always. My head laying on his chest, but somehow, that night, it did not fit perfectly in place as it had used to. I had thought all the day long exactly how to ask him, and now that the moment was here, my once sharp mind had barred me from any ideas. Shut against me, raging at my traitor heart for what it was wanting. Somehow in my obsession with Philippe, I had utterly lost my magic, and I no longer held sway over the waters and had lost the friendship of the forest. Something in his power over me had weakened my abilities, and my soul rebelled against the treason of my feelings. My nature understanding what was wrong for me, even when my heart could not.

He had been speaking of how soon his brigade would be departing from the Mackinac shores, and abruptly, I interrupted, the words I had tried to calculate tumbling over themselves like a toddling child.

"Philippe, I do not want you to go. You cannot leave again. I forbid it!"

"Ahh she is feisty, my wild forest sprite. You may not want me to go, but go I must, and go I will."

His eyes flicked to mine, in warning, daring me to contradict him.

I am certain he saw anger in my eyes, but I knew I must steel myself. I knew I must show myself a worthy adversary and not a weak woman to be controlled. I thought of all of the times I had snuck in and snuck out of my father's house for this man. I remembered the feeling of my obsidian ringlets still damp against my skin as I sat sweetly at the breakfast table. Every moment of this summer I had betrayed my father's trust, my own powers, and the nature of the island itself. I thought of the pained look on Jean-Luc's face when I saw him in town or one of the few times I came upon him in the forest. A look I had seen, but not registered until that very moment, when I needed it most to fuel my anger. A look of longing, a look that said he knew what I had done, but did not understand my choice.

I felt hot tears betraying me, showing my loss of strength, threatening to spill from the gambler's mask I so dearly needed when bargaining with Philippe.

"You will stay on this island. You will marry me. You will love me as you should. If you do not agree, I will make it so anyway. You know I have the powers of this island at my will."

I looked at him coolly, resolute and unyielding, daring him to laugh. But he did not. Instead he grew still with anger. And it was his stillness that scared me most.

"Sorcière, I have known you since we were children, and since I was a boy, you have made my pulse quicken with your enchantments over this woodland, and perhaps over myself as well. I was taken with your fearlessness and your wildness, and I only did seek you out because I believed your blood was as tempestuous as my own. But, I see now that you have been tamed by this island. If you weren't, you would understand that I cannot be locked into the prison of this place. Nor could I ever care for a woman who would wish it so. So, adieu, Cora, my wild one. Let us forget one another, and instead remember the beauty of the days we had."

He stood up haughtily, a prince ridding himself of an irritating supplicant.

White hot anger boiled, and I could feel the cooling touch of the manitou, and of all of the island spirits upon me. I was filled with a strange peace, and regretted the neglect of my magic. I had forgotten the gift of it, something so much more lasting than passion. Magic that was not tied to a tribe, but instead flowed through me always, as *necessary to me as the breath in my body and the beat of my heart. The magic of the island that I had cast aside as Philippe was now casting me aside. Still, I made one last appeal, for this was no longer just me.*

"Philippe, you must stay. I love you and I do not seek to imprison you. But neither do I wish our baby to never know his father."

The words were out. Words I had never planned on using, words that were beneath me. I was not one of those women who caught men in their nets with a child as bait. I had wanted him to agree to stay for love, for love of myself only.

His face did not change. Not a flicker. Not despair, nor excitement, nor fear. Simply nothing. And it was again, his stillness that was the most frightening to me.

"Do you imagine that you are the first woman who has shot these words at me? An arrow pointed to my good nature and sense of duty? You have no target, Mademoiselle. I already have a squaw waiting for me at my post, back at the Lake of the Woods. She has probably already delivered by now. Even she was clever enough to know I would not bring her with me, nor make her my wife. And she is content to see me on my return. I belong to no one save myself. So I say again, adieu, Cora, we are finished."

His eyes challenged mine one last time, a master giving his dog one final kick, as I placed a hand protectively to my still flat stomach. The right words sprang from deep within me, coursing through my blood out my lips.

"None of us, monsieur, belong to anyone but ourselves. But, love is not a prison except to the selfish and cold-hearted. It is the freeing of two souls, the recognition of the possibilities of great happiness that lies within another. So, as you say, farewell, Philippe, I pity your blindness."

I turned my back on him and strolled from the woods, sending a swirl of leaves to carpet my steps and to float around me protectively as I walked. I cursed him as I left, cursed him to never leave the island. Pleading with the spirits to hear me and keep him here. Begging the Manitou to make this man that I loved, love me in return, and to help me raise this child. Our child born of the island. To change him and make him worthy of me. I walked away from him, my head high and my back straight, loath to show any weakness, without even a backward glance. I could never have known that I would never see Philippe alive again."

She closed up the book just as Jean-Luc came into the cabin. She breathed out heavily, a great burden lifting from her breast and coming to rest on the pages she had trusted the words to. She saw his eyes fall on her own with concern.

"Mon Dieu, but you are the only woman who looks strongest when she has been weeping. I would ask if you are alright, but the steel in your eyes tells me that there is no need. You are healing yourself with every passing moment."

He bent to kiss her on the forehead, and without thinking, Cora tilted her head back in order to meet his lips with her own instead. His mouth opened to hers, and she tasted his cinnamon sweetness. Their kiss ended, with both of them bewildered at its happening at all, and at how much desire had been locked within them.

He stood up, awkwardly, and adjusted his buff coat, his tongue playing over his bottom lip, as if he was still trying to determine if it had been real. His mind fumbled to remember the words he had come in to say, his thoughts thrown into a hundred directions from the kiss that still lingered on his lips.

"Oui, well, it seems that a storm is brewing, and so I came down here to pass it with you. I have been talking at length with Monsieur Rast, and to be quite honest, I wanted to get your thoughts, if you can be troubled to offer them to me."

He looked back at her with his slow-moving smile, and Cora felt her breath catch. Their moments together were unusual and somehow mysterious, but she could not deny that she was, indeed, in love with her husband. The realization made her heart race, albeit in a different way than Philippe had made her blood sing. But this feeling was warmer, born of kindness and kinship. Her heart raced nonetheless, with the pace of her heart, however, there was also the undeniable presence of fear. If he knew all, how could he ever forgive her? How would he trust her love if he ever guessed what she had done?

Dismissing these thoughts, she rose and picked up her skirts to allow her to skip over and join her husband sitting on the bed, honored that he wanted her advice. Beaming with quiet happiness that she held the heart of a man who found her thoughts and ideas to be important.

But for how long?

:12:

Nicholas

After a short, fitful nap, he awoke. Nicholas was buzzing with the restlessness and panic of too much sleep. It took him a moment to recall that he was on a ship, bound back for Mackinac. Every moment, every brimming wave, carried him farther away from the charmed life he had built for himself on the continent. The closer the *Starlight* came to the shores of the island, the more he felt himself crumbling into the scared boy he had been the last time he had seen the swelling landscape of his home, the great tortoise sunning itself under the wide blue sky.

He fumbled about in his sheets for his pipe, and shakily stood up, all the while worrying the soft, well-loved, dark wood grain with his hands, thinking of the man that had given it to him and how dearly he wished for his guidance. Although, if Edward was here to guide him, then he wouldn't be on this ship to begin with. He shook his head to clear the confusing thoughts that buzzed in his mind.

As Nicholas dressed, his stomach heaved with sickness remembering the threats of the angry men at his bedside a few hours before. Although fear and disgust crept over his skin, he was resolved not to cower in his room like an old woman any longer. Adjusting the buckles on his shoes and the fit of his breeches, he only wished he had brought something to wear other than these *a la mode* styles so prized in the most fashionable circles in England. He saw now that as grand a figure he may cut in London or Florence, he was certainly not dressed for the hardy, rough life that bespeaks manhood in this wild place. Buttoning his fine shirt sleeves, he blushingly admitted to himself that though he knew his clothes singled him out, he was still unable to quash his pride in his appearance. A thought which only set him to shaking his head again.

He paused and breathed out heavily, taking comfort in the coolness of the pipe and the weight of it in his hand. It was always strangely wintry in his hot palms, like a stone from the bottom of a stream. No matter how desperately Nicholas clung to it, or how often his fingers had traced its curves, it never warmed to his touch, a soothing talisman to his burning soul. He filled with shame for trying to be rid of it. It was all there was left of Edward in this world, the Edward he remembered, anyway.

Excepting, Jean-Luc. Nicholas considered a moment, he did seem a bit like Edward, didn't he? True, he had been keen enough before to tell him of his brother, and he had been careful and kind enough not to mention the...the unfortunate event that had led to Nicholas' exile. So, perhaps he would do well to befriend this strong, considerate man.

He quickly finished dressing and oiled his hair to gleaming, as bright as a new penny. He noticed that the bruise on his cheek was deepening and the cut on his lip was angry, but no matter. He was a man sorely in need of friends, and dearly in need of forgiveness, perhaps looking a touch pitiful might help his cause. Turning from the looking glass, he had a singular aim, and that was to make Jean-Luc his confidant. And through him, to win himself the respect of those on the island through the companionship of a man they knew and trusted.

His hand reached out to un-bolt the door and his confidence faltered. Was this goal disingenuous? Was he, in fact, the villainous, insensitive man he knew they all feared him to be? Was he hoping to use this friendship for his own gain, or was he sincerely committed to change? He did not know, but only wished, again, that he had tarried a little longer in reading that ill-omened, odious letter from his mother. That his eyes had never traced the familiar loops of her handwriting, that his mind would have remained barren of all thoughts of this past life. This life that must now be his future. A great chill passed through his frame, and doubt enveloped him in its smoky embrace.

He heard it again. The same maddening voice as yesterday, fanning the flames of his temper, confronting him with doubt. He stopped where he stood, hand still on the handle of his cabin door, in order to make out the words cutting into his sanity. What was this invisible voice that spoke to his greatest fears? This shadowed specter that knew every ache in his heart, who mocked him without any thought or care? The words, although incomprehensible, tugged at him, stabbed at him, filled his mind with dread and anger. The voice was familiar, but like the words, he could not quite identify it. The whispers rang louder, filling his head, violently squeezing out thought and confidence, leaving him bereft. He had a sudden urge to throw himself overboard or to plunge his pocket knife into his heart. He swelled with an unknown unimaginable anger, but the voices seemed to swirl still more powerfully in his mind. He realized he was losing control, a prisoner in his own body. He could feel himself growing heavy, feel his knees shake and buckle beneath him, his vision was naught but blackness. Subconsciously, his hand reached for his pocket and with a single touch, the coolness of the pipe brought him back to his senses. Once again, the late afternoon sunlight poured through his small window, warming his shoulders and back. His breathing became regular, and he felt straight and strong. The cruel, mocking voice was gone as completely as if he had imagined it. He shook his head, to clear the malice of the unbidden encounter, and gave a small hollow laugh, his hands still shaking violently.

More than ever he was resolved to seek asylum from his damaged mind and damaged reputation in a friendship with Jean-Luc. He had become a kind of beacon to Nicholas, for whatever reason, he was a symbol of safety and tolerance, and Nicholas felt he needed both. He had no brother to cling to, or to speak for him, and so he would toss his fortunes in with this man, if he would have him, for he understood now that he could not make it on his own.

As for the bewitching Mrs. Delacroix, and the effect she had upon Nicholas? He would put her out of his mind completely. It wasn't attraction that drew him to her exactly, but instead more like a kindredness. A counterpoint to something inside of him, but he hadn't the faculties for sorting it all out presently.

He rushed on deck, though he knew that to any observing him that he appeared a madman, wild-eyed and red-faced. But he was bent on telling his tale to Jean-Luc, to unburden himself, and relax into the absolution the full confession would bring. He knew that no punishment could be worse than the silence of his secret, which was a cacophony in his own tortured soul. And no judgement of him could be worse than his own. He would lay himself bare before the playmate of his youth, as he should have with Edward. And perhaps Jean-Luc's courage would lend itself to Nicholas, or his condemnation of him would confirm that he could never, and should never have thought to return.

Stepping onto the deck, he felt a suffocating tightness in the air as his eyes darted about the ship, feverishly, in order to locate Jean-Luc. Before he was able to call out his name, Jean-Luc caught his eye and offered him a swift, good-natured acknowledgment with a tilt of his head. Nicholas bounded to his side and realized he had been holding his breath since arriving on deck. He exhaled heavily, and noticed the confusion on the face of a man standing alongside of Jean-Luc. He instantly saw his mistake. Jean-Luc had been in conversation with this other man, and he had rudely interrupted, already flawing his plan for greater popularity in his bumbling. Jean-Luc, the single curl of a smile in his direction, called an excuse to the other man and took Nicholas by the arm, leading him away.

"Monsieur Rast, what is the matter? You look as a man haunted."

His expression was good-natured, even if his words revealed the truth.

"I wanted to apologize, Jean. I find myself a stranger in my own homeland, and I fear that I know not who I am, or where I belong. I can't help but understand why most would be reluctant to accept me back into their society."

He frowned deeply, but Jean-Luc waved him off.

"Non, forget all about it. There is not a word to be said. It was long ago and everything was different then. Everyone will soon forget the past, mon ami. They *must*."

His words were said consolingly, but Nicholas saw that the man's eyes were lost in the horizon, and that the proclamation was meant to convince himself as much as

Nicholas. What in the world could Jean-Luc be trying to leave behind in the past?

"Before, you were speaking of Edward. The two of you...you were friends then?"

Jean-Luc considered this, and tilting his head to the side, his eyes still on the horizon, he shrugged his shoulders.

"In a way, perhaps. Your brother was a good man, and I admired him very much. But, we had...drifted apart from the closeness we had in our youth. It was around the time you left, I suppose. Of course, I still saw him from time to time, to go fishing in the canoe or to stop and converse in the street, but I would be lying if I said we were close. There was just something that was lost between us, trapped in time, that did not carry over in our lives as we became men. Since the time you left, my life has been Cross Shipping and Cora Ravensdale, with very little else, I'm afraid."

He absentmindedly opened up his snuff box, and seeing it was empty, closed it back up and returned it to his pocket. Nicholas felt the press of his own story begin to slacken in his old friend's company, his interest in his own problems falling away in his curiosity of this elder Delacroix's life, and that of his younger brother. Both men stood silently for a moment, both feeling a fond type of intimacy forming between them, the kind only brought about by shared experiences and common memories. Both were returning to the island of their birth under strange circumstances, Nicholas could see that now. He could not guess, nor could he ask what reason had precipitated Jean-Luc's departure, but he felt the waves of anxiety regarding his return flowing from him now, and was surprised he had not felt the man's nervousness before.

And, they both had lost a brother. Nicholas was seized by the impulse to inquire after the nature of Philippe's death, and could not catch himself before the words came tumbling out.

"Please, you've spoken of Edward, and his final act of heroism and bravery in death. It is these tales of him and his consuming goodness that strike the most pain into me. Knowing that my closest blood and only friend will not be there on the shore to meet me. But, I would ask about another..."

Jean-Luc cut in before Nicholas could finish his ill-framed question.

"He certainly displayed great courage. Not many of us jumped in that day to lend aid. And those of us who did knew it to be a fool's errand the moment our flesh plumbed the raging lake. Edward will be remembered as a hero. But, I know he would be proud to see you returned to take your place amongst your family."

Nicholas was nodding his head, glad of the sentiments, but eager for the conversation to move on.

"I like to think so. And might I say that I thank providence that one of you made it out of the storm alive."

He did not reply to this and Nicholas felt awkward at his inability to grasp Jean-Luc's mood. He fidgeted for a moment before posing his question straight out.

"I am to infer then, that Philippe...well, that Philippe perished in the same fashion? Did he, too, attempt to save those drowning in the waves?"

It was Jean-Luc's turn to look awkward. His eyes pierced into Nicholas', startled. On his face was written a hundred horrors that appeared very much like guilt. It passed, quickly, but Nicholas felt himself seize with chills at the sight.

"Indeed, no. Philippe did leave this earth a fortnight before your brother. And under much less admirable conditions."

His eyes took on the same faraway look again from earlier, and something in his manner said that he would brook no more questions. His face was colder, and

Nicholas feared he had offended in some way. They stood silently, again, each man lost to their own thoughts and confronting the realities of their situations. Finally, it was Nicholas who broke the uneasy quiet.

"I meant to apologize a moment ago for rudely interrupting your conversation, and for my behavior on deck yesterday. I am not customarily one for brawling. I do not know what came over me, truly, I was a man possessed. Thinking back on my actions, frankly, I am appalled. The same as I am appalled concerning my….inactions in another circumstance…"

Their eyes met as his voice trailed off. Jean-Luc made to brush away his apologies as unnecessary, but Nicholas pressed on. His brow was covered with a mixture of sweat and rainwater, as the first raindrops that had been threatening to fall had finally made their glistening debut. For these island men though, the wet was hardly noticeable, even while the rest of the passengers ducked snugly below deck and the crew came scurrying to the wooden planks, readying the *Starlight* for whatever nature may toss her way.

Their eyes were still locked as Jean-Luc anticipated the question that would soon fall like blood from Nicholas' broken lips. He waited though. Waited for Nicholas to say the words, waited to answer a question he did not desire to be asked. Part of him felt he shared the blame for what had happened, as any child feels guilty when something befalls a playmate that has been left behind.

"Come, my old friend. Tell me what you have heard. Tell me what is said to have happened that day, that last day of my childhood. The day that I learned the agony of life's choices. So that I might be prepared to face those on Mackinac."

He had attempted to sound glib, but a shudder had gripped him as soon as the words were spoken. In his mind's eye, again and again, he watched Beshkno's eyes dilate with fear as he fell from the tree. He watched as his body broke mercilessly in the bracken, and heard the sickening crack of splintering bones, breaking like limbs from a sapling. He felt himself grow faint, and slipped his hand into his pocket to grasp his beloved totem. In a moment, the horror had passed and he was able to guard his features. But the concerned look on his friend's face told him the episode had not passed quickly enough to go unnoticed. Jean-Luc's eyes softened, as though seeing Nicholas for the first time, and he grasped the younger man's arm at the elbow, looking into his eyes.

"It does not matter what they say. Not a bit of it. Our lives are our own, do you hear? Mon Dieu! Do not worry about the clucking of a few hens! Those who care for you think not a single word against you. We will take them on together, you and I."

This pronouncement was far kinder than he had expected, or even hoped for. But still, the question lingered and he must have an answer.

"Jean-Luc, your words touch my very soul. I have had naught but nightmares at the thought of coming home since sailing from England. To have a friend, if I may call you such, at my side, is the perfect panacea for my misgivings. I am afraid though, that besides your friendship, so recently rediscovered, I have no other to claim. I still would know what is said, so that I might prepare myself for the cruelty of those who would besmirch my name before I am able to show myself a changed man."

Nicholas guarded his tone. Trying his best to hide any of the pleading that he felt, from his words. He knew his marred appearance would already speak volumes about his character to those who would see him disembark. His purple contused cheek, and his split mouth preceding him as evilly as his reputation earned as a scared young boy.

"You are wrong of course, my friend. Your mother and father love you well, though you may not know it. No, do not contradict me, for I have seen the proof of their regard many times, in their pride over your many accomplishments abroad. They are known to call them out loudly to all, keen for the island to see you in a new light. As for your question, I must admit I am loath to answer it, but I see you will not discontinue wondering if I do not. So, I suppose I must oblige."

He cleared his throat and looked to Nicholas, judging one last time if he must really discuss the slander charged against him as a youth of some twelve years. Seeing it was so, he cleared his throat once more, ran a hand over his sandy hair, and continued.

"Some say you pushed the boy into the pit. Still others say you beat him mercilessly with a fallen bough or a cudgel of some kind. And then there are those that say, well, they say that you forced him to his death through... sinister means."

"What type of sinister means?" Nicholas asked. His whole body filled with the sickening blackness of fear.

"Well, they say you, magicked him to his death, I suppose."

Nicholas felt a low moan escape his throat. A sound that came from him and at the same time could not be coming from him. A hollow haunting wail that reverberated through his whole being. Jean-Luc swung an arm around his shoulders, as the rain began to fall in earnest. He made to hustle the young man back below deck, him being in no position to remain out in the storm, and Nicholas' reaction had admittedly frightened him terribly.

Nicholas only felt strong arms leading him back down, out of the elements. He hadn't realized how wet he had become from the downpour. He heard a calming, brotherly voice reassuring him. His heart went out to his lost Edward, such a sound as he had longed to hear for far too long. Nicholas was led gently back to his cabin, and Jean-Luc gave him promises to continue their conversation when Nicholas had the time to fully sort through this news, with assurances he would return in a few hours. Jean-Luc had just stepped into the doorway when Nicholas called him back.

"Jean-Luc, stay! Stay a moment, I pray you. It has set as a stone on my heart for ten years, and now I find that if I do not speak of it, the stone shall fall through and collapse my heart, my lungs and my being completely."

Seeing that he had Jean-Luc's attention, he gathered his courage to continue his confession, for once and all.

"That boy, he was my friend. Our playmate. I wished him no ill-will, felt for him nothing but friendship. But in my heart, I have torn myself to pieces for wondering if I did, somehow, cause it."

His eyes looked imploringly into Jean-Luc's, beseeching him to understand.

"I saw him fall. I saw it in my mind and then as if I had seen the boy's destiny play before me, I powerlessly, watched in true time as Beshkno fell to the earth. I had a vision of his death...and then it...it happened. At first, I could not believe it. It seemed a nightmare...but when I looked down into the pit and saw his bones, sticking out cruelly, white splinters on bronze skin, I knew that he was dead. Truly dead. I ran from him in my terror. In my horror that I had somehow willed it to happen simply by thinking it. I left the boy to die alone, and I too, died a little at my own cowardice."

Nicholas fell back against his pillows, spent from his confession. Feeling an unexpected relief from some of the strain of carrying the burden of the secret around with him nearly half of his short life. When he looked to Jean-Luc's even features, though, his eyes were lit up strangely, excited about something in the terrible tale Nicholas had related. When he replied, his words came rapidly, tumbling over each other in his hurry.

"A vision you say? So, a kind of magic perhaps, after all? Yes, I think so."

He muttered enthusiastically to himself. "Don't trouble yourself about this at all, my friend. In fact, I may know someone who can elucidate all of this for you. But tell me, do you still retain this power of prophecy to any extent? Any visions or feelings about objects or people? Are you sensitive to moods?"

The light in his eyes grew even brighter, two green flames in the semi-darkness of the cabin.

Nicholas was about to object to the absurdity of the conjectures, when he remembered the voice in his mind yesterday and today. He recalled the burns on his hands from reading that fateful letter. His mind drifted to the way he could recall every word of the Indian legends of his childhood. He remembered the way he had always known when it would rain on his uncle's country estate and knew just by looking at them which foals would not last the winter. He recalled many a gentleman's club and the way he knew which cards would be played, and how much would be wagered. All of these truths flitted through his mind, and his eyes suddenly locked onto Jean-Luc's, as a silent understanding passed between them.

Jean-Luc had been standing in profile before Nicholas, and now turned around completely to face him. In a kind of trance, Nicholas felt the image of the island spring before his eyes, and for the first time since his exile, the image was not hateful to him. He spoke.

"Often I have returned to Mackinac in memory. My mind skims over the rocky cliffs and through the leaves of the verdant forest. My boy's legs scramble up a tree, or race around the wood in pursuit, trying to find my friends that are hiding in sport. Always knowing where each playmate was hidden before I even opened my eyes. All save you,

Philippe and Cora. You were always obscured from me as in a fog."

The realization pricked at him, an idea he could not quite verbalize, as if the word itself was one he had never heard before.

"Now, my mind takes me to the beach where we swam in the sun, all of us boys coming home as brown as the spring-tapped maple syrup, kissed by the light from the clouds. Then, I see my own house before me. I can see the lilac trees that my mother so lovingly tended, and can smell their soft sweetness. The house is gleaming brightly with its new white wash of the season. My feet dance up the cobblestone walk, but I am always afraid to knock on the oak door. I bring my fist up to rap upon it, and realizing it is my own home, the corners of my mouth lift, and instead I grab for the handle, feeling foolish to knock on my own front door. At this point, my mind freezes and a grey fog descends. I know not if my own family is inside, or if it is peopled with rogues who have murdered them in their beds. I am afraid that those inside will be unfamiliar to me, and will cast me out. I look to the house and cannot tell if it is whole and solid, or if the white is scorched with smoke. My eye does not know if it sees the pain of the past, the reality of the present or a prediction of a tragic future.

I know that I will walk that path again, and soon, Jean-Luc, but this time, not traveling in memory. This time I will walk in true time, and in the winds of the island. What does it portend? What does it mean? What will I find on that path back home?"

Jean-Luc took a step toward the bed and regarded Nicholas steadily.

"I cannot say, mon frer. But I think it is naught but love you will find in that house. Rest now, and do not let cares overtake you. I must see to my wife, but next we speak, I know I shall have words to ease your doubts."

With those words, he walked purposefully out the door, leaving Nicholas more comfortable than he had been since the moment he had seen the letter from his mother, all those months ago, but also with more questions. He nestled in to rest, emotionally taxed from his day of confessions and altercations. Having a sudden thought, he opened an eye, and noticed the unlocked door, which he promptly jumped up and bolted before plunging himself into his own personal sea of sheets.

:13:
Walter

As the first drops fell, Walter looked on, fatherly, as the passengers scattered like children dismissed from their lessons, quickly scurrying back to their dry cabins. They would snuggle up and watch hopefully out their porthole windows, waiting out this irritating patter of rainfall. He could not help but chuckle to himself at the absurdity of it. Here they were, on a great gleaming vessel, surrounded on all sides by water. Traveling upon this great inland sea, glorying in the wet, and yet, a few lowly raindrops could send trepidation into the hearts of the lot of them. His smile broad, his head shaking in disbelief, he noticed, still chuckling, that young Rast and Delacroix were not among those retreating to dryness. Instead they stood, heads together, whispering conspiratorially, oblivious to the falling droplets donning their bare heads and wetting their collars. The sight of the two of them gave Captain Alberts a strange, paternal surge of pride, and for a moment all of his concern for the two men fell away. No amount of gossip, or drama, or disparaging whispers on the island could touch them. He believed truly, here in the beginnings of this tiny tempest, that all of their secrets and sins, whatever they were, were washing clean. A new start for this next generation of Mackinac men.

Even in the midst of his duties, now that the wind had changed, his mind journeyed quietly back to his own young manhood, and how he had conversed just so with a young Pierre Delacroix. Two young men, excited about the world and the possibilities that they both knew lay in wait for them. This was when they were newly married, before they had both welcomed mewling children into the world. And, most definitely before they also both, in turn, buried some of those beautiful children, which had made the infinite possibilities and adventures in front of them seem very limiting indeed.

He frowned as he pulled on the rigging, alongside of Big Charlie and another fellow from his crew, a newer addition whose unlikely name was Percy Beauregard Fitzwilliam, but was known to the crew as simply, "Leathers". He was a genial man, forever smiling, and whistling and slapping men on the back, quick with a joke and a ready ear for a story. Captain Alberts liked the man, as it was difficult not to, but was not satisfied with his story of himself. The Captain had asked his connections in port and inquired among the crew and other captains, but had trouble discovering much about his origins or his people. Most captains would not mind so long as the men on his crew proved to be skilled sailors who did not cause trouble, but Alberts was meticulous when it came to choosing the men for his ship. His friend, his employer, Pierre Delacroix had long left off questioning his methods and had learned to trust his good judgement.

Leathers grunted with exertion next to him and then shook his head, scattering the dribbles of rain from his hair and onto the men around him, seemingly luxuriating in the growing winds. The crew was singing merrily as they adjusted the sails and the captain tried to join in to the jolly mood. But, as he re-checked his instruments, he noticed the winds had shifted again, this time violently, whipping about him ferociously, hungry for destruction. The rain too, had begun to fall more rapidly and with greater force, each raindrop becoming a painful poke in his flesh. The songs of the crew began to quiet and then subside. Captain Alberts' brow creased with worry. Something troubled his conscience, something inexplicable about the ferocity of the onslaught that niggled at his brain, reminding him of the unsettling calm of the day before. Just what was happening on his *Starlight?*

With the falling drops misting his vision, he watched as the blue sky of a hazy, late afternoon turned grey and then black before his very eyes. Startled at the swiftness of the change, he saw Jean-Luc and Nicholas finally retreating to the safety and dry of the cabins. Jean-Luc's arm was around the younger man, and just before he disappeared from the deck, his head turned back, face catching the rain, and threw Captain Alberts a look that spoke of many things. Of alarm, and responsibility and worry for the ship and for the man he was aiding. His head turned back around, and tucking his arm more tightly around Rast, they continued below. Walter marveled for a moment at just how much Jean-Luc seemed like Pierre. He had seen the very same look of concentration, focus and action on the older man's face, an attitude and bearing that placed him above others, a man that others could lean on and follow. He hardly had time to consider what had befallen Nicholas that would call for M. Delacroix's support, but instead, spoke up to give orders to the men.

The ship would not stay the course in these contrary winds, and their situation grew only more precarious. The time had come for Captain Alberts to take his place and inspire courage in the hearts of his crew, and spur them on through whatever this storm would blow at them. He steeled his resolve and called out a list of commands that sent the men running to their respective posts. His usually calm voice carried in the storm, a booming cannon exploding out onto the deck, every man aboard heeding his orders the moment they were issued.

This should have been his element, but, he could not shake his earlier misgivings. Walter did not like the smell of this storm; it burned his nostrils, not the clear lake smell he was used to, but something acrid and sickening lingering in the air. He took his handkerchief from the inside of his sopping coat pocket and passed it hurriedly over his drenched face, any remaining dry spot on the handkerchief as wet as the lake itself, rendering its further use impossible. He picked his cap up and felt the water fall from his salt and pepper hair, and replaced the hat, which was useless as well. Still gripping the handkerchief, his thumb ran over his wife's initials, so neatly stitched. He was wondering if the same rain was falling on their little house in town as well, and what she was doing in that moment. Pressing it to his lips softly, he thrust it back into his pocket and stepped into a semi-covered corner on deck, attempting to stay out of the rain as much as possible in order to better read his instruments.

It did not matter, he finally admitted to himself, after several minutes of jostling to stay supported as he tried to make out the numbers and directions, repeatedly wiping water off the unreadable devices. The rocking and swaying of the schooner, as it tossed and tumbled through the raging blue, the waves growing larger with every scream of the wind. The instruments were worthless in conditions like these, and so instead he would fall back on his experience and captain's confidence. He could not help but begin to fill with something very much like fear, which he knew from years on the lakes was the friend of any true sailor. Men without fear were taken into the water, claimed by the waves, as the inland seas are fed by the fearlessness of foolish, incautious men.

He shivered and realized that it would be a miracle to bring everyone alive out of a storm like this. Even if the winds passed and the rain stopped, death by chill would still threaten his passengers and crew. There were many ways to die on the lake, and Captain Alberts had seen more than his share of them. He charged out from the corner, the rain coming in thick sheets, covering the men bodily, the schooner seeming as though it had already capsized. Surely, there could be no more water below them than there was, right now, on deck. He had seen many gales in his time, had faced devastation and lost good men, but he had never experienced nor heard tell of a storm to rival this. Water pooled on deck so that every step was a sloshing swim, the wood swollen from the saturation, the mast creaked and all about him, the crew was performing their tasks admirably. All aboard were violently tossed, and Walter knew to keep a tight grip on the wood, as one would a scared horse, lest he be tossed into the blue oblivion.

The lightning began then, just as he was feeling as though he was beginning to be on the right side of things. A bolt of bright white in the sky, illuminating each raindrop, a thousand, hundred thousand, a million of them twinkling gaily in the menacing night. Walter was truly a blind man, directing the ship through will alone, calling upon the Lord and all of the spirits of the lake to help guide him. The waves were now treacherous peaks and valleys as the ship traversed the rapidly altering heights, somehow retaining its balance under Captain Albert's steering and intuition. Every crack of thunder in the sky seemed cruel laughter, the world itself mocking him and his efforts. But, this was his ship, and his crew and he would not give up. His arms, he knew, would be aching on the morrow, and his legs too, from holding himself in place as he spun the wheel this way and that, somehow staying atop the waves. It seemed unbelievable that this had all begun with a small, winking sun-shower, harmless glitter on a happy afternoon.

It seemed to go on and on, the storm spinning dangerously, end upon end. The wind and rain could have been threatening to blow the *Starlight* over for minutes or hours, Walter had no idea of time. He had only focus for the task at hand, a concerned father with a sickly child, his place was in the thick of things, with his love, his ship. Sometime during the melee, Jean-Luc suddenly appeared at his side shouting, pleading for occupation. Captain Alberts gripped his shoulder, and shouted into his ear.

"My boy! Your occupation is to be the heir to this shipping company! I need you below decks, reassuring passengers and staying *alive,* so that my crew and myself have future employment! Forgive me, sir, but this ship is in the hands of powers greater than my skill and your strong back combined. I beg you back below deck, sir!"

Captain Alberts could not help but admire the young man's audacity, but all that he had told him, unfortunately, was true. It would help not at all to have him on deck, he was needed below. Jean-Luc clasped his arm and with a nod of his head, was gone again.

With the disappearance of M. Delacroix, Alberts felt all at once, very alone. He could see the frenzied shapes of his crew in the rigging and bailing the ever rising water from the deck, but he could not make out their faces in the weather. Nor could they hear his voice, or he theirs, through the deafening shrieking of the wind.

His mind went back to his wife, Agnes, his daughter, Caroline and wee James. Caroline would be married in late summer and James, his miracle, healthy and hearty after losing two other boys, was just taking his first wobbling steps on pudgy pink legs. James hadn't even been aboard a ship yet! Agnes, his sweet Agnes, who was both mother and father while he was away, sailing the lakes of the Michigan territory. Damn it all! Come what may, he would return to them. He threw his head back, water hitting his face with such force he felt that he was drowning, and he laughed in the eye of the tempest. He laughed long and hard, while his arms instinctively controlled the sailing of his beautiful, indomitable lady, his gorgeous, flying *Starlight*.

His laugh was cut short by the sound of canvas dissevered, a mangled tatter of fabric, hanging useless. The fore topsail was naught but shredded, white ghosts soaring in the wind. A lightning strike lit up the lake and he saw clearly the expressions of terror on the men's faces. This spelled trouble indeed, unnatural trouble that he could not but feel was blatantly working against his voyage.

Alberts stepped away from the ship's wheel, passing it to his first mate, and ran to his men on deck, shouting encouragements, a general with his army. The men took heart and continued tirelessly as the ship buckled and swayed, threatening to turn on its side at the slightest provocation.

Alberts hurriedly returned to his post, steering gravely through the wall of drenched night. He felt more confident, could feel the tiller respond to his commands, he was one with the ship. He was still afraid and he was soaked down to his very bones, the rain refusing to let up. But, spirits were still high, and as long as he could keep them from flagging, surely he could pull them through this. The storm could not go on forever, could it? It reminded him of Mackinac's creation story, the storm raging for three days and nights before passing, revealing the island. What would be revealed at the close of this? Perhaps they would be swept all the way back to the shores of Mackinac, her rich spring greenness providing a haven from this damnable night.

Lightning flashed again, and in the light he saw Big Charlie striding up to Leathers, who was growing weak from holding fast to the rigging and bailing the never-ending water. Big Charlie reached out to the smaller man, assisting him to stand. Darkness fell as the light from the sky disappeared, and then the light lit the ship again, and Charlie was gone. Vanished. Leathers was barely hanging on to the railing, in danger of falling into the swirl himself.

Captain Alberts was upon him in a blink, and others nearby had rushed to aid. The usually good-natured man was stricken dumb.

Alberts ordered his first mate, Reynolds, to take the wheel and Alberts hauled Leathers into his captains quarters, plying him with brandy. The small figure heavy with sodden coat and trousers, more lake than man. The captain demanded to know what had just transpired. Leathers opened and shut his mouth a few times, uselessly, like a fish pulled from the water, unable to breathe in the foreign environment.

"Speak man! Did he fall in?" Ordinarily, Walter would not have troubled himself with the storm's victims until it had passed, but something had caught his attention in that sliver of darkness. Something in Leather's eyes forced the inquiry. Finally, the man swallowed several times, loudly, and looked at Alberts with wild, unseeing eyes.

"Murdered, sir. He was pulled in, he was! I'll never forget it, 'til the end of my days. A man, sir. All in black with black hair, the devil himself! He reached out for Charlie's hand, and then he was gone, and Charlie with him! Gone! Murdered! Murdered!"

His cries were hysterical and growing increasingly more so with each breath. And although Alberts knew that none aboard could hear him over the driving rain and wailing winds, he still slapped Leathers to quiet him. Either he'd gone mad, imagined the whole thing, or something devilish really was tearing his ship apart. In any case, his wailing would help nothing. When he didn't cease his cries of "Murder", Alberts gave him a stiff thunk on the head with the brandy bottle, effectively knocking him out. He then took a swig for himself to quiet the memory of the man's cries from his own mind. Stepping over the prone figure of Leathers, he grabbed a flask and filled it and thought to find a cloth to wipe his sodden face, but chuckling manically to himself, realized it would matter not.

He stumbled back on deck to find the rain was still falling heavily, but it had slackened in violence. He went to relieve Reynolds, and passing him the flask, the man drank greedily before speaking.

"She's sailing true and steady, Captain. Steadier since Charlie fell overboard, though it seems that the lake has demanded a very dear price this night for our passage. A more unwilling tribute I've never seen."

The Captain's face was immovable as stone. He did not like to speak aloud thus, as it sounded like woman's tales in his ears, though he had been thinking the same himself. He considered for a moment before replying.

"Big Charlie will be missed. A fine man and a better sailor. His family will be cared for and make no mistake."

Now it was Reynolds' turn at confusion.

"Oh, but Captain, sir, then you do not know? Derry and Blankenship are lost as well, and M. Delacroix, sir, he is unconscious."

Walter's mouth dropped in bewilderment as his first mate went on to explain.

"The fore boom, sir, caught him. I daresay it was soundless and invisible in the rain"

Captain Alberts looked at Reynolds dumbly, as he heard the same cruel laughter of the thunder overhead.

"Is he very hurt? When did it happen?" He demanded of the exhausted man.

"I'm sorry, sir. But, I do not know. I had not seen him come on deck. But, he seemed to be on his way back down when he was struck, though no one will admit to having been near, or on, the boom. Big Charlie was first to him, rest his soul, and was the one who picked him up and carried him to the new doctor. It was strange to see a big man like that, carrying a man as tall and muscled as M. Delacroix, as gently as if he had been a new babe. He's with Dr. Gordon now, sir."

Captain Alberts' face was a mask of helplessness as the rain, mocked him by falling still more gently. Big Charlie had carried Jean-Luc to safety, and had in turn been carried to the jaws of death himself. The whole night rang too close to his terrible nightmare, and no amount of brandy would shake the images from his mind. He asked himself, not for the first time, just what was happening on this voyage. What was tormenting this ship?

Reynolds left him to walk the deck and talk to the remaining crew. Alberts, though, stood there, muttering to himself and steering lazily as the wind died down and the rain ceased. The skies remained hard and black but no longer ominous, a fitting black mourning for his dead men. The long, horrific day had at some point slipped into the serenity of night.

It was over, but with a heavy price paid, too high a toll extracted. Breathing heavily, releasing some of his own pent up exhaustion. He gave the wheel over to Reynolds on his return and headed to his cabin to change quickly out of his sopping clothes, lest he catch a chill and add to the growing death toll. He saw with some satisfaction and a little guilt that whether from the knock on the head or exhaustion from the events of the storm, that Leathers was as good as unconscious himself. He stepped back out on deck, and saw that the top sail was already being repaired by the crew, though it might take a few more dark hours before it was again whole. It would need replacing when they reached Mackinac. The lost men would need replacing as well, though, he knew good men were much more difficult to substitute. The rest of the crew were painstakingly removing the excess water and cleaning the ship, offering him a respectful nod as he passed before them continuing with their work.

He made to visit Jean-Luc and ascertain the gravity of his injury. It would not do for his future employer to be struck on his own ship, it really wouldn't. He slipped below deck and his feet picked the way toward the Delacroix cabin, when a heart-wrenching scream stopped his tread.

"He's gone!"

The owner of the voice was outside of the captain's vision, but his heart dropped in his chest just the same. They had to be speaking of Jean-Luc. Alberts felt for the first time that day as if he could not bear to go on, and his breath caught in his chest. The voice, unaware of the captain's presence in the corridor, continued a little less shrilly, to whomever she was speaking to.

"It's Nicholas! He has vanished!"

Walter, seized by a completely different horror, burst into the room to find a ghostly white Cora Delacroix, fainting onto the bed next to the bandaged and pale form of her husband.

:14:

Julia

She found the letter precisely where she had stowed it, tucked into a small cubbyhole in her escritoire. Julia Rast had reached her long fingers into the space, tentatively, terrified she would not feel the soft, well-loved paper. The letter from Nicholas, her baby, though a boy no more, was dearer to her than any of her fine furs or any of the brooches or delicate exotic knick-knacks her husband imported through the fur company. The letter was precious because of the hand that had written it, and the mind that had conceived the words.

Not that the words were particularly loving, if anything he sounded in turns stricken about returning home, and then annoyed to leave the life he had made for himself amongst his relatives. She could see the unfairness of it, but she couldn't separate her own feelings about the matter. She was ready to gaze upon his oft-imagined face. It was finally time, her boy—returning home!

There had been reports of the ship's delay and strange weather conditions on the lake, but she would be patient. Ironically, the last few months had been harder to bear than all of the last nine and half years before. But, now that she was right on the cusp of seeing Nicholas again, though she urged herself to be patient, she felt she could hardly bear another moment.

Her heavy hair was loosening, the pins not quite holding the thick braided rope in place. Julia walked to the mirror and took a long look at herself, an action that was unusual for her. As she had gotten older, she found little pleasure in confronting what was to be found in the looking glass. Her once fine, tawny and butterscotch hair was now streaked with silver, and her heart shaped face now appeared strained and gaunt. Only a faint gleam still burned in her quicksilver colored eyes. It was not age itself that troubled her, for she knew all must fall into it after the bloom of youth, but instead what it signified about what she had lost in those years. She was so very different than the woman who had stepped upon the island, full of hope, nearly thirty years ago. Two children buried, a stillborn girl a year after her marriage, and then Edward. Edward, the delight of his father's eyes. Hardworking, ambitious, kind, all of the things a parent dreams for in a son, but she had always had a special fondness for Nicholas. Perhaps because he had seemed a little lost, or because she knew he was no one else's favorite, and so he had been hers.

She felt in him the same connection to the island as she held, a stirring in the blood, a gasp at the clearness of the air. Edward was his father's perfect son, and Nicholas was her loving boy.

Julia shook her head, a tear slipping down her fair cheeks, her eyes beginning to darken like clouds in a sudden storm. She bit her lip, pushing away all of her weaker thoughts. She set hew jaw, gave her hair a final pin, adjusted the sleeves of her dress, the same color as the spring lilacs outside the window, and sent all scurrying clouds of feeling from her visage. She set her face as one would compose a letter. Making sure it conveyed the exact message she wanted others to read. She had a house to run, and some ribbons to fetch from town. Everyone knew that Nicholas was returning, and everyone had their opinion about it. It was Julia's intention to make them fully understand that their opinions were as unwanted as they were inappropriate.

"He was only a boy!" She couldn't help but whisper aloud, convincing herself of the idiocy and prejudice of small minded neighbors.

A knock on her door, and her efficient little maid, Josette, stepped in. Josette was young, perhaps Nicholas' age, though Julia could not imagine seeing her son so tall —or taller! Josette offered her a curtsey and then waited for madam to speak.

"Yes, Josette, what is it?"

"Mademoiselle Ravensdale, to see you, Madam."

Josette spoke with her eyes cast downward, a change in her demeanor that Julia had noticed since it became known that the youngest and last Rast was returning. She wondered briefly if this was owed to servant's gossip, or from the girl's family. Josette was part Huron, and so had probably heard talk...for a moment she considered asking the girl what she had heard, but was shocked by her own thoughts of impropriety. Scandalous!

"Give her tea, and tell her I will be with her directly." The maid was about to close the door, when a thought occurred to Julia.

"Josette, it is Mademoiselle *Rosalind* Ravensdale, then?"

The girl's face colored warmly, an attractive shade of red on her dark bronze face.

"Oui, Madam. I have heard that Madam Cora is retuning on the next schooner from Detroit, the same as

Master Rast, if I am not mistaken."

Julia had forgotten, although the flight of Mme. Ravensdale and M. Delacroix, so soon after the young Delacroix's death was all anyone in town could talk about, Julia had been too raw in her grief over the loss of Edward to care a fig for gossip. Not that she really ever cared for it, not since Nicholas anyway, it shocked her how cruel people could be.

She felt her face pucker at the thought of Rosalind Ravensdale. She was a sweet girl, young, with a kind of lost, forlorn look. Her face was milk and her hair the dark amber of maple syrup, fresh and pretty. But, when receiving guests at all, which she was loath to do, she had preferred the strength and glowing vitality of the elder sister. A forthright manner than brooked no meaningless pleasantries, skin that was always just a shade too-sunned for a well-bred lady. All combined with a stare as bold as any man's, and those cascading black curls, that she didn't bother to pin up, damn what the townspeople thought. It hadn't surprised Julia to hear of the couple's unexpected elopement, that is, when she did come to hear of it. It seemed exactly the type of thing this wild and vivacious young woman would do. Her reasons were her own, and Julia could not help but admire her daring.

Those thoughts danced in her mind as she approached the parlor. She was pleased, upon entering, to see that Josette had used their finest china tea service. She was always careful to play her best cards when it came to the commandant's family.

"Mlle. Ravensdale! Good Morning, what do I owe…"

She looked at the young woman's face and gasped. Her cheeks were flushed and her eyes a pleading agony.

"Rosalind! What is it? What is wrong, child?"

"Oh, Madam, I am come to ask if you've had any news? Or if Mr. Rast has heard anything at the fur company? M. Delacroix paid us a call this morning, and they've had some terrible squalls on the lake, causing a few smaller ships to capsize! No one has seen the *Starlight* since she left port three days ago. We knew there would be a delay, as we had word of the calms, but this sudden storm —they say it came from nowhere, and seemed to be driven at the helm by the devil himself! There is talk amongst some, of their being wicked magic on the lake."

Her face colored a little rosier, knowing she sounded silly to speak of magic to a grown woman, but Julia was used to the way the two, magic and religion, seemed to blend on the island. Julia folded in closer to the young girl, and enveloped her in a warm, motherly embrace. She remembered that Rosalind's mother had died in childbirth, delivering the shaking girl now in Julia's arms. How strange, that Rosalind had never known a mother, and her own heart was broken from the loss of her first darling girl, and then two strong boys. Thank God that one of them was returning to her, whatever the past may have held. She felt a tenderness for the girl and her young sweetness suddenly appeared as a kind of strength, instead of a lack.

She unfolded Rosalind from her arms.

"There, there, do not fret. We have heard nothing but that there is strange weather. Captain Alberts is as able as any captain as ever sailed the lakes. They hold no tricks he hasn't seen before. And, I know, in my heart, that my son will be restored to me. Between our Lord in heaven and your Gitchi Manitou on this island, we will see all of our loved ones safely on these shores."

The girl's eyes had perked up and a piqued interest had dappled her features at the mention of the great island spirit.

"Yes, child. Nicholas told me all of your nurse's stories. They were a part of him, I think. He saw the truth in every ripple in the water, and every flight of the robin from her nest. Because of this, they came to live in my heart too, all those years ago."

Rosalind smiled at Julia as if they shared a great secret. The look gave her features a new light, a hidden intelligence.

"We all shared the stories, and Nicholas remembered every word, Mrs. Rast. He listened to each one so carefully, and if any of us wanted to hear it again, we only had to ask him. He could do all of the voices and knew when to change his tone for the dramatic parts. It was like the story was living inside of him."

They shared another smile, this time Julia felt real warmth. She couldn't remember a time she'd felt so happy, so light…surely it hadn't been since the time when she'd had two boys in this house. It couldn't be that long, could it?

Julia took a long look at this young girl who just moments before had been an unwelcome interruption to her day. Sorrow could be a very binding force though, and Julia felt keenly joined to this younger woman, who was holding the same fears in her heart. They both sat silently for a moment, awkwardly reaching for their teacups, both attempting to determine the right tack of conversation. To continue on in the same vein, or to pretend the words unsaid? They smiled at each other, and avoided one another's gaze, until finally, Rosalind cleared her throat and licked her lips, determined to speak.

"Excuse me for saying so, Madam, as I mean to cause no harm, but that day…that day when it happened. Well, I've always wished I had stayed to play with Nicholas and the other children. Or that I could have been with him when he was alone and hiding. I'm sorry, I can see now that I am distressing you, but… he was our friend. And, we were so very young…I can't imagine any child that would not hide from that."

Her words were so plain, so maddeningly simple. But, Julia felt that it was the most wonderful thing she had heard. The girl found no shame in his actions on that faraway day. And was instead in despair that his companions had not been with him. She had waited ten years for words of kindness like this, unguarded, unjudged. Julia placed her hand over Rosalind's small, white fingers and grasped them warmly.

"Thank you, my dear. You've no idea what a comfort that is to a mother."

Rosalind brightened.

"Well, then, we have both of us comforted the other this morning. Thank you. But, I'm afraid my time is short. I must away, I have a few things to purchase in town before it is time to bring papa his lunch."

She gestured to a small basket near her and stood up, making to leave. Julia found she was unable to contain her words.

"Rosalind, I myself have a few items to gather from town, would you care to walk with me?" In a single moment she had crushed her self-sentenced term of solitude.

Rosalind heartily agreed to the company, as Julia knew she would. To think, to have lived on the island for thirty long years, and to just now to have made a friend!

The two women walked into town, their dresses swishing cheerily in the early spring sunshine. Julia felt foolishly like a girl again, and almost wished to run into her husband, desiring to share her new found glow with he who was used to seeing her only in sadness for so long. She could hardly account for the change, such small words from this fragile bird of a girl, but so strong was their physic to her broken heart.

Every colored ribbon, the pure white of the sugar in the barrels, and the yards of airy spring fabrics, all appearing so fresh and welcoming after the hard winter. She had been so used to the drab, heavy winter woolens and black mourning clothes she had been wrapping herself in these months, and so she was pleased to see that the items on offer matched her sunny mood. Her fingers played softly through the intricate lace, the sheerness of the muslins, and the lightness of the linens, each touch evoking memories of summers past, and two freckled boys with curling copper hair chasing each other in the sunshine.

Recalling herself to the present, she asked the proprietor, Mr. Jenkins, for a few lengths of the fabric on a whim, and the ribbons she had originally come for. Rosalind was gathering the items she needed from the younger Mr. Jenkins, and also earning herself the adoring appraisal of the young man as he fetched her potatoes and a heavy jar of last year's maple syrup. Julia realized that this year's maple sugar party had just passed, an island event she had left her husband alone to attend the past few years. Perhaps next year she would join him, and Nicholas would come. Perhaps this year many things would change for her.

Mr. Jenkins was ringing them up and could not help himself from offering them tobacco for the men in their homes. The bell on the little wooden store rang merrily as the door swung open heavily casting glaring yellow sunlight into the little space, shaking the peaceful, heady mood Julia had been luxuriating in all morning. When her eyes adjusted to the light, she found the eyes of her husband boring into her own.

Alexander, usually so precise with his gleaming gold pocket watch, and austere bespectacled face enlivened by tidy whiskers, that face was now twisted into an expression she had not seen there before. She realized that it was fear. Rosalind's cherry mouth fell open as if she was reading the bad news coming off of him in waves as strong as the lake.

"Storm." He said. But he filled the word with more meaning than Julia had realized it could contain. His mouth pursed tightly together as if he was trying to control it, and his eyes bulged wide. His hand dashed to his pocket for his handkerchief and then passed quickly over his forehead. Instead of replacing it in his pocket, his eyes looked down at it in his hands. His fingers crinkled the edges, seemingly drawing resolve to continue from the fabric. He looked back into Julia's eyes, as if no one else was present.

"There's been a terrible storm, the ship is feared lost as it is three days now since she's been sighted."

"But, Alexander, we'd already been told of the foul weather, I'm certain…"

"No, my dear, this is a new report. I came to find you the moment I heard it from the harbormaster that M. Delacroix sent around. When you weren't at home, they told me at the house you had come here, and here I have come in all haste. This new report proclaims a new storm, something fiercer and more diabolical than had been seen on the lake all this spring. All of the other ships have put into port along the coast, or have gone down beneath the waves. The *Starlight* has not put in. She has not been found!"

Julia's features hardened and flames of anger and resolve flicked hungrily at her insides. She wouldn't hear another word.

"Not yet. She has not put in *yet*, Alexander. I don't care if the devil himself has cast an eye on the ship, it will arrive in port safely. Nothing will keep me from Nicholas again, I swear it."

No matter how she turned in in her mind, she knew the words to be the truth, and not just her own wishes given voice.

Rosalind was clearly shaken, tears falling down her creamy face looking to Mr. and Mrs. Rast in turn. Alexander raised his hands in what seemed like a kind of supplication, awed by the vehemence and confidence exhibited by his usually stoic and resigned wife.

"Quite right. Quite right, my dear. I'll…I'll just be leaving. We'll discuss it more later, I suppose. Good morning, Jenkins, Miss Ravensdale."

He moved quickly, grasped her hand tightly, then offering them both a little bow, backed out of the store, leaving all inside in a different attitude than he had found them.

A collective sigh seemed to echo through the shop, like the building itself had held its breath in those unusual, tense moments. It had been waiting expectantly for the outcome of his news, and the response of the ladies who received it.

Mr. Jenkins shook his head quickly, clearing the moment from his mind, already having catalogued the scene to spread on to the gossipmongers of the town. He hastily packed up all of their purchases and was giving his son instructions for their delivery as the ladies stepped out the door.

Julia noticed that Rosalind was still shaken, her pale countenance a shade too pale.

"Do not trouble yourself about the news. No matter what they say. The schooner will arrive. Just make ready for your sister. But oh, that reminds me, she is a married woman now. Where will the couple be living?"

The change of subject and opportunity to give her own news, brought a flush of real pleasure to Rosalind's countenance. The path they were taking to the fort wasn't the most direct one, but instead wandered close to the water, and then cut a path between a few of the houses in town. It was June, but still chilly when one was close to the lake, the winds coming in strongly to swirl around the island. The lilacs were blooming and at their most purple perfection, the heady scent of them drifting after the ladies as they breezed past.

"Papa had a letter from Cora just a fortnight ago, announcing their final plans and saying that Jean-Luc, I mean, M. Delacroix has asked his father to engage old Mr. Ashworth's house to let, or for purchase if Mr. Laborie will agree to sell. The house would suit them perfectly, I think. On the very edge of town, almost in the forest itself."

Rosalind included this last sentence quietly, a whispered revelation of her inner thoughts. Julia thought again how sweet a disposition this mild girl had, always considering the happiness of those she loved. She wondered if her own daughter would have been as kind, she wondered if Nicholas was.

"Yes, Mr. Ashworth, rest his soul. I had forgotten he had passed. Never much in town, always combing the woods at all hours with his ghastly dogs. A lonely spot out there for a house though. Unless, of course, one likes the solace."

Her eyes skipped over to meet Rosalind's before she continued.

"But your sister isn't the type to feel lonely, I think. So she should be very happy. As long as she likes her husband's company!"

Rosalind's face turned bright at the idea of her sister's contentment and then pale again at the mention of her husband. Julia was aware she had trekked into territory that was somehow unresolved between the sisters, and certainly not her business.

She changed topics once again, this time to sewing patterns and the need for a partner to practice her French. They passed smartly dressed American soldiers, crisp uniformed and proud faced. The older woman could not but remember the other uniforms, worn just as proudly, by the French and British, on this same island in earlier days. The boys never changed, just their colors, to reflect the times. Always too young, so ready to fight, and bloody themselves, and cause their mothers grief.

She left the girl at the door to her father's office. With a tight squeeze to her pretty white fingers and a promise extracted for tea on the morrow, she took her leave.

It was on the path back, the wind threatening to relieve her heavy hair from its pins, that her palms began to itch. Her steps quickened as she hastily rushed home.

Her confidence of earlier had begun to ebb and fail her, and all she could think about was holding that frail, soft paper in her hands again. To trace the swirls of the handwriting that were made by the same hand she used to hold so tightly in her own, so many years ago.

:15:

Jean-Luc

The soft yellow glow of candlelight resembled a miniature star in the darkness of the cabin. Besides the faint bud of light given off from the candle, and the calming, familiar scent of dripping wax, the room was unnervingly dark. He had lain there for some seconds unmoving, trying to discern if he was awake or dreaming. Upon realization that he was no longer asleep, he began to sort out his muddled mind. He remembered the storm and his talk with Nicholas and all of the events that preceded it. Briefly, he remembered Cora, but all other memories were swirling remnants with no discernible shape or meaning.

Still frozen in place, he felt the presence of his wife beside him, which calmed him, and he heard the sweet melody of her rhythmic breathing. He now sensed the presence of others in the room, and finally, he shifted to perceive their identity. The movement of his head was greeted with a sharp, throbbing pain at his temple.

The candle was picked up and the light moved closer to the bed, until the holder of the light was standing directly over him.

"Easy, my friend. Easy. You've had a nasty knock and have laid unconscious these past hours. I'm heartily glad to see you awake."

The doctor's voice was quiet and had taken on a more reserved, professional tone. Though he scarcely recognized the voice from the amused, friendly one he had grown used to, it did seem more appropriate and heartening given the circumstances. He turned his eyes to the doctor, hopeful of further explanation, while his hand came to the place where he felt so much pain. He felt a large, ugly knot, and the skin was tender. Speaking softly in mimic of the doctor, he inquired as to what calamity had befallen him.

Jasper laughed silently and squeezed his shoulder fondly.

"I can't believe that I am your attending physician so soon, though I wish it was not so. I do not have the full story, but I will tell you what I do know of the tragedies on deck. But first, I must ask you a few questions. Hold a moment, the good news of your awakening must be passed on."

The doctor walked across the room with the candle, leaving Jean-Luc in darkness. He saw him approach another figure, who looked to be the first mate, and shook the man to waking. They spoke for a moment, with many gestures in his direction, and then quietly the man stood up and slipped from the cabin. The doctor and his glowing light came back into focus and Jasper now pulled up a chair alongside Jean-Luc's bed. Setting the candle down, he stretched his arms overhead, briefly, and then met Jean-Luc's confused eyes.

"You remember nothing after the storm began, hm?"

His eyes appeared grave, as they searched Jean-Luc, no longer the lazy blue eyes of this past afternoon, this was the look of a focused man, hard at work. Jean-Luc thought a minute, considering his question.

"I was upon the deck with M. Rast, and then he…he took poorly. I accompanied him to his cabin where we spoke for a few moments. I… returned here, to the cabin to pass the storm with Cora. But, after an hour or so the rain had grown dangerous and the wind shifted unnaturally. I decided I would volunteer myself on deck, for fear that in the crew's exhaustion we would all be lost. Cora…she begged against it, but I put on my mackinaw jacket and I believe that I went on deck."

He paused, and shook his head.

"I'm afraid that is the end of my recollections, and they are foggy for all that. The next I remember is waking up in this bed and seeing your candle."

Jean-Luc felt robbed, of his thoughts, of his memory —it pained him to have lost track of himself.

"Well, M. Delacroix, I will tell you what I know. You *did* make it on deck and succeeded in finding the captain. But, he most prudently sent you back below, fearing for your safety in the thrall of the storm. Apparently, you were not as successful at returning to your cabin. You were hit, at any rate, sometime after speaking to the captain. You knocked your head on the boom. Such was the force of the impact that you fell immediately unconscious. Because it was a head wound, you bled profusely, causing your injury to appear more dangerous than it really was. Though, truthfully, all blows to the head are a serious business. A giant of a man, calling himself 'Big Charlie', brought me to tend to ,you, before going back out into the storm himself."

Jean-Luc found himself shaking his head again, the doctor telling him strange tales of himself that were incomprehensible.

"You are a lucky man, M. Delacroix. Your wife is a most capable and kind nurse, and the captain himself has been down to see you no less than three times before posting his fist mate here to alert him upon your waking. I've sent him now to the captain, but with instructions to wait until morning to speak with you."

He heard every word that the doctor was speaking, but somehow it didn't seem like reality. Try as he might, he could not remember anything about what had happened or the hit itself. He felt guilty for taking a man away from his work on deck. During a storm of that magnitude, the ship needed every man it could get, and so his expedition topside had resulted in more problems for the *Starlight*, instead of the aid he had intended. He could not account for any of this though and he felt a very lost man indeed. Selfishly, he wished Cora would wake up, so that he could share his weakness with her and convert it into strength.

"Thank you, Dr. Gordon, for your most excellent care. I'm not completely myself as of yet, but I owe you and Big Charlie my health. I'll be sure to thank the man myself in the morning."

Jean-Luc smiled wide, feigning a joy he did not yet feel, expecting to see his good humor reflected in the doctor's eyes. But, his grin was greeted with a grim expression and the sound of Dr. Gordon awkwardly clearing his throat.

"Forgive me, but unfortunately, that will be quite impossible. Mr. Charlie perished in the storm, along with two other members of the crew. And your friend, Mr. Rast, has been injured most grievously."

Jean-Luc blanched and then opened and closed his mouth in succession, unable to form words.

"Dead! But, that is terrible! A terrible loss for their families and for the crew. I'm....well, frankly, I'm shocked. And, what of Nicholas? What has happened to him? What foolhardy thing has he done?"

It was strange. Too much had happened. Too many tragedies, too many deaths, too many injuries both bodily and emotionally had taken place on this ship. He could not understand it all. His eyes had grown wild in his hopelessness, and also wide with surprise in his regard and worry over the friend from his youth.

"It would seem that he fancied himself a hero, just as you had done. But, he disguised himself with more success, if you will beg my pardon for saying it. He found an extra coat hung amongst the crew's belongings, and a rough hat. He set himself to bailing water for hours on end, alongside the men. These acts being completely unknown to me, I had sent your wife to his cabin to be sure he was well. You were unconscious but comfortable and stable, and I thought a diversion from your condition would do her good. It was she who discovered he was missing, and fearing the worst, she became hysterical."

"Yes, but how was he injured?!"

Jean-Luc asked the question hurriedly and a trifle over-loud. Cora stirred next to him and he felt immediately sorry for his outburst.

"Shhh. Pray, do not wake her. She worked fervently and with the strength and fortitude equal to any doctor or soldier I've known. When she saw that the young man was missing she fainted, and I've since given her a very mild sedative to aid her much needed rest."

Dr. Gordon looked at her admiringly for a minute, a look of pride and respect on his tired face.

"As to your query, when the man was not found, not in his cabin nor below decks anywhere, he was finally located on deck. By the time he was discovered, a few crew members had already gathered about him. Sometime when the violent waves were rocking the ship, he was apparently propelled bodily into the railing, him being less sure-footed than a seasoned sailor. The collision has broken a few ribs and added some bruises to those he had earned from his scrapping the other day. But he succeeded in his efforts, as the crew has dubbed him, 'brave'."

Wild-eyed, Jean-Luc listened. He had missed a great deal, obviously, much excitement, but also he had missed the worry too. Though he felt anxious to think he had caused Cora any distress. This voyage only got more unusual and inexplicable with each passing wave. This was supposed to be a two day journey at most!

Suddenly, he noticed something. Something that made his stomach drop, and bile rise in his throat. Would it never end? He lifted his head to the doctor.

"So, now we are again in a calm, then?"

Doctor Gordon looked to him with obvious confusion, and then sensing the truth, nodded in confirmation.

"By God, you're right. Though, I hadn't noticed. We have stopped once again."

He didn't frown, which made Jean-Luc admire him the more. He respected the doctor's even-keeled attitude and laid back acceptance of the plans of the universe.

"Yes, well. I suppose we'll wait here now, hm? And be on our way when the time is right. I have given you much to think on, and I am heartily sorry for the burden, but I will leave you now to rest. I think we needn't fear for you any longer."

The doctor gave him his hand, becoming simply Jasper Gordon once more, instead of a man of medicine. Jean-Luc murmured many expressions of gratitude and friendship. The doctor left and took any chance of further rest right out the door with him. As the glowing light of the candle drifted out the door, Jean-Luc once again reached up to test the pain in his skull. The skin was broken, but only slightly, and he could tell that the swollen bump on his temple would be ugly. Still, he had been saved. Whether by luck, or magic, or design, he only knew that he was unaccountably fortunate.

He looked over to Cora, and though he could not see her in the absolute darkness, he could picture the way her night-black curls splayed across the pillow, and see the play of pink on her olive cheeks. Yes, he was indeed a fortunate man.

He stretched his palms and placed them beneath his head, now certain that all traces of sleep had slithered out the door, trailing Dr. Jasper Gordon. They had forgotten all about Jean-Luc, enrobed in the earliest hours of the new day, so new that the sun hadn't begun to awaken yet. He stared upward, though his eyes could still see nothing. It was unnerving, the account of his injuries and the loss of men from the crew. A terrible, ugly thought crept into his mind and he wondered, fleetingly, if Cora had caused this storm. He dismissed the thought, ashamed that he had entertained it, even for the shortest of moments.

Her sway with nature was great and undeniable, but he had never known her to use it in such a way. Never to harm or to kill. His head rocked slowly from side to side in disbelief. It almost was as if more had happened in these last few days sailing than had happened all of the past year hiding out in Detroit.

Hiding. Another arrow of shame pierced his heart. He could not believe he was using such a word to describe his actions, but what else could one call it? Why did everything have to be so confounded complicated? If only Philippe had not died, or rather, if he had not killed him.

Every time he thought the words, they stole his breath. He felt his face twitch with sorrow, and he turned his body away from his wife. Thrice shamed by his thoughts in the past few minutes. He tried to block out the memories, or at least dilute their potency. He could hardly bear much more pain in this dizzying darkness. But he knew they would come. They always did, and it disgraced him further to know that the grief of losing his younger brother, of killing his first friend and confidante... would pale in comparison to the anguish he would feel in losing Cora. Which he surely would if she found out what he had done. So many secrets that they shared between them. Those that she kept from him, and that he had hidden from her. How long could they continue in their pretending? Or would these whispers break them apart?

Jean-Luc breathed deeply and he sensed Cora shift closer to him in slumber, unaware of the thousand thoughts racing through his mind. She was seeking his warmth, and he hoped seeking the comfort of his body. Every touch of her was a thrill, a sweet drop of summer wine on his senses. His mind drifted, filling with sunlight, the blackness of the cabin forgotten. The wind sighing through the beech trees and the pines of the island. The two of them sitting on a fallen trunk, he heard the bubble of her laughter and felt the touch of her palm in his own. The words came unbidden to his mind.

"She walks in beauty like the night,
of cloudless climes and starry skies;
and all that's best of dark and bright
meets in her aspect and her eyes..."

He smiled to himself, laying in bed. How he had read and reread the poem! His mother, bless her, held Byron as a great favorite, and upon reading the lines in one of her prized collections, he had imagined it was written with his own beloved in mind, for he could not have phrased a description of her more perfectly. Her midnight curls and golden daybreak eyes, and how her smile possessed him. He'd memorized the lines, stanza by stanza, and had recited them to her, pink-faced, on that fallen tree, on that spring day. She had laughed and admonished him for making her vain. Her full red lips had met his own, oh so briefly! A blink and it was over, their first kiss and he'd hoped it held the promise of more. That day had been his way of declaring himself and his intentions. But, he'd often wondered later if he should have used his own words to make himself understood, instead of Lord Byron's. Would it have even made a difference? But that day all was glittering and beautiful in the world, and he had decided to have the poem copied by a lady in the town that did such work, having an elegant and graceful hand. He had thought to present it to Cora as a gift. It had taken some time though, and when it was finally ready, it was too late. Philippe was returned home and Jean-Luc had lost. The poem was still in a drawer in his room at home. He wondered if his mother had stumbled upon it, when she had, no doubt, rifled through his belongings in an effort to understand his sudden disappearance.

And there it was, tugging on his conscience, Philippe. Every reason that they had fled had been a result of Philippe's death and little did Cora know of his hand in it.

His mind drifted again, but this time, not to sunshine and the warmth of Cora Ravensdale, but instead to the clean wood and lake scent of his office. His head was bent earnestly over the documents and projects before him. His father, unusually, had absented himself from business, and Jean-Luc had the reins of Cross Shipping Company firmly in hand. The whole summer had been a nightmare. His father and mother astonished by the changes that had come over Philippe. He was crass, his rudeness was unforgivable. He was never at home and continually slunk to breakfast after the family had finished, and only Jean-Luc had known the truth. It had been a knife in his heart, twisting every moment. Worse, Philippe knew his feelings and dared to wink at him upon his morning arrival home. Or he would cast Jean-Luc looks in the evening as he walked out the door, delighting in his misery, and never telling their father and mother where he was headed or if he would return.

Their maman had cried for weeks and their papa was angrier than he'd seen him. And he? Jean-Luc was shattered on the inside. He had been so sure that she felt the same for him, certain that her feelings were growing in warmth with the weather. But, Philippe had returned and something within her changed, just as something within his brother had. She seemed dimmer somehow, and he brighter for feeding off of her glow.

Try as Jean-Luc might, he could not un-love her, and so could not reveal Philippe's comings and goings, for fear of blackening Cora's name. He knew he should cast aside this woman for loving his brother, but it was love, after all, and could not be easily altered. He had fallen for her grace and her wit, and the deep well of her thoughts, her soul. And he could not believe she had given this to Philippe, because he would not know what to do with such a treasure.

In his memory then, in the comfort and familiarity of his office, he had been suddenly torn from a ship's manifest to see the form of his brother in the doorway. His hair was as wild as the deep blue of his eyes, and it struck Jean-Luc as peculiar that a person with so much water in them could also contain so much fire. Jean-Luc had no time to speak before Philippe cut in with angry words, full of venom and seeking to puncture any who were nearby.

"Well, mon frer, you have the last laugh, after all. I should have left the wooing of society ladies to you, I suppose."

Laying in his bed in the silence of the ship cabin, he could still perfectly see Philippe's cold eyes freezing into his own, as if blaming Jean-Luc for his troubles.

He had arisen from his desk, allowing his greater height and broader chest to lend him confidence in this strange conversation with his brother.

"I do not appreciate your tone, your mockery, nor this disruption, and I will have to ask you to speak with respect when referring to any young lady on the island."

Their eyes had locked and held a silly, boy's game of challenge.

"Well, this woman is no lady. I can assure you of that."

Philippe's eyes had flicked down and a vicious smile flashed on his face.

"Do you come to gloat? You are her choice, but still I will not allow you to speak of her so. Come, Philippe, you have better manners than these."

Jean-Luc's voice had gone a little higher on this last sentence, betraying his own feelings about his brother, about Cora, and the summer. Philippe cocked his head to the right, and looking into Jean-Luc's eyes, his own began to lose their wrath. He seemed more like himself in that moment than Jean-Luc had seen him all summer.

"Peace, brother. You are right. I came here, after all, for advice. But, you look so stuffy and caged in this prison cell you call an office, that it fairly drives me mad. But, peace, I would speak with you."

"Well, mon Dieu! Of course, advice, let's hear it then. Is everything all right?"

Philippe pursed his lips then rocked back and forth on his heels. "No, I fear that our old friend may make problems for me. I am not sure when I will be able to return to the island after my brigade leaves. You see...she is with child."

He punctuated his explosive statement by a lift of his eyebrows and a shrug of his shoulders, as if this was a silly problem. Like he had forgotten maman's birthday or he was caught wrestling in the schoolyard.

Jean-Luc's mouth had hung open, and even remembering the scene, he could feel his heart beat so fast he was surprised it didn't waken Cora.

"Mon Dieu! Not come back? Why, you will not leave at all! You will marry her, of course. You will marry her and be a father to your child, and no more go gallivanting about the lakes. The world is now about more than just your desires."

Jean-Luc was horrified that Philippe could be given such a gift and look for nothing but to escape it. But was more aghast still at his brother's cold response.

"You would plan my whole life for me then, would you? You are as bad as she! Marry her? I will not! You must know that there is no anchor in my canoe, only oars."

The brothers had faced each other, and for the first time truly saw that they were nothing alike. Not in features or in attitude or in action. Nevertheless, Jean-Luc understood that Philippe *had* loved Cora in his way, for what it was worth. But he also knew that the only way to really love, is to love more than you love yourself, and this he could not do.

Instead, Philippe had hunted her. He had wanted her as he wanted the finest black fur of the sable. To take pleasure in its capture, and the knowledge that his possessing it meant that no one else might do the same, giving him prominence over others.

Jean-Luc had never been a man for brutal words or hasty anger. He considered it base and beneath his dignity. But he had not kept their liaisons a secret, all summer long, dying in his heart each day, protecting her, just to see Philippe now ruin her.

Their eyes never wavered, until Jean-Luc stepped forward and struck him with an animal force, felling Philippe and his look of contempt to the floor. Jean-Luc stood over him as his brother covered his face, expecting more blows.

"You are right, then. There *will* be some trouble in your returning, so see that you do not. You are not brother, nor kin, nor friend to me, and if I see you again you'd do best to hide yourself quickly. I'm not easily riled to hatred, but this one is absolute and everlasting. You are dead to me, and I wish you dead to the world, so that in your absence life itself would seem the brighter. Never return."

With those words spoken, he had felt a low growl escape his throat, and he had plucked Philippe up by the arms as if he weighed less than a feather, a piece of refuse to be tossed aside. He had thrown him over his shoulder and pitched him out the door of Cross Shipping.

Philippe would die that night, and Jean-Luc would have a part in it. His own angry curses coming to life as Philippe's drained away in the alley behind the public house. The weight of his ugly words and deeds would sit with him for eternity. He could not think on that now. Not yet. Not again, not with all of this new pain rubbing him raw. And now he suffered the memories alone.

"Dieu, forgive me" he thought. When time had come to be truthful, when he'd had the opportunity to take Cora into his confidence, he had instead told her a lie, looking directly into her eyes. A thing he did not think he could ever do without flinching, but it had been natural. He had come to her the morning after Philippe's death, seeing her face, usually so full of strength and character, now drained of all but excruciating agony. And so he had told her the fiction, that had somehow set her free. The deception that lay even now as a bedfellow between them. But, with every sweet rise and fall of her chest, under the blanket, he knew given the choice, he would tell it again.

At last the first pale threads of daylight began to weave into the cabin, and with them, Cora's eyes came open. Her smile was bright and as bold as the new day, taking its time in dawning. It chased the phantoms of the past from his mind. He could only look into her eyes and finish the stanza he had spoken in his mind earlier, but this time he said them aloud.

"Thus mellow'd to that tender light
which heaven to gaudy day derives"

And in her smile he found hope. Even with the uncertainty of a ship in a calm, somehow, they would make it home. Somehow, they would learn to love beyond secrets. Surely, they must.

:16:
Cora

If her baby had lived, he would be a few weeks old by this time. He would have been born in the early spring, arriving with the rest of the budding flowers and new green of the season.

Cora often had nightmares that her child was alive and that she had lost him somewhere. She would spend her sleeping hours wandering aimlessly in her mind, searching desperately for her lost boy. Upon waking, she would place a hand gently on her stomach and the flatness of it seemed to mock her. As if it had never housed a growing soul at all.

Thankfully, other nights her dreams could be pleasant and filled with love; this morning was one of those times. Perhaps due to a release from the stress and fear of the night before, or the tincture administered by the doctor. In either case, she had dreamed that Jean-Luc had woken from his injury and that he was holding the baby in his arms, gazing at him tenderly, and smoothing his downy hair.

She had opened her eyes to see that Jean-Luc was indeed awake, but of course the baby still only existed in her memories, or her imagination. She had smiled anyway, absurdly and inexplicably happy to see that part of her dream had come true. But what if? How deep would her happiness be if they were returning to Mackinac as a family?

But, no. He had promised and vowed to love and father the child. He had sworn the baby was as much his blood as any child could be, and for as much hope as she had that all could be well and that they could truly be a family, it was not to be. She wondered still if it was a kind of blessing, or if it was instead a blight on their union. It was most probably a bit of both, as were most events in one's life.

Soon after they had arrived in Detroit, Cora was distressed to discover that the early glow and flush of her pregnancy was beginning to fade. Instead, she had felt weak, and more and more she felt Philippe surrounding her. She felt him hovering over her every move, his breath in her ear, his hands on her growing belly. One night, she had awoken in terror. As she lay sleeping, the baby was born and was being held by his father. Philippe was cooing at him, and the baby was twisting his father's curls around his chubby fist. The baby began to whimper and she watched as Philippe's face twisted into laughter. He had stood up from the end of the bed, still laughing, and had taken a step away from where she lay. No matter how much she stretched her arms and cried out, he had only carried the baby farther and farther away, ignoring her anguished screams.

Jean-Luc had shaken her awake that night, for she had been screaming not only in her nightmare, but aloud in their bedchamber. She was soaked in angry, red blood; her nightdress, their sheets, and Jean-Luc himself covered in the blood that had been her child. But instead of fleeing from her, or showing disgust, he had only held her tightly as she wept, waiting for her to calm before summoning a servant to fetch the doctor. Jean-Luc stroked her long black curls and kissed her brow tenderly, as one would a small child. She had felt terrible loss. Even if the babe had been unwanted, and in a secret part of herself, she might have even felt a breath of relief, still, she was utterly broken.

She could not but allow the darkness to close upon her in the realization that it had all been for naught. Her curse on Philippe, and the hurried escape from Mackinac, all for nothing, all of her grand plans and schemes had flowed out of her body with the loss of the child. And worst of all, she was now guilty of having trapped Jean-Luc in a marriage that he need never have entered into at all. Even if it was a marriage she was now glad to be locked into, did this make her deception more wicked? Or less?

It was still that faint, early morning time. In the sky outside the window casements, just a breath of light was brave enough to cut into the all encompassing night. Just this hint of sun, still considering if it was indeed time to rise.

Jean-Luc was reciting poetry to her, or to himself, and only in pieces, as if he had begun before her eyes had opened. She reached up to feel his head, gently with the barest brush of her hand, and frowned at the feeling of battered skin beneath her fingertips. He brought those same fingers to his lips, and warmth flooded her body. With this small affection, an idea entered her mind. A brash idea, a bold idea, the kind of thinking that a younger Cora would have already put into action.

While considering how to convince him, she sat up and leaned in close to his injury. She summoned all of the warmth, love and joy she had felt since waking, and drew her lips into a kissing-bow shape. A small smile began to cross his face as she carefully blew a puff of the magic thoughts from herself into the ugly break in his flesh.

"There's nothing I can do to heal it, but there should be enough enchantment in there to chase the pain, and to give the appearance of healing."

Jean-Luc's face broke into a wide smile and he thanked her. "It's perfect, mon coeur. Although, you might have saved your breath, as one look at you this morning has given me the all physick I require."

She couldn't help but laugh at his early morning flattery, but it gave her the courage to suggest her plan.

"Do you think there is anyone yet awake, Jean?"

"Oui, I am sure someone is manning the ship, even if it does not stir in this calm. But the man is likely half dozing. All the other crew members will be fast asleep from last night's storm."

They spoke quietly, both unwilling to break the hush of the new, not-quite day. About what had happened the night prior, there were no words. The joy of seeing the other whole and well upon waking, said what a thousand words could not.

They laid there, on the thin-stuffed mattress, a bed that had begun to feel familiar. Her head fit evenly on his chest, both lost briefly in thought of death and storms and spilled blood. Forces beyond their control swirled around them, daring them to lose hold of one another. She couldn't bear it, nor would she wallow in despair as she knew the phantasms hoped she would. She sat back up and sprightly hopped from the bed.

Cora began pulling up and fastening the ties on her oldest gown. It was frayed in spots and so faded one could hardly tell it had ever been a wild shade of leaf green. The very first yawning rays of sunlight were sneaking stealthily into the cabin, not bright enough to be considered light, but just enough to lend a slight illumination to the room. Jean-Luc now sat up also, a puzzled look on his face.

"What are you about, mon amour? The moment you

left the bed the sun decided to begin its rise also!"

She shot him a mischievous smirk, and skipped to the bedside, grasping hold of his large, warm hands.

"Do you feel terribly unwell still, or have I truly healed you?"

"No, in truth I am quite recovered…and a bit restless. What can you be thinking of?"

Her eyes searched his, and she bit her lip in decision, giving herself one final moment to change her own mind. Was this a selfish whim? Was this too much like the thoughtless Cora of last summer? No, it felt right somehow. Last night she had understood fully the pain of losing him—a thousand daggers in her heart and infinitely more painful than the loss of Philippe or even of the baby. To lose Jean-Luc was to lose her past, her future, her very self. She did not have the courage, or the words to communicate this. Such things, she believed, were best understood in the whisper of the wind through the trees, or when covered lovingly in the embrace of the water. She was resolved then.

Her smile grew brighter and she squeezed his fingertips in her own, hoping to impart some of her feeling.

"A swim. If you're up to it. I find that I have been too long without a bath, and long for the lake's sweet kiss."

With these words she dipped down to press her lips to his, giving urgency to her request. His hand had caught her head gently, and he intertwined his fingers through her hair, pulling her down deeper to him, prolonging the sweetness of the kiss and flooding her body with longing.

Cora would never understand how odd, yet how marvelous his touch was to her. And she couldn't comprehend why it had taken her so long to realize it. If only she had seen him for what he was *before*. But, instead she had seen only a handsome chest, without opening it and revealing the treasure within.

Their faces were still close and when their eyes met, he whispered, "Oui, we will swim. It seems that I will drown in you whether I go or stay. But we must be quiet."

The wind was calm again, the ship's sails no longer unfurled but instead laid in the same sleepy stupor she had just awoken from. Cora knew that some aboard, the captain for sure, and perhaps even her husband, would be troubled by the calm and feel that it was yet another sign of rotten luck or evil forces. But, the ship was a broken thing and the crew a broken band. The storm of the night before had dashed them to their graves and had shown Cora the violence that was the enemy, her former lover.

She could feel Philippe's anger flowing around and through her, weakening her. The only force that was stronger was the connection between Jean-Luc and herself. A love that was vibrant and alive, even if they both tried to conceal the depth of their feelings. Their love was a power that reenforced and gave strength to her natural magic, her communion with the world around her.

Since Cora had first left Mackinac's shores, she had struggled to unlock her power, which had lain dormant when she was in Philippe's thrall. Detroit was a busier place than Mackinac, and the same enchantments she had so easily employed on the island, took enormous effort and energy in the bustle of the city. It had been an extreme exercise of her magic just to keep Philippe at bay.

Did she need to make a full confession to Jean-Luc? Was this the only way to reclaim her former self? Need she bare her soul of all of her nefarious deeds and curses? The more she fought within herself, the stronger Philippe grew, like dark clouds gathering in the rain. But Cora would not allow that to happen again. No more tempests. No more tragedies because Philippe willed it so. She would need to gather her strength, banish the past that lived so completely in her present, and sail the *Starlight* safely home.

So lost in thought, Cora had not noticed that Jean-Luc had risen from bed and was now dressing haphazardly. They both knew their clothes would be discarded on deck, so there was no reason to attire themselves properly. She could hardly contain her glee at seeing him, so much like the childhood swims they had all taken, filled with innocence, so many years ago.

He took her hand and gave her one of their private looks. A shiver passed through her, and she realized that all that may have been innocent in bathing in the lake together was now gone. She was surprised to discover just how dearly she held him, a mere whisper of his flesh on her own stirred her deeply.

And so they walked, quietly out of the cabin, and she willed the wood in the boards to remain silent under their tread. Jean-Luc crept cat-like up to the main deck, and paused briefly to bask in the stillness. A hush not only of the calm, but of this particular time of pre-dawn. The world itself is being reborn with the day, within it lie all possibilities, all futures. His wounded face was upturned toward the sky, the last scattering of stars twinkling dimly, refusing to be chased from their rightful places. But she was impatient, the water called to her, strongly, rousing her blood. She squeezed his hand and they moved together toward the railing, and together hitched the fraying rope-ladder over the side.

A cursory glance around revealed a drowsing look-out, who raised one sleepy, curious eye in their direction, before Jean-Luc signaled him for quiet. The man discreetly turned his body in the other direction, before slumping over against the helm. Cora was already undressing, and by the time Jean-Luc looked back at her, smiling his lazy smile, she was nude, clad only in the earliest of lights and the shadows that still lingered from the darkness.

His mouth fell agape, but for her this was not a brazen act, nor an affront to modestly. The lake was so near, and its call was so distinct; she merely wanted nothing between the blanket of water and her own skin. Cora reached for his hand and pulled it softly to her full lips, bestowing a gentle kiss upon him. Dropping it gently, she climbed down, hand over hand, before turning and diving evenly into the water. She became a part of the water, not even the smallest ripple greeting her entrance. Cora felt her skin illuminating, glowing with health now that she was wholly connected to that inland sea once again, a prodigal daughter returned. Just as soundlessly, Jean-Luc had snuck in, and now looked at her, awe-struck as her skin glistened and glimmered, the water swirling and rippling around her body, even as it lay still everywhere else.

Invisible, except for a ghost of grey on the horizon, the first herald of the arriving dawn, the sun now appeared bashfully at the edge of the world. The sky above them began to flash with the same radiance as Cora's naked flesh. The lake turned from a dark granite pool to a brighter blue glass, unmoving in the absence of wind, save for what waves caressed her skin.

Treading water, they swam separately about, their eyes never leaving the burgeoning sun, afraid they would miss its rise lest they remove their gaze. The morning was silent, only the sound of their own limbs parting the water, and the rocking groan of the *Starlight*. Cora felt all of her cares fall away, washed clean in her lake home. Her black curls spread out on the surface of the spinning waves surrounding her, like a train from a fine gown following behind her strong swimmer's arms. They still had not spoken. It was the first time Jean-Luc and Cora had been able to fully escape the world. This furtive bath was healing in a few short moments what months secreted in Detroit had been unable.

Freedom. Freedom from the past and the future, existing only in these moments of atonements and beauty and stillness.

Cora swam closer to Jean-Luc, both cautious to remain close to the ship. The expression on his face, however, stopped her progress. The same expression she had seen in their first meeting in the woods, and her mind was called back, just as it had been on deck, to the boy he was, all those years ago. The look spoke of great character and kindness. It was the expression that had first tied them together, the first real welcome she had felt on the island.

Suddenly, she wanted nothing more than to be anchored to him. Their eyes came to rest in the solace of the other, and wordlessly, she took his hand once more, bringing him toward the *Starlight*. Back to the side of the great oak ship, to the rungs of the shaky ladder. At first, Jean-Luc mistook her intentions and reached his hand up to climb. Instinctively, Cora ran a hand over his smooth, strong stomach, and he lowered himself down to face her. Their bodies barely skimming in the water. His hand floated down her bare back, knees slightly touching, her hand on his hip and the other softly caressing his face. They were bare to each other, completely, for the first time. No walls between them. No thoughts of Philippe. No clever waltz around awkward intimacy. It was vulnerable, and Cora was astonished at how erotic this defenselessness was.

She had been laid bare before him the morning after Philippe's death. Pregnant, devastated, guilty and ruined. He had been unguarded before her every day of their courtship before Philippe had returned to Mackinac, before having to conceal the depths of his feeling. But now, they were both faced with their inner torments, their imperfections mirrored perfectly in their eyes, and neither of them could bear to look away.

Cora felt an overwhelming love for this man who had been her constant. Truer than a north star for sailors, he had guided her with friendship and love for the whole of her life. Saving her from ruin and also saving her from herself. They held each other and the water held them.

She did not know the precise moment, but some time in the first sliver of brilliant orange sun winking on the horizon, it happened.

Her mouth moved forward and found his, and their bodies, though unused to each other, fit together effortlessly, as if they had longed for each other all the while, before even their own hearts knew of it. The lovemaking was slow, the water encasing it in shadow, a lilting dance for which they alone knew the movements. They had only one other experience together, but it had been drunken, clumsy, filled with sadness, and never thought of again until this moment. And even now to think of it was only to dissever the memory and replace it with this one.

He filled her utterly. He was on her lips, and in her arms and moving sweetly inside of her. Jean-Luc's skin pressed tightly against her own and Cora had never felt so strong. They were not two people becoming one, but rather, two lost people, becoming whole once again.

The movements quickened and then slowed, and they clung to one another tightly, lost in the bliss of the moment. Together they watched the dawn burst brightly with the promise of a vibrant day.

"Mon amour, how dearly I treasure you."

The world had flipped for them many times this morning, changing the way they saw and loved the other. Strange, how much can be stirred up in the silence of a calm.

Later, back snugly in their cabin with not a soul on board the wiser, Jean-Luc and Cora had added a new look to their secret language. One that spoke of love and trust. He had given it to her eagerly, along with a kiss, after shaving and dressing properly. He absented himself in order to pay a call on the injured Mr. Rast. Cora had likewise wrung the water from her curls and dressed simply in light yellow with a sheer chemisette around her collar, echoing the lightness of her mood. She combed through her curls and added just a touch of beeswax to her full red mouth. Thus attired, she sat down at the miniature desk, and opened her book. She had much to say this morning.

"For those with few cares and no set schedule, there are far worse things than a ship becalmed. To some it would seem a drowsy, floating holiday of sunshine and the glittering lake.

Ah, to be without care! I almost cannot recall a time when I was not burdened with the stresses of an innumerable number of things. Before returning to Mackinac, there was life in Detroit and the constant ghostly reminder of Philippe, always at my elbow or behind my back. Before this, was the pregnancy and the poisonous, living Philippe. And even earlier than all of these, was the winter sickness on the island. It would seem with adulthood comes anxiety and worry. What I would give for a simple summer of untroubled youth. But, back then, all I could think on was being the young woman I am now. I suppose that as long as we are living we are never truly happy…except for stolen moments, scattered throughout the hours, never altogether at one time.

Looking back at the pages I have written previously, I see that I have come near to the end of my sad story. And that, in truth, I am edging closer in my narrative to the present moment. But only when all is told within these leather covers can we return, and I pray most fervently to any and all good spirits to give me the guidance I so desperately require. If only the gitchi manitou could look kindly on his wayward daughter and tell her just what her next step should be…

And so, I had walked away from Philippe for the last time. Though, I did not know then that those last hateful words from my lips would be the curse that killed him.

Returning home, I had kept to my room, refusing food and drink, too furious to even grieve. I was a ruined woman. Is it too bold for me to say that I did not care? I know I would still have the love of my family and my old nurse, what more society would I need? But,

I was not blind to how my situation would affect that same family. Mackinac may be a small northern place, but we had our share of society and morals. One ruined daughter would taint the other by association, and so Rosalind would suffer for my sin. My papa, too, would be looked down upon by his peers and fellow officers. It was this that hurt me. Not because I was so unselfish—no, it was because I worried how it would poison their regard for me. My wayward boldness would turn from a pleasing facet of my character to a symbol of the family's downfall. This could not be, yet...I was powerless to change it.

I stayed in my chamber the whole day through, plotting and planning, each idea cast aside even as it was conceived (As I wished the baby had been!). I had no relatives to fly to for safety, nor to visit, save a distant aristocratic cousin in England. Our family was as much an island as Mackinac. And so it came to be that I was no closer to any sort of decision at suppertime than I had been at breakfast. I had finally allowed a concerned Rosalind into the room with a venison broth and a calming tea made with herbs from Waseya's garden. I had gone to sleep that night with a heavy heart weighed down by the kindness of a family I had betrayed.

The knocking on the front door rained down like thunder, each strike a lightning bolt to my brain. The whole house was awakened as we each flew to the sound, wild to know the matter. Papa, looking as dignified as possible in his sleeping cap, opened the door to reveal a young soldier from the fort. Rosalind and I pressed together on the stair, listening closely, our hair falling out of our night braids. We knew from experience that it could be a problem in the village or the fort, as my father had requested to be alerted to emergencies in either. The young man saluted, but when his eyes fixed on my father in his night clothes, he seemed to have briefly forgotten his errand. A pointed glance from Papa soon remedied it, however, and the soldier thrust a note in papa's direction.

He opened it quickly and I could not make out the words from where I stood, but I could see that it had been hastily scrawled.

"Any reply, Commandant Ravensdale?"

"No, private, come in. Tarry a moment, I will accompany you back to the fort."

Papa took a step toward the staircase, still holding the note, when suddenly he paused and looked back to the soldier, a thought having occurred to him.

"Have his parents been told?"

The young soldier had shifted uncomfortably before answering. "No, sir. I am charged to go there next."

"In that case, I will make that visit with you as well. Bad tidings should come from a friend. I shall only be a moment."

Rosalind and I were frozen to the railing, standing in our nightshifts, dripping with questions. What had happened? And to whom? Papa had turned back to us, had placed a somber foot on the stair to climb back to his chamber and make ready for this mysterious task. His head lifted and he peered deeply into our eyes.

"My darlings, I'm afraid you too, must hear troubling news from a friend. I must ask you to brace yourselves and take a seat for these tidings."

Keeping his eyes on the both of us, he swallowed with difficulty and continued.

"It has occurred to me that this poor soul is almost as family to the both of you as well. I would be remiss in withholding the information from you both."

Rosalind, usually so quiet, had grabbed a hold of me, and I of her, before replying boldly. "We have each other, Papa, and have no need of chairs. Pray, speak your worst."

A fiery glint of pride shone in his eyes. "Yes, well, be brave my dear ones. The great playfellow of your youth, and your boon companion, Monsieur Delacroix, is dead."

Both of us reeled as if shot with a cannon. I could feel the blood pumping in my heart and it surprised me, for I felt that it would have stopped at the news. Perhaps I should have understood my true feelings, because the well of my grief was filled…but because I had thought Papa was speaking of Jean-Luc.

Rosalind maintained a calm I could hardly credit. This sweet sister of mine was showing strength I had not dreamed she possessed. She was able to master herself and ask the question that I had not even formed in my mind.

"Papa, in either case, my heart melts with sadness, but, please **which** M. Delacroix has been so cruelly felled? And by what means?"

Her quiet voice was the first time I had considered it might be Philippe. A whole different range of emotions surged through me, and none of them the dead and broken ones I felt when I had thought it was Jean-Luc who was gone from the world.

Papa looked again to the note so tightly held in his fingers, searching it for the information upon realizing he also did not know. Not finding that which he was seeking, his eyes looked questioningly at the young soldier.

"Forgive me, sir, and ladies, but it is my understanding that it is the younger M. Delacroix, given name, Philippe. And I am told it was due to a disagreement in a tavern."

I may have imagined it, but I could swear I felt Rosalind's embrace tighten for just a moment, and then I felt myself begin to swoon. Papa had taken a step toward us to offer comfort, but Rosalind already had a hand up.

"Please, Papa, give us a moment. Please, go and make ready. The Delacroix's should not have to await the news a moment longer."

She had quickly led me off the stair, past papa, and into the parlor. She gently steered me to the sofa and I felt again a swoon come upon me and as the room faded into oblivion, I felt a hard slap from my docile sister.

"None of that now, Cora. I don't have a clue what has been into you as of late, but no fainting. I need you well, sister. Stay here, and I will get you something cool to drink. Then perhaps, we can mingle our sorrows together."

She left the room and I raised my hand to feel my cheek, still warm from the swat.

I must confess, I had no desire to join my sadness to hers. My *overwhelming feeling was not grief, but guilt. I had wished him dead all day, or wished that he would never leave the island. I had entreated the soul of the island and called on the manitou himself to make him stay with me. I had cursed him with all of the magic I had, and now, so soon, it had come to pass. My wish had been granted. It occurred to me then that not only was I guilty of killing a childhood friend and father of my unborn child, but that his death had changed nothing in my situation. He had still cast me off, and I was still ruined. Ironically, he would forever stay on this island.*

Though, later I would come to know that it was only his body that might remain, and his spirit would trail my steps wherever I should go. How could I have ever wished for such a thing?

With this whirling tornado of emotions spinning inside my breast, I slipped to my bedchamber and put on a sturdy black dress with a fitted bodice and wide waistband with small puffed sleeves. It was a mourning dress I had not worn since the death of Waseya's husband. I left my black hair down, as a veil trailing behind me, the opposite creature from a bride. I heard Rosalind calling to me in another room as I snuck quietly out the back door, oddly, for the last time. Though, again, I did not know it would be the last at the time.

Without thought, my feet brought me to the clearing in the forest, and when I arrived my only thought was to destroy myself..."

Cora, hearing Jean-Luc's unmistakable footfall, slammed the little book shut with such force that it rang like a thunderclap. She hastily covered it up with a handkerchief just as the man himself walked into the cabin. She was bringing it all to a close, the purging of her soul was almost complete.

"Mon Dieu, cher! You gave me such a fright. Are you shooting pistols in here? What was that sound?"

His voice was merry and he had already swung his great arms about her waist. She immediately recalled the fevered passion of the morning and her cheeks grew hot with blushing. She pressed her face to his chest, and wondered if all of this soul searching would truly bring her peace.

:17:
Jasper

Sleep was still an elusive phantom for the doctor. Instead of seeking his own rest, he had merely swapped one sick room for another. He had been tempted to look in on his wife in repose, but had thought better of it. The sight would only prove a cruel tease to his own weary bones.

He had been sitting in the cabin with a snoring Mr. Rast for the past hour or so, and had only recently shooed the ship's doctor to his bed. The man was old, and had seen many ships at storm and their tragedies, no doubt, but Jasper was ashamed to have chosen Jean-Luc's sickbed over young Rast's. And so he would take over the watch until the young man stirred.

Mr. Nicholas Rast was most definitely the more gravely injured, but Jasper was wary of him and his erratic behavior. It was for this reason that he chose Jean-Luc's sick room, and that he had formed the beginnings of a friendship with M. Delacroix and his wife. She was a touch forward, it was true, but knowing his own wife's temperament, he thought Madame Delacroix a suitable companion for her, and hoped they would be friends. He felt badly enough about taking Isobel away from family and then so quickly snatching her from the acquaintances she had made in Boston. Would that she was happy in Mackinac—and he hoped too that the disappointment, anger and tears he had caused his family would all be for naught. He hoped a little time, separation and success would prove them wrong.

But as it was, he had welcomed the setbacks in the journey, and not with the good-natured indifference others aboard had believed to him to have. The series of calms had forestalled his uncertain future, a welcome reprieve from the unknown.

All of the time spent at his patient's bedside he had been free to brood over these thoughts, some time set aside that was his own. No longer having to decorate his face with bright smiles or plaster his expression with little-held confidence and enthusiasm. If only he could feel the way he pretended, if only life were that simple.

Standing up, Jasper was sorely in need of a stretch for his cramped muscles and knackered bones. His arms raised up high above his head and his ears were greeted by a series of loud pops and creaks, which caused his patient to turn in his sleep. Bending back down over the bed, Jasper heard more loud protests from his joints as he gently made certain that Nicholas had not turned in any way that would further injure his broken body. He stood back up and looked about him. Jasper did not intend to pry, poking into another man's possessions was not one of his vices. But, he did have to admit that Mr. Rast seemed a great mystery to him. His poor conduct on board a few days past, namely, fighting—and in front of ladies! His rude demeanor in interrupting the conversation between Jasper and M. Delacroix. And then…having the courage to go on deck and aid the crew in their hour of need. What sort of man acted so contrarily in such a short space of time?

Jasper had also noticed that the Delacroixs both treated this strange young man with special regard, a wayward pet, or as a younger brother. It was all puzzling to Jasper, and because he was dead on his feet with exhaustion and weary of waiting on his charge, he decided that perhaps poking about *could* be added to his sins.

Clothes were folded smartly in a small, open traveling trunk, and stacks of correspondence lay close by. Dr. Gordon would not further demean himself by reading the man's letters, and so his eyes passed over this quickly, and came to rest on the dressing table. A small upright looking glass, a razor, a shaving cup and a pipe.

Jasper brought the candle over and glanced at himself in the mirror. He saw a haggard face with deep circles under brown eyes. His auburn hair was not retaining the red lights of his early youth, but was fading to a medium brown, and at the moment it was disheveled and dirty. He scowled at the reflection and the overwhelming blandness that he saw there. Still peering into the mirror, he reached for the pipe, and bringing it to his nose he wondered absently what kind of tobacco this English dandy preferred. Upon sniffing, however, he found that it only smelled like wood. Jasper turned the pipe over in his hands —another mystery! The pipe had been well-handled and the wood was almost rubbed out of its original shape in some places. What man keeps a pipe so close at hand—a pipe that has never been smoked?

Shaking his head, he sat back down for his vigil. He was ashamed of his snooping, especially as it had further baffled his understanding instead of elucidating it. This Mr. Rast had a striking, almost feminine type of beauty, which would have been more distinct if his features were not so marred by bruises and scrapes from his recent activities. A type of appearance in a male that is not often seen past boyhood, after which men are generally given to harsher angles. Though he had gathered from talk that the young man was returning to the island as his home, Jasper could not for the life of him place Mr. Rast there. These hands were more befitting a life of billiard playing and croquet than a life of harsh northern winters. Again he mused, who *was* this strange man who belonged more than Jasper, yet was completely out of place?

Dr. Gordon thought he heard footsteps in the corridor but could not imagine anyone was already awake. He stood up to peek out the door, when a rustle from the bed caught his attention. He spun around to find his patient awake and groaning. Quickly, he stepped back to his seat by the bedside and hastily rolled his sleeves. Nicholas turned to face him and his eyes first lit with confusion, which then drifted to recognition, and then aloofness. He was in too much pain to care who was in the room.

"Good Morning, though it is still just barely blossoming on the horizon."

"Yes, quite. Hello, Doctor. I seem to be in worse shape than last we saw one another." Mr. Rast made a feeble attempt at a smile which ended in a grimace of pain. "Oh...the pain is everywhere. Indeed...even in places I did not know could cause discomfort!"

Jasper Gordon set his face in a hard line, and reached to feel the places on the ribcage that had been injured. He already had his wife make up a poultice before sending her to bed those long hours ago. This he then applied gently, all the while studying the young man's face.

"You are studying me, Doctor. Am I very terrible to look at? Was I much hurt?"

Nicholas' visage took on a shade of alarm, and a vigorous shake of Jasper's head seemed to allay the sudden fear. He considered for a moment before replying. In truth, Rast's face was open and friendly, and while there was a trace of haughtiness in his manner, his easy speech and demeanor all but silenced it. A cloak he had worn so long that he himself did not notice its weight.

"In all honesty, sir, I have been considering your character and finding that it does not agree with your actions. In conclusion, I am perplexed."

Nicholas laughed. "A good American answer, that. It is good to ask a question and have it answered with such forthrightness. Though I blush to imagine your earlier thoughts of my character. Now, tell me true, am I very hurt?"

It was Jasper's turn to smile. "Ah, you will mend. Time as they say, is a great healer, hm?"

"Yes but it takes as long as it wants!" Nicholas laughed again, more easily this time. "So, Doctor Gordon, you have been given a post at Mackinac. How does it suit you?"

Jasper, who had been near to drowsing before, was now fully awake. Something in Rast's attitude was engaging.

"I suppose it must and so it will. And yourself? Are you glad to be returning home?"

Nicholas cringed as though he was once again being tossed about by the storm. The sudden change surprised Jasper and he moved quickly to ascertain that there were no more injured bones, but he was waved off.

"No, no, Doctor. There is no panacea for this injury. I am inspired by your candor to return the same; in short, I'm not pleased to return home. I am heartily glad of the delays. I think an angel must have sent them for they are prolonging the time before my destiny must unfold. This is a happy limbo for me, though I wish I was in greater comfort at the moment."

Dr. Gordon was stunned to hear his own thoughts so parroted. He looked again at this winsome young man, and tried to see him more closely.

"So, then, if I may be so bold, why do you return?"

Nicholas' eyes flicked downward, and a spasm of agony shuddered though his body. He took a breath in and released it out, taking his time. Jasper was amazed by the turn their conversation had taken thus far. From untrusting strangers to confidantes, it seemed. There was something so lost and pathetic about the aspect and person of this battered and bloodied soul, something that intrigued Jasper both professionally and personally. He found that he saw shade of his own difficulties in this man.

Nicholas finally turned his eyes back up to meet Jasper's.

"Well, Doctor, that is the question I've been asking myself since the moment I stepped onto the first ship in England. I suppose you've already heard a fair number of whispers about me?"

When Dr. Gordon nodded in agreement, a look of determined concentration on his features, Nicholas echoed the expression and gently pulled his hand up to his face, covering his mouth and chin. The story was swarming inside of him and he had been so very careful to keep it there. Jasper could see the war raging inside and waited patiently. It was the hallmark of a doctor, the ability to wait things out. Sometimes time could cure all kinds of illness and pain.

"So, I will not endeavor to go into detail about the long past. I have gutted myself of it already and not too long ago— so I am loath to do so again. It is better staying where it belongs. But, to answer your questions without hemming and hawing, I will say that I was called to return because my brother, Edward, perished in a storm last summer."

Jasper began his words of condolence only to be waved off yet again.

"Tut, I have not yet finished. I had promised to be honest, so I must be fully truthful. I beg you to remember this when ugly things are circulated about me on the island. Remember that I was open and earnest with you when I did not have to be. Hear me, even if I had not been called home, I would have had to return. My relatives had cast me out."

His eyes opened a little wider at this proclamation and Jasper, felt himself lean a little more forward to the story. He could not control his usual guarded expression. He reasoned that it wasn't that surprising given what he had seen thus far of Nicholas, but still, the young man before him seemed such a muddled combination of opposites. He paid closer attention to every word Nicholas was saying now, as he continued with his story, unable to pause once he had begun.

"I ran into some trouble in London, you understand. I…I have a talent with cards. A gift… a second sight one might say. I always seem to know what card my opponents were wont to play, and could read their many moods during a hand…"

A lopsided smile spread over his contused features.

"At any rate, I also have a violent temper when being accused of cheating. My companions and I had a bit of a falling out as a result of these skills, and believe it or not, my face did look worse than it does now. Somehow their gambling debts to me turned into my debts to them. Combine that with an ill-considered seduction of one of my cousin's dearest friends…and, well, my uncle gave me the boot. I went from wildly popular in my new life, to privately discarded by all those that I thought were my near and dear. I return home, a prodigal."

He sat back against the bed, wearied from the words. Jasper was silent for a moment, mulling over the tale. Where this young man went, trouble soon followed.

"You could not have remained in England then? Or are you relieved to work with your father? I have heard it said that he is an important man on the island, hm?"

Nicholas sat up a little straighter, angling himself out of the direct early beams of the new day.

"Goodness, no. I'm not cut out for the office of the fur company. Though many stand in awe of my father's relationship to Mr. Astor, frankly, the whole business frightens me. As for your other thought, I am certain that I could have stayed, as my uncle's attitude toward me had already begun to melt. If I had pressed the issue I am sure it could have come out differently. My aunt and uncle loved me dearly, as did my cousins. I was welcome in any salon I walked into on the continent or in England. But, when the news came, my charm turned off and I was diminished. Edward was...he was the greatest man I knew. I couldn't imagine a world where a man like him is taken, and a man like me survives. I dread to return, but I am honor bound for love of a brother, though he will not be there to meet me when I arrive."

He looked wistful, his eyes clouded over concealing the bright glimmer that had been there before. Jasper could sense he was in another time, and decided to employ, once again, his most useful tactic of waiting. When he could no longer bear the silence, though, even this skill failed him.

"You said you had a gift with cards, and a way of charming people. Would you care to elaborate?"

Nicholas stirred, sitting up in his sheets, his midsection bandaged and beginning to turn shades of purple where the bandages did not cover him. He smiled.

"Yes, a great gift that I squandered. I have a sense of nature, and people you might say, but sadly, used on the the wrong things. I've been told that I am a formidable storyteller as well."

Before he could stop himself Jasper blurted,

"Like Madame Delacroix then." But Nicholas barely noticed the interjection.

"Yes, just so. We had the same tutor for telling tales...

all those years ago." His eyes took on a faraway look again, and Jasper began to think he had better take his leave. Suddenly, though, Nicholas looked him square in the eye.

"Well, well, well. I reckon that you have a secret too. It's fairly screaming to escape your lips."

Jasper's eyes grew wide in alarm. Was it possible? He has just been thinking of his own past...how could this man know? A lucky guess or...something else?

Sunlight timidly had begun to illuminate the room, showing the untarnished copper brilliance of Nicholas' hair. He pulled the sheets up, covering his broken body and looked to Jasper expectantly, ready to hear his confession.

He could feel his expression betraying him and the chair he had been occupying all this while was growing unaccountably more uncomfortable. His hands twisted in his lap, and he resolved to speak. Even though he didn't yet know what he thought of him, or if he liked the man or not, Nicholas Rast had succeeded in sniffing him out.

"You are right of course. And, I must say, if that is in fact, some skill of yours, I am duly impressed."

He stopped, and Nicholas motioned him to continue, holding up two fingers to the side and rotating them in a circle, a rolling motion to stir up Jasper's words.

"Ah, where to begin? I will keep it short, as I am not a man to tarry on details, but...well, you've seen my wife?"

Nicholas nodded and Dr. Gordon continued.

"I fairly worship her now, but...there was a time when the idea of marrying her was abominable to me. We have been betrothed since we were young, a bit of an old fashioned idea for an American family, but my mother was keen to keep the family connection in England. We are second cousins, Isobel and I, and sweethearts for a short while when we knew one another as children."

He stood up, Rast's unnerving gaze had begun to discomfit him, and movement felt better with his thoughts.

"As I grew older, I began to resent a lot of the decisions my parents had made for me. My father was a lawyer, and I was to be one too."

The look on Nicholas' face stalled his pacing, until Jasper realized what it was for.

"Yes, we have that in common. But, I obviously did not take over the family business. I struck out on my own and even…"

His next words died in his throat. He could not believe what he was close to admitting to this unruly boy he had never even properly met. But the line had been cast out, he would have to untangle it now.

"That is, I even had made an offer of marriage and had been accepted by the daughter of a physician I worked under. I felt a proper rebel, my own man with my own choices."

Nicholas spoke, "What happened then? You are thankfully, for my sake, not a lawyer. But your wife is from Devon, if I am not mistaken in her accent."

Jasper smiled, the first true smile of the day.

"Yes, hm. My parents had written and sent for her when it was clear that I had abandoned my law studies. They had thought to bring me to heel by sending for my intended. When I told them of the engagement, they were in hysterics, as was I at the thought of Isobel in Boston. We were great correspondents, you understand, but I had not thought of her romantically since I was young."

It was now his turn to find himself with cloudy eyes, recalling those early days of youth and stolen kisses away from their parent's sight. His reverie was interrupted though, with a cough. Jasper looked up dreamily.

"Well, Doctor?"

"To bring my story to a close, they insisted that if I was going to go through with my own choice for marriage, than I would need to greet Isobel at the dock and break the news to her myself."

He paused again, letting the flood of memories wash over him. The jostling of the buggy on the Boston streets, rehearsing all of his explanations to Isobel.

"But, when I arrived at the dock...I was a boy again seeing Isobel for the first time. The harbor, and ships and all of Boston disappeared. She was...brilliant. I have no other word. Obviously all the plans changed and we were married in a fortnight. Of course, there was an ensuing scandal in the town in reaction to my changeable behavior, and I volunteered for army service. I knew it would be the only way to shield my wife from the unpleasantness of wagging tongues. No sooner was the ink dry that I was assigned to Fort Mackinac. My parents were heartily glad that I honored the engagement to Isobel, but were devastated that we were leaving. My new wife, my new career and all my future is now on this boat. "

Nicholas tilted his head to the side and nodded his chin up and down. "Well, at the very least, you learned that perhaps parents do know best...some of the time."

Jasper agreed. "It would seem so." And quietly he added, "And as I said, I shamed myself in Boston for my behavior and treatment of the other young lady, but I know that people are much more forgiving of folly than we give them credit for."

His eyes burned meaningfully in Nicholas' direction. The young man flinched, as if the words cut him, but soon he was nodding his head again.

"Well, you might be right for all that. Everyone seems to tell me the same thing, so mayhap it is true."

The two men sat silent for some moments, their eyes fixed on the window, and then Jasper stood up. It was time for him to get some rest.

"Well, Mr. Rast, let's neither of us speak these confidences. The ship has stopped, as the wind must need rest from its wild swirling last night, as we all do."

"Thank you, Doctor. For your trust and your care."

"You are entirely welcome. Now, both of us needs to take a cue from the weather and rest ourselves. Let your body heal."

Jasper turned toward the door and gripped the handle. A question had been tugging at him, and he must ask it if he was to get any sleep. He spun around on his heel to see Nicholas already lying prone, seemingly dozing. He changed his mind, and was about to step out when Rast's voice spun him right back around.

"You were wondering why I ventured out into the storm. It wasn't to end myself like you've been thinking. I have seen the ugly thought dancing in your mind since you first sat down to watch over me. I went up because I could sense they needed help, and I could feel Cora's fear rising as she tried to control the storm herself. Somehow, I knew Jean-Luc was in pain…and, well, it seemed like something Edward would do. So, I disguised myself as member of the crew to lend the hand they needed."

He took a breath, and then added pointedly,

"Now, Doctor, if you could hand me that pipe you were so eagerly inspecting some time ago, I would be much obliged. I like not to be separated from it."

With that strange revelation, and pipe tucked securely in his palm, he rolled tenderly to the wall and said,

"Good Morning."

Closing the door behind him, Jasper stepped into the hallway and found his own cabin door. He couldn't believe the confessions he'd made and heard these past hours. He laid down next to his sweetly slumbering wife, but he couldn't shake the strangeness of these Mackinac folk, and how they all seemed to hold more mysteries than ever.

:18:

Walter

The sun shone so sweetly on to the top of Walter's cap, and he felt its soft kiss on his hands and cheeks as he strolled the deck. He was in no mood for it's cloying sweetness, though. His mood was black, indeed.

After Reynolds came in with the report of young Delacroix's returning health, the captain had slept fitfully, haphazardly waking and sleeping until the clock confirmed the grey light's message. He was free to awaken for good.

At first, he had not noticed that the wind had fled with the rest of the storm. But upon splashing his face in the basin with the lukewarm water in the stillness of the cabin, it became all too clear. His hands in the bowl, the sloshing of the water, and then the realization that the *Starlight* sailed no more. Instead, they were left to bob and sway impotently on the lake, crippled once more.

Captain Alberts walked the length of the deck now, and tried to conceal his frustration. He hoped the crew, now all awake and resuming their posts, would not notice. There was the sail to repair after all, and the lost men to mourn. He was certain that a fair few of his men were glad of the opportunity to mend all that was broken in their hearts and on the ship. But not Walter. He was bone-weary with the voyage. He missed his family. Captain Alberts had been born to the water, but he needed a night or two each week to lay his head to rest on his own bed. This morning he had been furious with the turn of events, this new difficulty thrown in his path. It was as though Jesus and all the saints, all the spirits of the north and any other power looking down, had abandoned him completely. The captain had dashed the basin to the floorboards, and gloried in its destruction—finally, something he could control.

If he thought he had fooled his sailors with his outward show of calm, he was very much mistaken. Most of them had served on this merchant ship with him for years and knew his moods better than did his wife. The set of their captain's jaw, the blankness of his stare, it jarred them to see him like this. It was this foul attitude that gave them the most alarm.

Standing at the prow, a loud groaning sigh made its escape from his chest. He wasn't just angry, he was afraid. The sheer ferocity of the storm, the loss of his men and the slightest taint of unseen, meddling forces. The fingers of evil had their grip on the *Starlight*, even in the morning sunshine, as friendly as it seemed. As a result, again and again, he felt his gaze searching out the shadows, anticipating the next lurking obstacle.

The captain looked downward and cursed the lazy water that laughed heartily at his expense. Less than seven hours with favorable wind and they would be in Mackinac. They weren't blown too devastatingly off course, and with a little wind, they could be in port before nightfall. But, the lake had failed them; right on the doorstep of home, they'd had the door cruelly slammed in their face.

Walter's brooding was cut short; something moved on deck. He heard a creak and turned to look over his right shoulder, yes, there it was. A shape, a glimpse of a bright red scarf, curly black hair, Alberts moved his lips to speak...

A tap on his left shoulder flicked his attention away. His confused gaze landed on Leathers, who managed to comport himself with more equanimity this morning than he had been able the night before. Giving the man a cursory expression that signalled he was to hold on a moment, Walter turned back to his right to speak with the other man behind him. But, the man was gone.

"Leathers, err..." What was the man's blasted name again? "That is, Fitzwilliam, who came with you just now? The sailor with the red scarf?"

"Not a soul, Captain. I...I came alone, sir. The men would like to know what you'd have them do, sir. And the orders for the lost crew, sir."

The captain was perplexed, and even more angry than he had been before. What did the man mean? He had just now seen a man behind him, with a voyageur's red scarf and curling, black hair...

Walter's eyes bulged and suddenly he felt nauseated, his stomach heaving angrily. He remembered Leathers' crazed laughter, and his description of Big Charlie's death and suddenly...his own nightmare from a few night's before came to mind.

Each scene from the dream returned to him with absolute clarity. So, there was a specter on his ship, killing his men, stirring the weather, and just now, the phantom had meant to meddle with him.

Walter slipped swiftly back to the moment, perturbed by the gaping mouth and ridiculous expression on Leathers's face. He reached forward, placing his hand beneath the man's lower jaw, and swatted it upward, rattling his teeth.

"Close your mouth, Fitzwilliam. You're a man, not a fish."

Captain Alberts marched back to the men, who all eyed him warily, uncertain if he was still in his mood.

"Listen here, sailors! There's a great deal of work to do on my beautiful lady. I want her gleaming and as brilliant as the goddess she is. I want no Irish pennants hanging from her sails, I want no tears in the canvas, I want to be able to kiss her very deck without soiling my coat. Fitzwilliam here, this anchor clanker, seems to have questions about the duties on this vessel. He said he was speaking for the lot of you, but I know that my crew knows better. So, hop to, and you, Smitty, belay the line there!"

He clapped Leathers on the back forcefully, sending him forward toward a bucket.

"That's the right idea, Fitzwilliam. Swab this deck 'til she shines. I want it all tip-top before the wind comes around, gentleman!"

The Captain's brisk manner had worked wonders on their faith and they fell to with abandon. The crew scrubbed and repaired and shined his *Starlight*. Now though, the tasks were performed with urgency, as they believed the wind might pick up any moment.

It was still morning, but already Captain Alberts needed a drink. He shot another sharp look at the men, resting finally on Leathers, who squirmed under the captain's harsh scrutiny. Walter narrowed his eyes meaningfully, being sure to impart the message that he remembered what had occurred the night before. This withering glance deflated Leathers, and his head hung down as his arms moved furiously at his task.

Regaining control of his ship was a step closer to regaining his own mood, and as the captain strode purposefully toward his quarters, he saw Jean-Luc emerge from below deck. Taking a few steps out of his intended route, Walter grasped him by the elbow to rouse his attention.

"M. Delacroix, please join me in my quarters, if you will. I fear we have much to discuss."

His hand dropped from its place on Jean-Luc's elbow and Captain Alberts continued his progress, certain that Jean-Luc would follow. When he got to the door, he saw with relief that he wasn't mistaken.

Stepping in, Walter was glad that he had left the slats open. Even without the wind, the new air floating throughout the space had chased out the smells of fear, confusion and storm from the night before. He smiled, and directed Jean-Luc to a chair.

"I am glad to see you up and about and healing. Will you have a drink? I have a nice malmsey that Mr. Rast, Alexander Rast that is, gifted me this past Christmas."

Jean-Luc shifted lazily in his chair. "No, I thank you, sir. It's too early for me, I'm afraid."

Ignoring him, Captain Alberts poured out two glasses and placed them on the table before taking a seat. He snatched his glass and downed it all in one draught, and quickly popped up to pour another. Sitting back down at the rough little table, he ran his hands over the marked and mottled wood, recalling past, unmemorable crossings, aiming to forget the topic at hand. He searched his mind to find anything that would enable him to divert his purpose for bringing the boy in. But, it was no use.

Now sitting forward in the straight-backed chair, Jean-Luc cleared his throat.

"You indicated that you had something to discuss, Captain?"

Sliding his eyes back into focus, Walter looked at Jean-Luc with no little surprise, nodding his head, inwardly convincing himself of something.

"Quite right, yes. I did. I did, indeed."

His head continued bobbing strangely, and Jean-Luc sat back against his chair, knowing that there was more to this conversation than he had originally thought. The captain's eyes finally found his, and Walter spoke.

"I can't tell you how relieved I am to see you on your feet and looking so well. I was frightened half to death about you, my boy."

"Thank you, Captain. And thank God your fears were groundless—and also for the fort's new doctor."

"Yes, indeed...new doctor, yes."

Walter felt his mind blur again and his eyes glaze. He took another sip of the wine and absently motioned for Jean-Luc to join him in drinking. He had so many words he wanted to say, and not a clue how to say them.

The seconds ticked by awkwardly, and the silence in the Captain's cabin was becoming uncomfortable. Alberts maintained the same posture, one hand on the glass, his other hand on the table, silently drumming his fingers on its marred surface. Jean-Luc sat ram-rod straight, drink untouched, patiently waiting on this man he knew and respected, to speak.

Finally, taking the glass and knocking back the malmsey within, the captain's eyes came to penetrate the depths of Jean-Luc's, an action that so surprised him that he sat up even straighter.

"A right terrible storm we had last night, eh? For myself, I've never seen nor heard of one like it, except in tales."

Walter looked deliberately at Jean-Luc, though he felt a coward to face him down thus. He was trying to read the boy, and was using his knowledge of his character to do so. Still, Jean-Luc did not fidget, remaining impassive.

"Yes, it was most unnatural. I am indebted to the actions of your crew, though the man that saved me, I am told, was lost."

His expression was sincere and Walter hated himself even more for the path of conversation he was traversing. But, he had to know. He was consumed by the need to understand what was happening around him. It was this feeling alone that drove him away from failure and despair; the possibility of altering the outcome of what was shaping up to be a doomed crossing.

"Yes, a great loss. The families will be cared for. Imagine, though, if some other misadventure had struck you, or Cora! Your father would be inconsolable. A terrible, awful business."

He shook his head, suddenly struck with melancholy over the losses to his crew, and also dismay at how to continue the conversation. Then, a thought suddenly occurred to him, something he'd heard that he could use.

"A moment ago you said, "unnatural", what did you mean in using that word precisely?"

The captain leaned forward, trying to gather every word, even those that were only being spoken in Jean-Luc's most secret heart. M. Delacroix hardly stirred, though the question hung menacingly over him. He went a little paler for a moment, before his normal sun-darkened coloring reappeared.

The young man met his eyes and there was a sadness inside of them.

"Oh, I'm sure I don't know, Walter. Can I call you by your given name? Father always does."

He paused for a moment and Captain Alberts nodded, his hand went to his pocket feeling for his pipe. Upon reaching in and feeling for the trusty thing, he remembered that the both of them had emptied their stores of tobacco in the last calm. How long ago that seemed! Was it really only two days prior? So much had happened to his body, his spirit, and his sanity in the past days that he could hardly credit the time. He took his hand from his pocket and placed it, empty, on the table.

"Let me tell you a story that my wife told me, Walter." Jean-Luc's face seemed to glow with the mention of her, and he settled more comfortably in his seat.

"Years ago, the Ravensdales came to the island. Waseya came to stay in their house, as you may know, to help the commandant with the girls, as their mother had died in childbed with Rosalind. She worked to teach them languages, and sewing, basic mathematics, and she taught them some musical skill on the pianoforte. She also started a small garden behind their fine townhouse. It was only a small patch, just to give the girls something to do, you understand."

Walter's resolve had begun to falter, and his patience wore as he listened. What *was* the boy talking about?

"Excuse me Jean, but, you said…"

"I know what I said, now allow me to finish. We are getting to that. In good time."

It was maddening. Jean-Luc was perfectly poised, as if the question wasn't hanging between them. As if Walter hadn't accused Jean-Luc of knowing more about these events than he let on.

"…a small plot of soil. They grew some beans of some kind and even a few wild strawberry buds were planted and seemed to flourish. Waseya, though, had been most eager about cultivating corn…"

"Corn?" Walter asked. He couldn't begin to understand what the boy was getting to. Perhaps he had been knocked harder in the head than the doctor realized.

"Mon Dieu! Oui, corn. In her tribe, it was only women who could touch the corn, a man's touch would spoil it. As is true of most things men touch, come to think of it. But, in any case, one night she had gathered the girls together, and they were to walk through the two or three rows of the new seedlings, unclothed. It was something to do with honoring the Manitou and the corn spirits."

He paused and gave Walter a sidelong glance. Walter wasn't sure what to think. Was this supposed to be racy? A lesson of some kind?

"Are you going to finish, Jean? Did it grow? Hand me your glass of malmsey if you're set on wasting it."

"Tut-tut. Wait for the end! Oui, it did grow, but that is not the story. The tale ends like this: Commandant Ravensdale betook himself outside after finding his daughter's empty bedchambers. He marched out to the garden, but Waseya met him at the edge, bold as you please, and ordered him inside. He was so stunned—he obeyed!"

Jean-Luc broke off to laugh at the thought and Walter could not help but join in. Battle hardened soldiers would not even dare to give the commandant orders, but a small, naked, chicot woman had!

"When they returned inside, having re-clad themselves modestly in their nightdresses and robes, Waseya sent the girls to bed. The girls had crouched, hidden on the stairs, to see if their father would send their beloved Waseya away. He had glared at her for a moment and then asked her to explain—here's that word again— her *unnatural* behavior. Before he could finish, she put a hand up, silencing him and said, 'It is only *unnatural* because you do not yet understand it. To me, your reaction is most unnatural—because it is foreign to my understanding. Something is not evil or wrong simply because we have no experience of it.' Then, she bid him goodnight and not another word was ever said of any of the new ideas she brought under their roof."

Jean-Luc relaxed his back even further into his chair,

and reached for his wine glass taking a teasing sip.

"A most excellent malmsey, Captain, très bien."

The captain looked at him mournfully, needing still to have his answer.

"I understand, Jean. But, please. I know what they say on the island about your wife, and I am not one to credit the jealous gossip of angry women, but I also know there was bad blood between you and Philippe. And…I have heard a few whispers that do not bear repeating about the night of his passing—may God rest his soul. Finally… there was some mystery about your flight to Detroit last autumn. It was so sudden…so strange…"

He looked deeply into the younger man's eyes, seething with violation. He could feel Jean-Luc's loathing crashing into him like waves, and it broke his heart.

"Believe me when I say that I do not care for gossip, and that I do not judge off hand. But I have injured passengers and crew members that will never again walk ashore in Mackinac. Good men who died in their duty during a harsh and sudden storm. We've had delays I've never even imagined in all my years sailing this lake. So, I ask, only out of my own confusion and sorrow. As a friend, and one that has looked on you as proudly as any father…"

The words hung and Jean-Luc's expression had softened, which gave Walter hope. He took a deep breath and asked,

"Does your wife have anything to do with these calms and storms? Does she traffic with spirits or the weather or any such thing that controls the destiny of this ship? Or is it your brother's spirit that roams my deck?"

His eyes were heavy and suddenly he felt horribly tired. In answer, Jean-Luc laughed and popped to his feet, making to leave. Though, his expression matched the captain's, not a trace of genuine mirth to be found.

"I wish I knew, Captain. But, even if she did, what would it matter? What would it change? And if Philippe *has* come here in spirit, I wish he would speak with me, I have a few questions myself."

His hand clasped the door as he turned to Walter one last time.

"But no. I fear that it is merely that the wind does not always blow the way the ship desires. Or, sometimes it does not blow at all."

And with that, Captain Alberts was left alone with two empty glasses...two empty glasses, and Jean-Luc had but taken a single sip.

·19·
Pierre

The window in his office looked out onto the waters of Mackinac. Nearly every day he had lived here, he had raised his head up from his ship manifests and captain's logs, and allowed his eyes to wander out over the the waves for a moment or two before happily returning to his work.

These past few days had altered that familiar routine. He was restless, red-eyed and instead of immersing himself in the business he had loved like a child, he would gaze for hours into the blue. His weary eyes flicked back and forth on the horizon, endlessly grasping for a glimpse of the *Starlight*. The ship carried his most important treasure, his son, Jean-Luc.

His other shipments, from the western lands across the lake and from St. Ignace had came and went, but the only ship that really mattered tarried, never coming close enough to land to even allow someone to sight it. He knew this because he had hired men to do exactly that, sending them down the most eastern points of the Michigan territory, but all was silent.

Which was the same attitude surrounding Cross Shipping. The clerks, when they spoke at all, spoke in veiled whispers and no one dared to pass too close to M. Pierre Delacroix's closed office doors. They respected their employer for his masterful control and great knowledge of all aspects of shipping on the Great Lakes. But they were also afraid of this lapse into listlessness, as it was so contrary to his usual good-natured enthusiasm. Some had even been heard to utter words like "cursed" and "supernatural", though they were careful to speak in hushed tones, lest it got back to M. Pierre. Though they might admire their employer, their feelings could not nip their speculations and gossip.

Pierre had been sitting in his chair since early morning, ostensibly browsing expenditures and revenue, but his eyes hadn't made it beyond the second line of figures. His gaze was directed out, seeing but unseeing, barely registering movement. His eyes had grown more lined with crimson and bags hung as heavy anchors beneath. His jaw had gone slack, and a small ribbon of saliva dangled from his slightly opened lips.

This was a man that would be unrecognizable to the people of the town. They would shudder to see his fire so utterly extinguished. As the spittle fell from his mouth to his trouser leg, he heard a sound at his door. The clamor brought his vision back into a hazy focus, and his head lifted.

He would normally have been surprised to see Marguerite at the office, he could count on two hands the times in their marriage she had stepped foot in Cross Shipping. But here she was, sweating delicately, the small bird-like bones of her arms quivering with exertion.

"Oh mon Dieu, but I came too fast!" her voice fully snapped him back to the moment, and he raised a hand up to his face, wiping the look of despair from it in one gesture.

"My dear, what are you doing here? Is something the matter?"

All at once, Pierre's fears reached a fever pitch, he was certain that she had come with news, news of their son...

"No, nothing different than has been the matter since this past autumn. One son buried, the other vanished to Detroit, and the both of them haunting me daily."

She was picking up a chair, for which he stood up to offer assistance, before being shooed back to his seat by his unflappable wife.

They were silent for some time, both of their eyes focused on the water before them. His melancholy from earlier couldn't quite envelop him as before, her arrival had chased it into a corner, waiting to reappear when he was alone.

"Why have you come then, Marguerite?"

He asked the question timidly, suddenly confused at the realization of how strange this visit was.

"Oh, I don't entirely know. I was sitting in the front window, fretting, thinking to maybe pay a call at Philippe's grave. But, I knew that your eyes were searching for the same sight as mine were, and that 'twould be better company to wait together."

She laid her hand on top of his and they smiled at one another. A sad smile that said many things, but mostly confirmed that neither of them had been fooling the other.

With the amount of worry that flooded between the two of them, Pierre was surprised to see how bright and clear the day was. The wind was slow and lazy, but he prayed it find its way to the *Starlight* and send her safely to harbor.

"Look!" Marguerite's face lit up as she pointed to the lake. He was caught for a moment by how the sunlight falling on her face at just this angle transported him back so effortlessly to the wisp of a girl he'd fallen in love with in a field of purple flowers, and how intrepid she had been to risk her life on this Mackinac gamble with him. He was blessed to have chosen such a woman, and doubly blessed that she had chosen him too.

A formation of canoes expertly handled by young natives was the sight that had caught her attention. There were many tribes living on the island, but still more came in the summer to receive their government payments. They came every year, and every year less and less departed in the cool of the autumn in those same canoes. Instead, over time, some members of the tribes had come to prefer a life opposite from the roaming existence of their people, and so they too, became part of Mackinac.

Pierre's brow filled with deep creases and furrows of worry. He had often looked forward to the return of the Ojibwa, the Huron, the Fox and the Potawatomi, but this year—this year he had heard there would be trouble with the agreed upon payments.

Marguerite though, she loved to see them return. She had longed for it and it had stirred her blood to see these noble people and their bright culture—so like the one she had left behind in France!—enliven the sleeping island every spring. She had led the boys out, holding each of their hands in hers, and had taken them to the shore, so they could watch them returning. It was something in her half Romani-gypsy blood that was set on fire with the idea of a free, roaming people.

Pierre had sometimes wondered if this was where Philippe's troubles had begun, if his blood was too wild, and it had ruined him. Pierre had been so lost in thought, he hadn't realized that someone else had strolled into his office, someone whom his wife was staring at with unbridled fury.

He turned to behold a man that appeared familiar to him, but he couldn't quite place. He scanned through his memory, as the intruder stood at the door, staring back at them.

"I'm sorry, can I assist you? Do we have an appointment?"

The man looked as if he was about to answer, when Marguerite cut in.

"Francois Gaillard" She threw the name at the man like it was an obscene word. She was regarding him with open disgust, such a sight was hardly to be believed for Pierre. He had always known his wife to be kind and above all, tolerant of others. Until, he realized that this man with his hateful smirk had been one of the men under Philippe's command in his brigade. This was the man who now wore the black feather of the Lake of the Woods.

Without being asked and still unspeaking, Francois took a seat, and without dropping his gaze, he leered at them.

Pierre and Marguerite exchanged looks and he could not remember a time he'd seen her so angry. Their attention was drawn back to their unwelcome guest as he cleared his throat, a sound like gravel and sand, and spoke.

"Bonjour, M. and Mme. Delacroix, how convenient to find you both here. I trust Claude is no trouble, non?"

He lazily gestured toward the door and Pierre recalled he had taken on the man's younger brother last summer, at Philippe's insistence. He had forgotten the connection.

The Gaillard family had come to Mackinac just a few years before from Canada, where they had been unsuccessful, and before that from somewhere near Paris. They had been unpopular in town for one reason or another, since almost the moment they had arrived. Marguerite suspected the father was violent and so she had lent help to the mother and her brood of neglected offspring. All had perished from smallpox two winters past, excepting the promising Claude, a younger sister, Odette, and this angry man before them.

Last summer he had been always in Philippe's shadow, until with Philippe's death, Francois had eclipsed him.

"Claude is a talented young man, I have no complaints. Excepting of course that his brother thinks it meet to barge into my office."

This only seemed to brighten the man's smile.

"Yes, forgive me, but after I saw that Mme. Delacroix was not at home, I thought it high time to come here."

Pierre looked to Marguerite in confusion and was taken aback once again by the waves of loathing that washed over her countenance.

"What is the meaning here? What is it you come for? I'm a busy man, M. Gaillard, and I have never cared for games."

"Ahh, a man after my own heart then. Just as I told your wife last autumn then, although I fear the price of my silence has increased with my absence this winter."

Hatred, like a lightning bolt lit up Marguerite's whole person, the force of it shaking Pierre. The man's words... what could they mean? He looked Francois over, taking in his wiry frame and loose, untidy brown hair, tied back into a knot. He looked hungry like a young and rangy wolf, and just as wily.

Responding to the reactions he was receiving, Francois snickered quietly and then reached into his pocket for his watch, and checking the time, feigned alarm.

"I too am a busy man, monsieur. And so, I will tell you what your wife has so obviously not, and then you will understand, my, let's call it, *generosity*, in keeping what I know in confidence, this long cold winter. Why, I'm hardly asking for anything. If these facts were to become known, well, I don't think any of these fine island gentry would be too pleased to have the stain of your friendship."

Francois' face was turned up into an unsettling grin, and his eyes flashed with excitement at the sense of unease he had been the architect of.

"I've had the good manners to visit your exquisite wife many times last autumn, and even once since the brigade's return. Each time I have gotten naught for my pains but harsh words and withering looks. I have come, this final time, to treat with you instead."

"What is it that you seek, M. Gaillard, and what is the nature of the information that you possess? Tell me plain, no more dances, sir."

Pierre had at first recoiled upon hearing that the man had been bothering his wife, and wondered why she had not spoken of it. He sensed that the man did have some kind of damaging secret, but his manner was growing tedious.

"Ah, so you're wife has told you nothing, I see. Tisk, tisk, Madam. Let us just say that in the brigade, Philippe and I had become like brothers..."

"Philippe had already a brother, Monsieur." Marguerite interrupted him, her eyes burning with abhorrence.

"Oui, though more of a puppet than a man, non?"

Marguerite was poised to strike again, but Francois put a hand up, dismissing her unspoken words.

"Though a mother would see his failings as virtues, I'm sure. Now, as I was saying..."

He paused, walked over to a small sideboard that had a few crystal bottles upon it. Pulling the stopper out, he took a long sniff and unceremoniously poured himself a drink from the decanter. Francois drank deeply from the glass and wiped his mouth with his sleeve.

"Dieu, but that is fine. I'd rather like a bottle myself." With the same foul grin he sat, and continued.

"Philippe and I were as brothers, and we shared all. Our drink, our furs, our women and our secrets. Last summer, though, we had a bit of a row. I found out he was no longer sharing his women or his secrets with his friend, Francois."

Pierre made a gesture of impatience. "Get to it, man. My wife does need to hear such filth. Spare the details. What is it that you know and what is it that you want for the information?"

His voice was calm and impassive, and he regarded Francois as one would a mosquito, an annoyance that was simply too close. Something in his tone gave Marguerite hope and flooded Francois with rage.

"The facts, *Monsieur,* are these. I know that your son, Philippe, was carrying on a carnal dalliance with the harlot that is now wife to your precious heir, Jean-Luc, and I also happen to have knowledge that Philippe had gotten her with child. Most damaging of all in this love triangle—I also know that it was none other than Jean-Luc Delacroix who brought about his own brother's death."

He finished speaking, spitting each word out carefully and cruelly, a judgement on the two people before him. He sat back into his chair and took another long draught of the warming whiskey, before recklessly tossing the glass behind him, shattering it into a thousand diamond drops on the floor. Francois was unnerved by his accusation and the lack of response he was getting, though he would not show it. Marguerite was clearly livid at the charges he had so violently thrown at her sons, but Pierre, however, simply appeared bored. He drummed his fingers on his knee and discreetly checked his pocket watch, before he too, walked over to pour himself a drink. His soft-soled leather shoes made a crunching noise with every shard he trampled and the room grew completely silent as he took a sip. Then, tilting his head and considering for a moment, he spoke.

"I see. Much of this was already known to me. But, I must ask again, what is it that you want?"

Francois now stood up, feeling at a disadvantage to be making demands from a lower position than the man he was requesting from. Pierre was a large man, built like his son. Some older men softened as they aged, the hard hewn muscles of youth disappearing into fatty, comfortable folds. But, Francois noted that although M. Delacroix's face was lined and his hair was growing snow and silver, he had retained his youthful vigor. Even at 60 he was a man to be respected and awed for his physical presence alone. Francois licked his lips and looked from husband to wife, and replied.

"I want, that is, I *require* very little. Just a partnership in Cross Shipping. It was what you wanted for Philippe and now Jean-Luc will have a partner. As I said, I am prepared to be most reasonable."

"Is that all?" Pierre asked. His face had finally found a smile. Marguerite, sitting in the same attitude blanched, and covered her face with her hands, and began to weep.

"Yes, that's all. Excepting, of course, some ready money—and perhaps the charming house M. and Mme. Jean-Luc Delacroix were to reside in. It may be better to keep the whole family under your roof, non?"

In response, Pierre simply noted, "It sounds as if you would like to become Philippe."

He uttered these words carefully, but Francois did not take offense. He supposed it was rather true, and he couldn't help but add, "Oui, but then I would also need to share Madame Cora's bed."

To his surprise, Pierre's smile grew even wider, even as Mme. Delacroix's shaking sobs grew stronger.

"Yes, you would, indeed. But as you said, for the transformation to be complete, Jean-Luc would then need to kill you."

Francois' stomach rolled as he felt the unease in the room melt into his being. Madame Delacroix now lifted her head from her hands, and he saw his mistake. She had not been grieving, but rather, laughing, and quite hysterically.

Pierre returned from standing at the sideboard and resumed his seat by his wife. Wordlessly his hand sought out hers, which he clasped tightly.

"Now that I presume you have quite done, I will explain why I must refuse your demands."

Pierre's voice was business-like and professional, never wavering or altering tone or volume. His eyes were neither piercing nor lazy, and the calm attitude in which he spoke snaked beneath Francois' skin and settled into dread in the pit of his gut.

Pierre rubbed his lips together and took another sip.

"The creature that returned last summer was not our son. We do not know what demon or *wendego* had so convincingly donned his skin, but we mourned his passing long before his body ceased to walk this earth. Secondly, Cora Delacroix has always been as a daughter to us, and the only quality she need possess to earn our love is that she is adored by our son. Nothing else in her character is our business nor our concern."

The corners of Pierre's mouth drew up, and his eyes wrinkled merrily for a moment. He was thoroughly enjoying himself.

Francois could not bear this insanity. The way the man was speaking was madness.

"You do not care that she will bear the bastard child of your dead son? You do not care that I will humiliate your family's name to any man, if I only but open my mouth?"

"Humiliate is a strange word. To make someone humble, they must be willing to be humbled. But, we will not argue vocabulary. No, I pray you, monsieur, do not interrupt, it is my turn to speak."

Pierre and Marguerite exchanged looks, annoyed at the rude interruption.

"To continue, as to your other charge, that Jean-Luc was somehow responsible for Philippe's death, you've offered no proof, and it seems by its very nature, to be more the business of our family than your own. Finally, as to your request. You have been witness to my wife's response, which was wholly appropriate. Unbridled hilarity is the only way to greet such a preposterous petition. Furthermore, you forget, *monsieur,* that I own a shipping company. A company that is respected all the way to New York, Boston and across the ocean to England and France…"

At this point, Francois quickly cut off the flow of Pierre's speech. "Monsieur, it is for that very reason, that respect for your company could be so easily lost…"

"Tais-toi, garçon! Hush! I am speaking. Now, Madame Delacroix and I are steadfast believers in changing one's surroundings in order to alter one's attitude. So, for you, I propose a journey."

Marguerite smiled sweetly at her husband and patted his arm affectionately. Francois truly began to suspect, that they were both, in fact, raving mad. His unease trebled to see how unaccountably merry this conversation had made them. He had not realized until now that he had so completely lost the upper hand. He scrambled to reclaim it as fear gripped his insides.

"I think not, M. Delacroix. I have made my desires known, and if my terms are not met, I will ruin you. I swear it. I will ruin your son and any future the Delacroix family had on this island."

He tossed the words like daggers, allowing his fury to take root and fill the room. He was dismayed then, to be greeted by the inane, raucous laughter of the two older people.

"Where do you think, my dear Marguerite?"

"Oh, I was thinking, perhaps, Hispaniola? Or didn't you just say a few night's back that there were some interesting things happening in Cuba?"

"Mon cœur, you are an angel. Oui, Cuba is having their own struggles for independence. A perfect place for the volatile M. Gaillard."

They both turned toward Francois, smiling widely. Pierre stood and took a step closer to him, appraising him and then a look of displeasure came over his features, and he lunged out, more quickly than Francois would have ever imagined. He grabbed the younger man by the collar of his newly purchased shirt, paid for with his voyageuring furs.

"Bon voyage, Monsiuer Gaillard. You will be enjoying some of the hospitality of Cross Shipping after all."

Before Francois could respond, a fist like a dropping anchor slammed into his jaw, knocking him backward into the scattered crystal pieces he had sprinkled so carelessly earlier, and all was darkness.

Pierre shook out his fist, and wrapped the broken and bleeding knuckles in his handkerchief. He went to the door of his office and opened it swiftly. His clerks and messengers could not hide their interest and curiosity, they appeared to be writing a little too quickly, their eyes darting from their work to their employer a touch too frequently.

"Claude, Robin, step into my office, please. Bring rope."

The two men popped up from their desks, Robin fetching a length of rope quickly from just outside near the docks. Together they bounded into M. Delacroix's office.

Glances were exchanged all around the outside office floor, but the hum of work never stopped. The two men had entered to find the fragments from a whiskey glass surrounding Francois like a cloud.

"Claude, tell your mother that your brother is going away on a trip."

The young man looked down, wide-eyed. "Is he...?" Not waiting for the young man to complete his thought, Pierre answered.

"Yes, he is going on a trip, and he'll be doing it alive, though he is currently not in full possession of his senses. Claude, bind his arms. Robin, we'll need our largest shipping crate. M. Gaillard had come to see us today with the aim of traveling somewhere exotic. He became so overwhelmed that he fainted. As I do not want him to miss his ship, and I would not want him to awake and harm himself, it is best if he is crated. I would like to include directions for the captain of the vessel explaining when it would be most advantageous, for his health of course, for M. Gaillard to be released."

Claude's expression was twisted into utter confusion. Pierre knew there was no love between the brothers, but the boy clearly knew that Francois would only come here with the intent to harm. Robin, though, had been with Cross Shipping longer, and knew and trusted his employer's orders.

"Yes, sir, M. Delacroix. I think I know exactly the right temporary sleeping quarters for this man, and on the *Lady Liberty*, who is leaving today. I'll draw up the instructions for her captain myself."

Without another word, they both bent down and carried Francois out, and Pierre could hear Robin explaining something to young Claude in hushed tones.

He took a hold on to the tops of their two chairs and brought them closer to the window. He sat down and resumed his watch on the water. Marguerite stood up, and crunched over the crystal, pouring one more glass of whiskey. Sitting down next to Pierre, she grasped his hand and pulled the handkerchief off, and then poured the liquor over the knuckles. She rewrapped the cloth over the injury and held his damaged hand gently in her own. Marguerite matched her gaze to his, staring silently out onto the lake.

He made to speak, but she squeezed his fingers lightly, never taking her eyes from the waves.

"Surely you and I do not need words or explanations for what happened. This is our family, and I have relied on your judgement since the day our feet touched this shore, and I have never been wrong to do so."

They both smiled, and though neither of them could see it, they both knew the smile was there. Silence fell over the room, their eyes locked on the deep blue of the straits.

:20:

Jean-Luc

He'd made his tread purposely overloud to give warning of his imminent intrusion into her solitude. The ruffle of paper and a sharp intake of breath on the other side of the door told him that he hadn't been quite noisy enough, or that perhaps she had been too absorbed in her writing.

He'd been to visit Nicholas, and it seemed to Jean-Luc that on each encounter they fell more easily together. All time apart forgotten, just two wild island boys speaking of the forest and recalling fond memories. Oui, he would be glad to have Nicholas back home. He was already twice the man he'd been since their first meeting on the *Starlight*. An English dandy no longer—but now a hearty Mackinac man.

He had opened the door to see her burying her commonplace book, though he suspected she was using it as a diary or confessional, haphazardly beneath some correspondence they hadn't the time to reply to yet. Her cheeks burned crimson, and he suppressed a laugh, how foolish that she should be ashamed to be writing her secrets!

Cora quickly sprang up and clung to him. She was in his arms, her head on his chest, and all thoughts of what had transpired earlier with the captain, and just now between himself and Nicholas vanished. Only their early dawn swim was left swirling in his mind. He loved the way she fit in his arms, loved the freedom of pulling her close without reserve, a gift so recently discovered. This woman, his wife, finally his to adore completely.

All too soon, the embrace ended, and they began to speak of the stresses awaiting them in Mackinac. They worried and discussed the work of settling everything into their new home. Realizations that their lives, their belongings, all of their pasts would need to be packed up and brought to this new space they would share, and from those pasts, they would somehow create a future. As they spoke, a weed of discord grew between them, adding an edge to the conversation. It teemed with words unsaid, secrets refusing to be revealed. He could feel the captain's accusations hanging heavy from his tongue, but he did not want to further spoil her mood, or sully their hard-won newfound intimacy. But the tighter he held the truth, the more it spilled out between them, mocking any belief he'd had that all was healed.

Jean-Luc noticed that she too, was concealing something. But what? She had not quitted the cabin since their swim this morning…and his mind flew briefly back once again, to that sunrise lovemaking, their bareness of souls. But, then the tension of expression, and her eyes looking somewhere just over his shoulder, ripped him back to the moment.

What was she hiding?

Conversation had ceased. Discussion of their new home and the awkwardness of quitting their parent's houses, draped a pall over their cheer. The thought of the gossip that would accompany their valuables and clothing leaving one roof for the other was not a happy thought.

She came forward again then, and embraced him, brushing her lips softly against his. He knew she was escaping from him, hoping to evade their mutual deceits by removing herself. As quickly as the veil between them had been tossed away, she arranged it again, artfully. Cora muttered something about seeing how Mrs. Gordon fared after last night's storm, and she rushed to open the door. How easily she slipped from his fingers! How cruelly she cut him! Jean-Luc could not resist calling out to her, calling her to account for herself once more before she left the room.

"Cora, how much longer must we sit in calm?"

One corner of her mouth twitched upward and she bit her lip.

"Soon, my love, soon. It is almost finished."

The door opened and closed again before he could say another word. He shook his head back and forth a few times and blinked his eyes as wide open as possible and shut them tightly with deliberation. No matter how many times he did so, the world he saw before him was the same. How could he have gained her so thoroughly and then lost her trust so completely all in a day?

He sat down in the little chair near the desk, the same that was so recently inhabited by Cora. He could still feel the warmth of her body on the seat. Wasn't that a kind of magic? Feeling a person's presence after they've left the room? Part of their own heat remaining to add to one's own? Jean-Luc mused, and chuckled at himself for the silliness of his thoughts.

Everything about her was enchantment to him. The sun reaching through the gaps in the tree leaves to dapple her hair, or the way the path cleared when she trod upon it. She could wade calf deep on the lake shore, and not a drop of water would stain her dress.

The real magic though, was in her stories, and in her eyes. It was the sound her laughter made in the darkness, and the flush of anger on her cheeks when she was wronged. With her, the whole world was more alive, and he could hardly believe there had ever been a Mackinac without her.

But, he was impatient to get home. He had spoken true to the captain, if Philippe *was* haunting the *Starlight*, he did have questions for him. Maybe just two. Why? Why had he changed so? What had happened to the brother he had known as well as himself?

His fingers had been absently prodding through the correspondence, searching for something to distract him from his increasingly ugly thoughts. Something more solid was beneath this last letter, and lifting it up revealed Cora's book. He held the small thing in his palm, and was glad that she had taken such a liking to this gift. He had seen it in a shop in those days before they were to leave, and it reminded him of a similar book he had given her as children. Then, he had hoped she would write him letters or recount some of Waseya's stories in it's pages. Now, he wasn't sure why he had purchased it. He didn't know what he thought she would write in it, but he had been captured in the memory of the past, when he'd presented a small, golden eyed girl with a gift, and she'd adored it. Perhaps he had been hoping to see a glimpse of that unbridled joy again. In this, blessedly, he had been right. For he had seen that life-drunk woman again, and it filled his soul.

Jean-Luc made to replace the book, but it dropped suddenly from his hand. It was odd, because he had been holding it firmly, closed between his thumb and fingers. It was almost as if…but no, he didn't really believe in such things. But… it did feel like someone had snatched it from his hand and dashed it to the floor. Peculiar.

He bent down to retrieve it, and the book was open. His hand gripped the edge in an effort to close it up before he lifted it, but it refused to budge, being held open by unseen hands. But, no...that was not possible. Shaking his head, he tried again, but to no avail. He did not mean to read it, but a few of the words had stung his eyes.

"As it is, I can still feel his expert hands sliding evenly down my naked back, to the curve of my waist, and lower, as the soft waves lapped against us like a lover's tongue"

Beads of sweat broke on his forehead and his arms were shaking. His brother was haunting him, Philippe would always live like this in her memory. Her first love, her grand passion— not ignited by her husband, the man who loved her, but by his fiend of a brother. A man that was Philippe, but was not. A man that had sworn to love her, but never had. A demon who had sown unhappiness in the lives of all he touched last summer.

Hot tears came from his eyes. It was not that he had thought he possessed her, nor had he ever doubted she had loved Philippe, but to see her own thoughts, revealed like this...it was agony. Was the love he felt this morning real? Or when she looked at him, did she only see his brother?

Laughter rang in his ear, cold, mocking laughter. The page that had been stuck before, the page that taunted him, suddenly turned, and the pages of the little book seemed to fly past of their own accord. The laughter continued, grew louder. Jean-Luc stared at the book in disbelief, raised his hands to his ears to block the derisive shrieks, but it grew louder, and the sound felt as if it was inside of him. Then, silence.

The pages of the book ceased their flipping and the mocking cackle had made an end. He looked about him, wondering if he'd imagined it, and he bent down to retrieve the book once again. As before, the words he saw stung him painfully, though this time for a different reason. It was her latest entry, and he guessed that this was the secret she had been concealing. The gap between them since this marriage had began, and he now held it in his hands. The words cut him, to think of her so desperate... so helpless. He had never imagined her thus.

"Without thought, my feet brought me to the clearing in the forest and when I arrived, my only thought was to destroy myself."

Destroy herself? The words slashed through him, a cold steel blade in his chest. That morning, the morning he had found her in the wood. He had been there all night, after he...after he killed Philippe. Jean-Luc read a little backward to discover that she blamed herself for Philippe's death. She attributed a curse, spoke in haste to his demise. Could she really believe this to be true? How many blows could a man withstand before he fell apart?

He dropped the book on the desk heavily and it made a satisfying thud. He thought for a moment, his eyes tracing the outlines of the shadows on the wall. The same sunshine he had basked in this morning, now seemed too bright to his newly opened eyes. He picked the little book back up. It looked so harmless, just leather and paper, stained with ink. Whoever thinks that words do not have the power to harm, oh, but how very wrong they are. Words cut in places that bleed continuously.

His hands shook as he flipped to the beginning of her last entry. There he read the details of the last moments she saw Philippe, felt her hot anger and the freezing of her heart against him.

Still holding the book, he heard the door. He did not lower himself further by hiding his desecration of her privacy. All would need to be brought into the light now. No more hiding, no more shoddily erected walls to keep the other out. This was not the way he would have wished to reveal his secrets. But, destiny chooses its own time and

Jean-Luc was but a servant to its capricious whims.

When she saw him, she blanched, her body falling back against the door for support. He looked at Cora pleadingly, though he did not know what he was begging for. Her color returned and she stood up tall, boldly, prepared now for the scene before her.

"You've read it then. Good. Now you know all. I wrote it more clearly than I could have spoken it. The truth I have tried so long to hide, that I longed to prevent from being discovered, so that you might somehow still love me. But, I knew it would out eventually, and you would despise that which before you had worshipped."

She paused, and he tried to speak, but Cora continued on, not wanting to hear what she was certain were condemnations of her.

"I will go away. I will leave you in peace and never trouble you. Please, I beg you though, not to speak of my shame. Not for my own sake, but for Rosalind and papa and…"

Jean-Luc had stood up and stopped her mouth with a firm kiss. It lingered and melted into something more passionate. When they finally broke apart, there were hot tears on both of their cheeks. Before she could speak, he shushed her with another light kiss, and then taking her over to the bed, they sat, facing one another.

"Mon amour, oui, I have read some of your diary. Only a page of a…personal nature…" He cringed, unable to stop himself.

"But also, the last entry in the book…and far from blaming you, I find that I must make a confession of my own. You see, I too, have been hiding an ugly secret. I too, have reason to worry that you will order me away."

Her hand reached out to clutch his and she started to protest against his concerns.

"Non, do not make promises yet, cher. Only, give me a moment and listen to my sins. Fit it together with your story, and only then tell me whether you will still have me."

His eyes searched hers earnestly, the golden irises revealed nothing though. Not judgement of him nor hope. Jean-Luc's mind stretched back, found the place in the narrative he needed and resigning himself, he began.

"Let me start at the end, and then I will wind my way around to the beginning. I saw you in the wood, in the clearing where we had spent so many beautiful sunlit hours. You were there, weeping softly. At the time, I thought it to be from heartache at losing the man you loved. I know now that it was that, but it was also for the guilt that you felt. When I saw you so broken, an idea sprang into my mind. I wanted to save you and I wanted you to save me. But I knew you would not have me if you thought I offered myself to you in anything other than honor. I knew you would refuse anything resembling sympathy or duty. So, instead, I told you that Philippe had told me all, and that I knew of your plans to marry. I told you anything I thought would make you agree. I said that Philippe had begged me to take care of you if anything should happen to him. We both knew it to be a lie, but I prayed that your pride would allow you to indulge in the deception, and that somehow you would believe that what I was saying was true, or that I believed it was."

Cora was crying now, silently, but with desperation. He had offered her the lie in the forest, hoping she would take it—and she had. He did not mean to shame her, he only needed all pretense between them laid bare. He pulled her hand to his heart and laid it there, waiting until her tears ebbed, before continuing.

"But, I must tell you that he had indeed come to the Cross Shipping office that day, but we both know it was not to share glad tidings, rather to tell me of his leaving. We had...words, heated words, as I did not agree with his decision. I was furious with him and sent him away with curses similar to yours."

Cora leaned forward whispering words of forgiveness, of kindness, but gently he pressed her back.

"Your words are balm to my guilt, but they are given too early. I have not done with the tale."

Her eyes flicked a shade deeper gold in surprise. But, she stayed still, listening intently.

"This is the memory that has haunted me every hour since that night. I have tried so hard to forgive myself! To forgive him that drove me to it. Cora, you cannot blame yourself for curses or ill wishes. This hand that presses so devotedly to your own, this is the hand that killed Philippe Delacroix!"

Her eyes widened in shock, and tears flowed freely unchecked down her cheeks. Yet, she did not let go, did not try to snatch her hand away in horror. He tried to shake her off, but she held fast.

"Release me! You heard my words! You cannot love me now!"

"I would know the end of the story, please. You promised the full truth and I will have it before I make any decisions."

Her voice was calm, her bearing, unyielding. Her hand remained intertwined with his own. Something in this steadfastness brought him out of his hysteria.

"Oh, I did promise. I do owe you the bare truth"

He took a deep breath, pressed his shoulders back, and brought forth the words he needed to purge himself of the deed.

"I had worked late after our altercation, I was loath to go home lest maman read the whole of what happened on my face. It had grown dark, and it was late indeed, before I locked my office door behind me. Still, I could not force my footsteps toward home. Instead, I kept to the path that led to the back of the tavern. I hoped to clear my head with a drink and fellowship.

Behind the tavern, I began to worry I would meet with Philippe and I had no desire to quarrel again. I thought instead then to return home after all. I turned to leave, and then from a dark corner I heard a laugh. A gurgling laugh that came from a pile of clothes rumpled against the wall.

I approached, hand on my blade, lest it was someone aiming to do me harm. Then, the same voice spoke.

'Ah, well met, mon frer.'

I crouched down to see his face more clearly in the darkness. 'Philippe, you are drunk.'

He laughed again, that demonic cackle.

'Would that I were, but no, this malady will not be gone in the morning.'

He sat up a little straighter from his slump, and pulled back his coat to reveal his red scarf. At first, I did not understand, but it quickly hit me. I realized the scarf was scarlet red with his blood, not the merry crimson of the cloth. I covered my mouth in horror, and sank to my knees before him.

'Philippe! Dieu! Who has done this?'

'Ah, it was accomplished between myself and Francois Gaillard. We had some disagreements on a few points regarding the brigade. But, ah, his point was sharper than mine, eh?'

He laughed at his own joke, the same blood-filled torturous sound.

We sat there, brothers, but I could not see the boy I had known and loved. That boy was already dead. Philippe looked at me with those icy blue eyes, gathering his strength to speak.

'Dieu, but this stings! I have become a hardened man, Jean. I know it. Do not ask me how or when, for it does not matter. In the end, your soft heart has carried the day, and you will win all.'

I made to disagree with him, I wanted to beg him to let me summon the doctor. But the blood was pooling and I knew as well as he that there would be no recovery.

'Jean, though I have sinned against you often and much, I must ask you for one final favor.'

'Anything.' I had naïvely replied. And in that moment, I know I would have done anything, no matter the request.

'Mon frer, if you have ever loved me as a brother, ever held me close to your heart, I pray you, unsheathe my dagger and end this suffering. I am too cowardly to do it myself, but would welcome death from my own trusty knife, and from one who has loved me well, even when I have done naught to deserve it.'

He closed his eyes, knowing I would not refuse him. It did not then, nor does it now feel like the bravery he pretended it was to render that service. But, I pulled out his naked blade, and I held him as I pressed it cleanly through his heart. He was gone... but he has been with me, and between us, ever since."

With this final sentence uttered, Jean-Luc's proud bearing slumped, the confession having stripped him of all dignity.

His sigh was audible, and he could faintly hear the mocking laughter of that faraway night. He wasn't sure if the laughter was inside as it was before Cora came in the room, or if it was the cruel memory. Cora, the woman he loved, the one he'd meant to save. Was it ever true? Or had he been trying to save himself all along, using her as shield against his wicked crime? It mattered not that Philippe had asked it of him. He had killed a man, his only brother. He should have found help, attempted at the very least to alter the moment. How she must despise him.

Then, she was everywhere. Her lips on his forehead and in his hair and at the end of his nose. "So brave", she was saying, over and over, the chant coming to life with her breath.

"How can you forgive? How can you ever think to love me?" Jean-Luc cried out in earnest. Could this be real? And why did she call him brave?

Cora answered his unasked question, as though it had been written plainly on his features.

"Philippe did not mean that you had courage enough to sink the knife in his chest. He trusted you had the mettle to live with his request and your fulfilling of it. He knew that your heart was dauntless enough to face the demons of it, even if his hand lacked the daring. And live you have, and through you, I have lived too. When I had thought to vanish into the darkness of death, you held the torch, guiding me into the light. And now I am strong enough to help shoulder your burden of grief, just as you have shouldered mine."

They were standing palm to palm, and air swirled around them, a whirlwind of light, enveloping them in its embrace. The smile on her face touched her eyes, and he returned it. This then, was the true fuel of magic. Happiness and love.

"Come now, husband. Let us have one more night on this ship, one final farewell to the past, and let it be buried in this spot on the lake. Tomorrow, the waves will carry us on."

They walked hand in hand, out of their cabin to join the others for the scanty supper meal. The feeling between them had warmed, burning away the icy taint of the spirit that remained glowering behind them, sitting in the little desk chair.

:21:

Nicholas

Dawn crept in on pink satin slippers. Nicholas' eyes popped open greedily at the sight of it. He had been waiting for some time for the light of morning to arrive and end his dark vigil. He had slept in stops and starts, as invalids do, too long in bed without the necessary movement to make him drowsy.

Nicholas had lain in bed the whole previous day. Sometime in the dark hours of the night, after Dr. Gordon had come to see how he fared one last time, he had decided that when the sun rose, he would too. And so, he raised his arms above his supine form and he nearly cried out in pain. It shot through his damaged ribs and seared like a flame. Lowering a hand down, he traced the bandages under his linen night shirt. His fingers then drifted to his battered face which had begun to whisker. He hadn't been two mornings without a shave since he was a boy, and he chuckled at the thought. He stretched again, more carefully this time, but paused with his arms extended above him, he was sure he had heard something at the door.

This was not the jolly knock of a friend announcing their visit, or the doctor come back to check on him. Instead, it was footsteps and low angry voices outside in the passageway. Had members of the crew come to threaten him again? He shuddered involuntarily, defeated to think he hadn't managed to earn any of their respect with his aid in the storm. Nicholas' palms began to sweat in anticipation. Should he cry out? Or would that further brand him a coward? The voices continued for a moment, then stopped abruptly and his door swung in.

In the doorway stood a solitary hooded figure, holding a finger to their shadowed lips, gesturing for silence. The door shut silently behind the dark silhouette, closed by unseen hands.

"Who is it? What do you want?" Nicholas croaked timidly.

A woman's voice, bold and clear, answered him quietly.

"To see how you fared, and if I could bring you comfort."

"Who is it? Who else is with you?" Nicholas' voice strained ever higher. The apparition before him was otherworldly and strange to his senses. Somehow as familiar as his own shadow, yet different too.

Taking a step forward, the hooded woman removed her covering, revealing the cascading raven tresses and glittering golden eyes of Cora Delacroix. She smirked mischievously at him.

"Why, Cora, you gave me such a fright coming in like a phantom from a nightmare!" He blushed scarlet and then added, "Did Jean-Luc accompany you? I heard two voices just now."

Nicholas had drawn himself up gently to sitting, embarrassed of his unshaven face and various ugly injuries. Cora sat down gingerly in the chair beside his sickbed. She reached out a hand, and as he grasped her cool palm, he remembered that this was the first time they had spoken since they were children. He had conversed with Jean-Luc many times on this journey, but never until now, with Cora. His heart warmed to her, for she had grown into a beautiful woman, but he was glad to see she had retained something of the wild curiosity of childhood in her features.

They studied one another for a few long moments, until she spoke, breaking the eerie quiet.

"No, I am come alone. Philippe did want to enter your room with me, but I forbid it."

She spoke of spirits? And so freely! She was either quite mad, or he hadn't been mistaken as a child to think her powerful. The more he considered the calm of her features, the greater the feeling grew in him that he had known there was a presence aboard this ship since he had boarded. A sense of unease, a trembling in his soul. Her face remained open and curious, as his mind picked over these revelations, a farmer at a vast, puzzling harvest.

"Is…is Philippe often with you?"

She sighed. "Yes. Nearly constantly since his death. Though he does not like to haunt me when Jean-Luc is by, and he has no qualms about leaving off bothering me if there is better mischief to be caused."

She looked at his bandages meaningfully, and Nicholas understood and nodded. For all of the talk of the crew about the oddities of the storm, he had thought them only to be superstitions. But no, it suddenly made sense that it was a violent, angry storm, brought about by the wrath of a spirit. He marveled at how she easily accepted these events, how evenly she spoke of them, as if they were discussing a neighbor's crop or a new brooch.

She smiled again gently.

"I knew you would understand. I have been waiting for the right time to speak with you, but I knew I must wait until you were yourself again. And here you are, Nicholas. We both have had a trying time with these gifts of ours, have we not? How wonderful it will be to have someone to confide in again."

The forgotten past dawned on him in that moment. In a flash, a flood of memories descended on him, long pushed back, of a little girl trailing blooming flowers in her wake, where none had been before. Whispered secrets between the two of them, and the joy of confounding their companions with tricks in the branches, and in their games. The stories that came alive when Waseya spoke them. Then, the day that Beshkno fell from the tree, and he had blamed his gifts, and laid them aside to tarnish. He only reached for them afterward to cheat men at cards or to charm a love interest, forgetting along the way the beauty of all he had learned on the island.

All of his struggles pulled away like stitches let out of an ill-fitting garment. He breathed deeply. What comfort lies in discovering that we are no longer alone. The whole morning brightened before him.

Suddenly, she stood from the chair and came quite close to his bed. She bent over, tenderly, and her forehead wrinkled in concentration. Her hands passed lightly over his face, and each place she touched burned hot and then tingled like snowflakes falling on his skin. His hand reached up to touch the places where he had felt the sensations, but found nothing amiss. Just the softness of his own flesh.

Before he could ask what she had done, she flicked her fingers toward the small looking-glass propped on his dressing table, and it sailed effortlessly to her waiting hand.

"How did you…?" Nicholas' mouth gaped.

"I confess, it is a trick I am just now learning. The frame, you see, is made from maple, and so, it responds to me, even as the growing maples do in the forest."

She grinned unabashedly.

"But, I think you will prefer this enchantment."

Cora raised the mirror until it reflected his smooth, unblemished reflection.

"Although the bruises and injuries themselves still need to mend, they are now unseen. We could not have you arriving home looking less than your best." She whispered.

Nicholas' eyes grew wide yet again.

"I can hardly speak. Nor barely believe what I am seeing. There are memories hidden from me, locked within my own mind. Memories of the island, and of happy children reveling in the magic of it. They are but shadows to me now."

"You will remember in time. Patience is indeed a great healer." She patted his hand blithely.

"No doubt. But, I thank you. You have restored my appearance, which, a few days ago meant a great deal more to me. But, you have given me back my pride, at least I can walk with my head high, back into the arms of my family, and my home. I cannot thank you enough, or Jean-Luc. It is good to find oneself back amongst friends."

She squeezed his hand once more, briefly, whispering, "No, it is good to find oneself back where one *belongs*."

She lifted her head and replaced her hood. Cora walked backward to the middle of the small room, and closed her eyes. Arms outstretched, palms up, she raised her hands high in the air, and as her arms moved higher, the air around the cabin began to spiral, flying this way and that. As the wind collected, her hands still up in the air, Nicholas could not take his eyes from her. The wind grew stronger and stronger, whipping her hair around her face and shoulders, and then quickly, she pulled her arms back down to her sides.

Cora gave Nicholas a wink, and suddenly, he felt wind begin to fill the sails of the ship. Sitting up, he looked out his casement windows and saw that it was true. The ship was, once again, pulling fiercely in the rolling waves.

When he managed to drag his eyes away from the sight before him, he stammered, "Cora, you've…", but he never finished his thought because she had disappeared. The door firmly shut, and all he could hear was hushed voices and footsteps in the hall.

He sat up tall, ignoring the protests of his pained body, his fingers once again traced over what had been his mottled flesh. While his face still ached, he knew the marks of his adventures aboard the ship were no longer written on his skin. He couldn't help but sneak one more look out his window, fairly disbelieving the truth of his eyes. It was incredible, but the *Starlight* was indeed sailing once more.

With new energy, he bounded from the bed, splashing his face with cold water in the basin, and hurriedly he shaved his few sprouting mustachios and the grizzle from his chin. He donned the plainest clothes he had, no longer desiring the fashionable, showy finery he had relied on to earn him praise and esteem. That version of himself was so foreign to him as not to be real at all.

He pulled on a pair of breeches in a light brown color with tall riding boots, and a plain white linen shirt with a stiff collar and a blue waistcoat. In London he would be regarded as a bumpkin, or at best, a country squire. Which was, he supposed, pretty close to the truth. Though, the realization no longer shamed him, but instead he felt proud. Proud of his Mackinac roots, and his place in the world.

He walked around his trunks and cases, gently bending to close them up tightly. His hand brushed the letter from his mother, and he was surprised to find it no longer burned him as it had whenever he'd had the courage to read it. Now, as his knuckles brushed over the paper, he saw her. She looked older than he recalled, but he could see her perfectly, sitting, writing at her desk. She was wearing mourning, and she paused from time to time to stare blankly ahead. She finished, and picked the letter up, kissing it, and tears began to fall on her black crinoline. The vision ended as abruptly as it had begun, and though it wasn't a happy sight, it did wonders for his soul. For not only was he missed by his family, as he had so often doubted, but he had rediscovered his gifts. He had only had faint remembrances of them, whispers of them in England, and now they bloomed. He felt it must be something in these waters so close to Mackinac Island that restored them. He wished then, for a moment, that he *had* seen Philippe's spirit this morning, as he had many questions he'd like to ask his old friend, and better times to reminisce over.

Buckling his valise, and securing the clasps of his trunks, Nicholas looked around the little cabin that had been his hideaway and his dungeon. Only one item had not been packed, and snatching the pipe from the rumpled sheets, he walked deliberately into the passage, and out onto the main deck.

He emerged in the glory of a full, warm sun, and a bracing lake wind. The sailors on deck smiled warmly at him, greeting him kindly with nods of their heads and claps on the back. It couldn't be imagined that these were the same men who had cheered on a fight they hoped would leave him dead or disfigured. These, the same men who had threatened him in his own cabin. Yet, it was so.

Nicholas hailed them affably, echoing their warmth, casting out all the hateful notions that had held him back too long. He was done with fear, and anger and spite. It was time to go home.

He stood at the stern, looking back on where he had come from, marveling in all that had changed on this journey—more than had changed in 10 long years. He was soon joined by Jean-Luc, who clapped him on the shoulder warmly.

"You are looking the wrong way, mon ami! To the bow if you wish to glimpse your future."

They were then met with Dr. Gordon, whose good-natured expression appeared to be contagious.

"Well, gentleman, seems we've nearly arrived, hm?"

Putting his hand to the sky and measuring the position of the sun, Jean-Luc nodded. "Oui, if the captain's instruments can be trusted for our location, we should be docking in the harbor by sunset."

"We are not too far off course then? Splendid. I hope you are right, for all of my shows of patience...I am nearly bursting to bring the journey to an end now. We are all of us on the doorstep, so close to coming home we can almost smell dinner!"

The doctor laughed at his own joke, and then turned serious.

"But, Mr. Rast, this voyage I have heard much of your island legends, but I have yet to hear one pass your lips. And Mme. Delacroix has said naught but how lovely you tell them. Let's have one, to welcome us to the island, hm?"

Nicholas raised his eyes from the blue and white wake, trailing the ship like a tail.

"Do you remember any of them, mon ami?" Jean-Luc looked into his young friend's eyes, a shadow of worry overtaking his features.

"As if they were written on my heart" was his reply.

Nicholas turned toward the other men, and then looked upward into the sky, considering a moment.

"Yes, I have the very one for a day such as this, and fitting for a man who has not yet the pleasure of Mackinac's shores."

His grey eyes went black, and when he spoke his voice was strangely animated. The stories had always lived inside of him, seeming to possess him, and were finally reawakened after so long lying dormant.

"Long, long ago, when the island was inhabited by the Gitchi Manitou, and the evil wendi-goes still haunted Devil's Kitchen. Back in the time when the Great Thunderbird Chief still made peace-pipes from the red island clay. In this time, the turtle spirits Neebing and his brother, Kisinaa decided to run a great race. Neebing was always first between them in feats of strength or speed, easily winning their contests by many lengths. When Neebing ran, the sun shone warmly and the trees, with their leaves of green, whispered encouragingly to him. The bear, the fox, the stoat and the birds called fondly after him, 'There is our champion! The mighty Manitou who brings summer with his steps!'

For many moons, he ran northward, bringing warmth and light. Soon, Kisinaa, grew angry with his losses and he ran more swiftly, trying to catch up. Through his efforts, he ran closer to his brother, and though he still could not catch him, Kisinaa saw for himself that where Neebing's feet touched the earth, flowers burst to life, and earth and sky were in harmony.

The sight inspired further rage, and Kisinaa decided to punish the earth. He called on the spirit of the east wind, and bid him bring floods, and he then called the south wind spirit to blow great heat and wither the crops. Soon after, he called the clouds to block the sun, hoping Neebing might become lost in the dark. But, Neebing was clever, and with a simple smile from him to the cloud, the sun reappeared, shining brighter than ever.

Seeing this, Kisinaa filled with fury. He called on the spirit of the north wind to bring sleet and snow. Neebing had now reached the Great Lakes, where he stopped to rest after his long run, and it was there that his brother flew past him in the night, bringing the full power of the wind. Realizing what had happened, Neebing leapt up, and dashed to overtake his brother, but only for a few short days, which are now called, 'Indian Summer'. At last, winter settled over the land, blanketing Mackinac in ice and snow.

Thus, when the weather changes rapidly on the island, it is still said that Neebing and Kisinaa are running their race."

Nicholas' eyes blinked and lightened to grey, and he turned his gaze back to the water.

"That was some tale! I felt I could see the race before my eyes. Why, you were another person entirely!" Dr. Gordon exclaimed, his eyes shining in wonder.

"The more that I hear of Mackinac, I can hardly credit it exists." He added, shaking his head in amazement.

"Oui, Doctor, it is indeed a lively place. Now, Jasper, Nicholas, would you like to join me at the bow? I want to be the first to glimpse the island!" Jean-Luc looked to both men. Dr. Gordon readily assented, but Nicholas demurred, begging their leave to join them in a few moments.

His eyes never left the swirling blue. He had always liked the legend he had told, had always seen himself and Edward in the roles of the two competing brothers. Nicholas had assigned himself the part of Kisinaa, jealous of his older brother, though he wondered now if that was still true. He couldn't help but think that he had never been in the story at all, that instead he had always been the teller of the legend, and never the man within it.

Warmth coursed through him, and his fingers closed over the coolness of the pipe in his pocket. Drawing it out, he rubbed his thumb over the familiar strength of the wood, before bending his arm back and throwing it into the churning lake foam.

His mind framed the words,

"Take it, Edward, you are alone and have need of its comfort. Keep it safe, until we meet again."

Nicholas had clung to it as a symbol of his brother and as a gesture of love and strength for far too long. Now, he gave that back to his brother's spirit, and he filled with peace.

Soon, he would be back in Mackinac, and he would be ready. He stepped away from the stern, and felt a firm tap on his shoulder. Turning around, startled, he saw nothing. Shaking his head he made to take another step toward his companions, but this time, not three feet from him was Philippe. He was not the gauzy phantom he had imagined, nor was he solid as a man—but, something in between. A smile, unbidden, came to Nicholas' mouth, in the joy at seeing an old friend he had thought lost forever. He recognized the tight black curls and the piercing blue eyes, but they held no malice.

In a voice as airy as the wind, he echoed Cora's words from earlier, saying simply, "Back where you belong..." before vanishing, leaving Nicholas alone with the whirling blue.

.22.

Marguerite

Resting on a small table positioned to be seen the moment one opened the door, Jean-Luc found a curious envelope. They had just approached their little house after alighting at the harbor. They had been greeted warmly by all who had gathered dockside, and said a hearty farewell to Nicholas, the Gordons, and to an emotional Captain Alberts. Commandant Ravensdale and the Delacroix's had wept and embraced them again and again.

His name was printed on the outside of the envelope in his mother's slanted, spidery hand. He broke the seal carefully, showed it to Cora, and began to read aloud.

My dearest son, Jean-Luc,

Is it possible for an island to be a whole world? Mon fils, I had never thought so.

As well you know, I grew up surrounded by the lavender fields of Provence, and my whole life had been an undulating sea of heady scent and sweeping purple. A fairyland, truly. Your father, (Oh, how young we were!) he swept into town one day with the north wind, this curious, merchant mariner from Marseilles, with a head full of dreams. What castles we built in the air, how easily his fantasies of life became my own. I had never been impulsive, you understand, not in the way that my Tsiganes-gypsy people historically have been. And when we arrived, most on the island could not understand why I had come to Mackinac. But, I tell you now, it was for love of your father, and the dreams of adventure that he'd shared with me.

Jean, how can I explain…it was as if every step from France, was a closing up of the world. Those blown wide open wishes of our courtship dimmed in the smallness of our new home. Your father could not have been happier, this island always seemed an untapped paradise to him. But, I must confess, I felt cheated. A princess locked away in a faraway tower, her heart ripped from her chest, and buried into a corner to wither. At the same time, your grandfather was so pleased to have your father to help him, and with Pierre at the helm, Cross Shipping thrived.

When you were born, the cage of the island seemed to swell to encompass the whole of existence. There was no other place but here, no other life than this. And with Philippe's birth, the island grew still larger. The ground my boys trod upon was my only home. You both had released me from any and all doubts I had weighted myself so heavily with.

You were so full of earth and trees, and you fell in love with the island, delighting in every piece of it. Philippe, so brimming with water, a child of the lake. And then Cora arrived, a mixture of light and dark, with her golden eyes and shadow hair. Can I say it? I felt whole. I even had the lilacs of spring to greet me in lieu of my lavender. Life was the dream Pierre had promised, thrice blessed with a loving husband, and two boisterous sons.

Don't fret, your maman has not lost her mind, I promise, this missive is coming to a point.

Knowing all I have just related, understand my pain last summer when Philippe returned. He was as a stranger, as you well know. My heart seemed shot through with a bullet, and there were times that I'd reach my chest in the night, to be certain that there was no hole. It will probably not surprise you to know that news of his death did not break me, for my son was already dead. In my mind, he had perished somewhere out on the rivers of the north, or at his winter post, long before he returned to these shores, a phantom of the man he had been. His death on the island was a ripping off of a scab. Painful, but never equal to the injury that had caused the laceration from the first.

Truth be told, your leaving did not undo me either. In fact, I was glad of it, which irked your father. I knew he was keeping a secret for you, but I did not need to know it, and I still do not. The only thing I needed was for you to return, and I had faith that you would, and if you are reading this letter, that faith was justified.

But, oui, I was happy. You needed a step away from this place, in order to see the world better. The world of the island.

When we received word you wanted to purchase this house, I began to pack up your belongings, and Rosalind began to sort Cora's. We wanted your new house to feel as a home from the moment you stepped in. I knew this house would suit you both, almost a part of the forest, and every year the wild of the wood grows ever closer to the back steps. As I cleaned and arranged this house myself, I would sing old songs from the south of France, pouring love into every room.

It was as I was going through the papers in your desk that I found the Byron poem, "She Walks in Beauty", one of his most stirring, I think. So beautifully it was copied out, with artistic representations of the moon and starry skies illuminated on the fine paper. It was obvious that it had been meant as a gift, but never given. I have taken the liberty of having it framed and it is now hung over your marriage bed, a fine oak masterpiece your father had hand-carved for you both.

All this letter, to tell you that I knew without hesitation that the poem was for Cora. It had always been for her, as you have doted on her since you were a boy.

At first, I had been irritated when you were young, a boy should *adore his mother for a few more years before falling in love—making a different female the center of his world after that. But, your feelings were so pure, that my own could only echo them. I fell in love with her too, as a daughter of my heart.*

I want you to understand that I know what it is to leave home, and to find another. I know what it is to turn my life upside down for a dream of love. It is pain, and loneliness, but it is also light and hope. Whatever did send you away is of no import. Your sails have come to rest, the Starlight is at anchor, and you have come to a home filled with love. Keep it always brimming.

Welcome home, mon fils.

Your truly affectionate maman.

Epilogue

It was unseasonably warm for late September. An Indian summer day that did seek to conceal from anyone basking in its glory, that autumn was on its way on stealthy tiptoes.

Cora was lazing beneath a willow tree in the forest clearing. Jean-Luc dozed softly next to her in the stolen sunshine, his body reclined on the soft green moss, and his sandy hair hanging loose over his eyes. With a flick of the wrist, she charmed the boughs of the tree in closer, making a haven around their daydream afternoon. She would need to waken him soon, as they both would require washing up before dinner at the Gordon's home in town. But not yet, not yet…she would let him sleep just a little longer.

The clearing in the wood lit up for her with memories. This was the place she had first met two young boys that would change her life. This was the place she had many a sweet rendezvous with the man who had become her husband, and the place that she had first set eyes on the new Philippe, the man who haunted her even now. Still, the memories were a balm to her spirit. Every rock, every branch, every inch of the space, brought to mind a flash of something. A look, a gesture, a joke, a forbidden dance, and a hurried proposal. This clearing was her life, this forest her home, and here was the place that her mind would always come to, when in need of repose.

She picked up their satchel, and dug around a minute for the jar of ink and the new steel nib her father had ordered for her, come all the way from London. Dreamily, she opened the small commonplace book she had begun writing in, so many months before.

Cora skimmed the pages, in turns shocked by her own words, and sometimes comforted by them. As of late, her entries had been less interesting. A recipe for jam, a recounting of a favorite legend she had all but forgotten, and a list of names she would like for a baby, or a kitten, whichever came to her first. There were only two pages left, and her husband had very kindly brought home a fresh, pristine, leather bound book for her to gild with her swooping, overly large handwriting. She couldn't imagine what words she would find to fill it.

She sighed, raised her pen and just as the nib hit the paper, she saw something from the corner of her eye; something that prompted her to look up, briefly forgetting her writing.

Two swirling leaves, the first of autumn. Both bright, sunburst and buttercup yellow. They danced and pirouetted, moving together in an unnatural but beautiful rhythm. Philippe came slowly into focus, and he grinned at her. No longer the cold, malicious smile she had come to know, but now, the expression had grown warmer, and friendly. A few more of the leaves changed as his ghostly figure passed over them, each shade more brilliant than the last. He approached the sleeping figure of his brother and crouched down. Cora watched as the phantom of Philippe began to transform from the man she had known and lost, back to the young boy she had first encountered in this space. His black curls surrounding his round face, his eyes a more innocent lake blue. He whispered something in his sleeping brother's ear, and though still dozing, Jean-Luc chuckled. Philippe laughed and melted from sight, the only clue he had been there at all was the the trail of new autumn leaves on the forest floor.

Taking a hand, she tenderly pushed Jean-Luc's hair out of his eyes, and gently kissed the tip of his nose. She took the nib up again and began to write.

Like the chapter in my life that is now closing, so too, will my entries in this book. I have come to an end of something, though I fear I will not know what it is for many years, and it will not be until I look back on this moment, or re-read these words at some later date, that it will become clear to me.

It is months now that we have been back to Mackinac, but on our return we both knew that the whole world was different for us. That we were now never alone to face the world, or to shoulder our sorrows without the other. It is a beautiful thing to be loved, there are too few among us who truly understand its power.

Speaking of this power, I have reason to think that this great force is to blame for Nicholas' unprecedented zeal for his work at the Fur Company. His father suffered a stroke this past July, and our young friend filled his father's position with such skill and enthusiasm that none could have predicted. Though, if one glimpses him when Rosalind is by, it is completely understandable why he would want to make a respectable man out of himself. I cannot help hope she looks on him the same way someday, and I am heartily glad that his troubles seem to be forgotten behind him.

As for my troubles, Philippe will always surround me, until the moment that I too cease to breathe on this earth. Though, thankfully, he no longer follows me about like a spaniel, and he cares less for mischief. In death, his spirit has found a healing calm on this island that he never experienced in life. It pains me though to see how he aches for Jean-Luc, though he cannot see Philippe. More and more, his spirit returns as the young man he once was, the man who worshipped his older brother. I pray that God grants him peace.

Although my tale seems to be heading this way, and I long to write that we are living happily ever after... alas, our life is not a fairytale, even if we are constantly surrounded by magic. This past summer has been difficult, and I cannot help but foretell that the situation here will grow worse. The government has cheated the tribes from their payments, and there is much unrest in the town and in the fort. There are new settlers here all the time, and they are not interested in the old ways, or in living in harmony with the native people. I weep to think that the legends and the magic of the island will one day be lost, but hope that in some way, and in some people, it can perhaps endure. As it lives in Nicholas… and within me.

Which brings me to the very end of this final page. I realize now that I will have many more adventures to recount in the sweet little book waiting for me at home. I have a suspicion that perhaps there is a little seed of magic growing for Jean and I, though it is still too soon to know for sure. If not now, then soon.

Our story, the tale of two people who found something lost, on a beam of Starlight made of strong oak, resting on a bed of lake glass, will become its own legend. Our story, will live on in this clearing, in these trees, and perhaps even in a beam of light, growing within me, even now.

Cora quickly caught a tear that threatened to smudge the page she had so feverishly written. It was getting late now, and the darkness would only come earlier and earlier until spring returned. She clasped the brass fastening on the front, and the click of the mechanism, though quiet, roused Jean-Luc. He opened one sleepy eye, and the corner of his mouth lifted at the sight of Cora and her ink-stained fingers. With another flick of her wrist, the boughs of the willow floated to their original position. He stood up and stretched, and dusted off his trousers. Gathering the satchel and her book, he slung the pack over his shoulder and took her hand, kissing it slowly.

On the walk home he recalled a dream he'd just had of Philippe, and a joke he had told him, and of yellow autumn leaves as bright as stars, dancing on the forest floor.

Further Reading

For further reading on the History of Mackinac, of the Great Lakes, or the legends of the island, please see the glorious works I used for reference in writing this novel.

They are a joy themselves, as the island really is a magical place.

Fuller, Iola. *The Loon Feather*. N.p.: Mariner, 1967. Print.

Gringhuis, Dirk. *Lore of the Great Turtle; Indian Legends of Mackinac Retold*. Mackinac Island, MI: Mackinac Island State Park Commission, 1970. Print.

Ratigan, William. *Great Lakes Shipwrecks & Survivals*. 3rd ed. N.p.: William B Eerdman's, 1977. Print.

Williams, Meade C. *Early Mackinac: A Sketch, Historical and Descriptive*. St. Louis, MO: Buschart, 1901. Print

Book Club Discussion Questions

- Each character in the book clings to something different: an object, person, or a part of the past. What is it for each of them, and what does it say about their character?

- How are Nicholas' and Cora's powers different?

- On the surface, Jean-Luc seems to be a "perfect" man. But, he is flawed. What are his character flaws, and why are they not as easily perceived?

- Cora is wildly different than most women of her time. What are some examples of her nature and characteristics that would have made her stick out from "proper" society? Why is it important that she is different?

- This book deals with opposites: in appearance, in actions and in nature. What are some of these opposites and what do they reveal?

- The elements play a substantial role in the book, and in some ways are a character in their own right. How does nature influence the plot? The characters?

- Which character seems the most complex? Why? Which seems the most simple? Why?

About The Author

ALEXANDRIA NOLAN hails from Michigan's second motor city, Flint. She is an alumna of the University of Michigan, where she earned a Bachelor of Arts in English.

She is the author of *Starlight Symphonies of Oak and Glass,* a novel of magic, folklore and natural history of Northern Michigan. *Wide, Wild, Everywhere,* a collection of fictional short travel tales, and *Shears of Fate,* a historical fiction novella set in a post-jazz age Traverse City, Michigan and Chicago. She maintains a lifestyle blog, *Greetings from Nolandia,* and is an avid travel & lifestyle contributor to various online and print publications.

She resides in Houston, Texas, with her husband, Terrence.

www.alexandrianolan.com

Made in the USA
Middletown, DE
08 July 2015